BY F. SCOTT FITZGERALD

NOVELS

The Last Tycoon (Unfinished)
with a Foreword by Edmund Wilson and Notes by the Author
Tender Is the Night
The Great Gatsby
The Beautiful and Damned
This Side of Paradise

STORIES

The Pat Hobby Stories
with an Introduction by Arnold Gingrich
Taps at Reveille
Six Tales of the Jazz Age and Other Stories
with an Introduction by Frances Fitzgerald Smith
Flappers and Philosophers
with an Introduction by Arthur Mizener
The Stories of F. Scott Fitzgerald
A Selection of 28 Stories, with an Introduction by Malcolm Cowley
Babylon Revisited and Other Stories

STORIES AND ESSAYS

Afternoon of an Author
with an Introduction and Notes by Arthur Mizener
The Fitzgerald Reader
with an Introduction by Arthur Mizener

LETTERS

The Letters of F. Scott Fitzgerald
with an Introduction by Andrew Turnbull
Letters to His Daughter
with an Introduction by Frances Fitzgerald Smith

AFTERNOON
OF AN AUTHOR

Afternoon of an Author

A Selection of
Uncollected Stories and Essays

By F. Scott
Fitzgerald

WITH AN INTRODUCTION AND NOTES

BY ARTHUR MIZENER

CHARLES SCRIBNER'S SONS

NEW YORK

*Originally published under the sponsorship of
the Friends of the Princeton University Library*

Printed in the United States of America
LIBRARY OF CONGRESS CATALOG CARD NUMBER 58-7519
SBN 684-10149-1 (trade cloth)
SBN 684-12734-2 (trade paper, SL)

35791113151719 C/P 2018161412108642
791113151719 C/C 20181614121086

CONTENTS

AFTERNOON
OF AN AUTHOR

INTRODUCTION

O<small>NE</small> of the most remarkable things about Scott Fitzgerald as a writer is the dual character of his self-knowledge, the curious way in which he combined the innocence of complete involvement with an almost scientific coolness of observation, so that he nearly always wrote about deeply felt personal experience, and nearly always as if the important use of personal experience was to illustrate general values. "Begin with an individual," he once wrote, "and before you know it you find you have created a type." As a general proposition, that may be exceedingly questionable, but as a comment on the character of Fitzgerald's best work it is very shrewd. This curious sense of experience is everywhere in Fitzgerald's work because it was the permanent foundation of his awareness of experience.

The special intensity of his work is, then, the product of an odd kind of irony. Even when we do not know the personal circumstances which lie behind a story like "One Trip Abroad," or " 'I Didn't Get Over,' " we experience their consequences as we read, feel all the force of the special case by participating in the story in the same way we participate in the recollection of an experience of our own which has meant a good deal to us. At the same time, we are always unusually aware with such stories that they are representative, that these people and their experiences are typical of a whole class and—often—typical of the crucial moments in their lives. However much he may be talking about himself, Fitzgerald is always talking also about a "young American couple," about what life in Paris or on the Riviera was like that year, about the characteristic wearing away of innocence to the point where it takes several drinks to light up the face.

The effect of this double perspective on a single occasion is analogous—at least in one respect—to the effect Henry James found with such delight "in a palpable imaginable *visitable* past—in the nearer distances and clearer mysteries, the marks and signs of a world we may reach over to as by making a long arm we grasp an object at the other end of our table. . . . That, to my imagination, is the past fragrant of all, or almost all, the poetry of the thing outlived and lost and gone, and yet in which the precious element of closeness, telling so of connexions but tasting so of differences, remains appreciable." Fitzgerald often got his double perspective by making precisely this long arm down the table of the past—characteristically, however, it is down the table of his own past, a past he has experienced personally, not of the historical past of which James was thinking (James is speaking of *The Aspern Papers*). The sense of his past is very sharp in Fitzgerald: his memory for the precise feelings of a time and for the objects to which these feelings cling is remarkable, as if he lived—to borrow a fine phrase from Malcolm Cowley—in a room full of clocks and calendars—or perhaps in an author's house like the one he describes in this book. The way Fitzgerald used this acute sense of the past is illustrated by "News of Paris—Fifteen Years Ago," where the doubleness is even in the title, in the clash between "News" and "Fifteen Years Ago."

But "News of Paris—Fifteen Years Ago" makes it quite clear that Fitzgerald is not aiming simply at creating for us a simultaneous sense of the pastness of the past and its presence, of its poetry and its closeness, any more than James was, for all his emphasis on these things, in *The Aspern Papers* or than Eliot usually is in his poetry. In all of them, the pastness of the past is really a clarity of vision about it, a power of making judgments of it of general moral significance. This is much easier to do with what is past. But the distancing of time is not necessary to such judgment, and sometimes Fitzgerald achieved it for events which were practically contemporary with his judgment of them. At his best, however, he could always give the events of his narrative "the precious element of closeness," whether the events were lost and gone or a part of the immediate present.

There is something peculiarly American, I think, about the irony of this clash between judgment and intimacy; or perhaps it is only that with us the gap between our public and our private selves is so great that we can bridge it at all only with irony, and ordinarily cannot bridge it at all, so that a writer who can has a special appeal for us. He shows us that the society which has produced the inhuman monsters of Mr. Reisman's *Lonely Crowd*, with their absurd concern with conformity to the moral standards set by their society, can also produce—frequently in the same person—its lonely men of conscience, its Strethers and Morris Gedges, its Gatsbys and Stahrs, with their deep concern for the moral imperatives of private, felt experience.

In any event, one of the consequences of the doubleness of Fitzgerald's perception is that, by making everything he wrote at once personal and public, it draws his fiction and his non-fiction very close together. There is little point, for instance, in trying to say whether even so small a piece as "Ten Years in the Advertising Business" is one or the other. Both of its incidents actually happened to Fitzgerald, almost exactly as he sets them down, but both are *written* here, created for us as invented incidents are in a good story, and they are fitted together so that they embody a "moral" which is by no means simple. Indeed, they are made to blur together as do events in the carefully calculated confusion of the fictional sleeptalker like Lady Macbeth and Molly Bloom—and this too is part of their "moral." This brief "essay" really works the way a skilfully constructed double metaphor works, and thus conforms to a design which Fitzgerald, with his acute feeling for the ironies of time, used with particular delight: this is the design of "The Lost Decade," for example, and, in a slightly different way, of "News of Paris—Fifteen Years Ago." Because the distinction between fiction and non-fiction is not, in Fitzgerald's case, of major significance, I have not tried to distinguish between the two in making the selections for this book.

The main purpose of these selections is to illustrate both the persistence of Fitzgerald's fundamental sense of experience and the way his uses of it varied as he matured in feeling and as his circumstances changed in time. For, though the fundamental perception remained constant from the beginning to the end of his career, he did mature; his ideas became more penetrating, his feelings more considered and less conventional, his craftsmanship more precise. Apart from the steady development of his craftsmanship, this maturing was overwhelmingly a matter of personal experience rather than of literary development in the narrow sense, and, given Fitzgerald's precision of recall, it is almost as important to notice the time about which he is writing in a given piece as it is to notice when he was writing about it if we wish to trace his development. Fortunately, he usually wrote close enough to the time of the events he is describing so that, with one major exception, it is possible to arrange these pieces according to the chronology of their writing and also to keep them in the chronological order of the events they describe.

The one considerable exception to this generalization is the first

Part of this collection, the pieces Fitzgerald wrote about his young manhood and about Princeton. These were written ten or fifteen years after the events they describe; in feeling and technique they belong at the end of Part II or the beginning of Part III of this book. But since all of them are saturated with the feelings of the times recalled and only occasionally give us a glimpse of the special, personal Fitzgerald feelings of the time they were written (the quality of the judgment in them is another thing), they are, I believe, more valuable if they are read as a kind of prologue to this collection, an account of how Basil Duke Lee, "like Grant, lolling in his general store in Galena," prepared for the "intricate destiny" that awaited Fitzgerald when, in 1920 (the year he wrote "Who's Who—and Why"), he became a public figure not merely in his imagination (where he had always been conscious of the actions that a man might play) but in incredible fact. The only other exceptions to a chronological arrangement in this book are minor ones made for reasons which are self-evident.

I have tried to include in this book only pieces which will serve its main purpose, to show the character of Fitzgerald's fundamental perception. Some of them are more obviously personal than others, but all of them derive their energy from some actual experience in which Fitzgerald was deeply involved. This is not least so of them when their superficial details are not, as they are not in beautiful late stories like "Design in Plaster" and "News of Paris—Fifteen Years Ago," literally biographical. All of them, too, were written, not simply because they were personal experiences, but because these experiences seemed to Fitzgerald fabulous. This is not least so of them when they are, as are "How to Live on $36,000 a Year" and "Afternoon of an Author," ostensibly autobiographical.

I have also tried to distribute these selections evenly over the twenty years of Fitzgerald's career as a writer so that they will demonstrate the typical uses he made of his perception in each period of his career. The selections in Part II belong to the period of *This Side of Paradise*, *The Beautiful and Damned*, and *The Great Gatsby*; the selections in Part III to the period which reached its climax in *Tender Is the Night* (for which "One Trip Abroad" is clearly a preliminary study); the selections in Part IV to the period which reached its climax in *The Last Tycoon*. I have also tried, incidentally, to fulfill another purpose.

One of the neglected aspects of Fitzgerald's achievement is that aspect he himself took such pride in (he mentions it several times here), the fact that he was a professional writer, that, for all the notorious irregularity of his life, he produced in his short career a remarkable quantity of work, nearly all of it professional in quality ("You do not," he once said in understandable irritation with some of his critics, "produce a short story for the *Saturday Evening Post* on a bottle"), and a surprising amount of it of very high quality indeed. It is an incidental intention of this book to suggest the quantity of good work Fitzgerald did, and it therefore includes nothing of his which has appeared in book form before.

To be sure, this is not the best way to do justice to this aspect of his achievement; the best way to do that would be to publish all Fitzgerald's good work in chronological order. But practically speaking, this way may be the only one available to us, for by a series of accidents for which everyone, including Fitzgerald himself, is to some extent to blame, it has become nearly impossible to make an orderly presentation of all his good work. One example of the way the career of his work has been bedevilled will illustrate the difficulties. Any number of people tried to get him to make the nine Basil Duke Lee stories into a book so that they would be permanently available to readers and so that their continuity and cumulative effect could be seen. But some queer anxiety about becoming like Booth Tarkington, a fear of "going into a personal debauch and coming out of it devitalized with no interest except an acute observation of the behavior of colored people, children and dogs," led Fitzgerald to refuse to put the stories together in a book. He always argued that he wanted to revise them before doing so, though when he finally did put five of them into *Taps at Reveille*, he made only very minor verbal revisions in them. The end result of this attitude on Fitzgerald's part is that only two of the nine stories are now in print at all. But since they are in print in the standard collection of his short stories edited by Malcolm Cowley, it would be difficult to print the whole series in another book. A seemingly endless series of similar accidents makes it probable that a representative selection of the forty-nine stories Fitzgerald wrote between his last collection of stories in 1935 and his death in 1940 will never be made into a book and that a fully representative selection of the one hundred and sixty stories he wrote over the twenty years of his career will not be made in the foreseeable future. The stories and essays which Mr. Cowley had necessarily to exclude from a volume which would simply not hold more than twenty-eight stories will get into print, if at all, helter-skelter, in books like this one which have some other purpose.

Only someone who has collected all of Fitzgerald's stories and essays—and I do not know anyone who has—or has had available to him the Princeton Library's wonderful collection of them and has thus been able to read his work straight through can have any idea of the professional care with which he wrote and rewrote even the least important thing he did. Only such a reader can fully understand the persistence of Fitzgerald's remarkable sense of experience, the variety and fullness with which he used it in his work, and the way in which his use of it improved as he matured. But the hope of this book is that something of all these purposes can be served by these selections. Some of the things they make clearer for us are, I think, fairly obvious when they are thus brought together.

The early Fitzgerald, who is directly represented here by "Who's Who—and Why" and indirectly represented by the Basil Duke Lee stories, believed very deeply not only in the ecstasy of happiness, which he knew by direct experience, but in the possibility of making it a habit and the object of one's life. His early stories are attempts to show what happiness, or at worst gaiety, is, even when they are implicit in the most evanescent or trivial experiences, as they are in early stories like "The Camel's Back" (1920) or "The Offshore Pirate" (1920) or "Bernice Bobs Her Hair" (1920). There was only a moment after he had achieved the heights where he thought happiness was to be found during which he could deceive himself into believing it was there. It always turns out, as Basil discovers in "The Captured Shadow," that you can share your ecstasy with no one; and it always turns out that you cannot sustain it yourself, as the Fitzgerald of "My Lost City" realized in 1920 almost as soon as he got to New York and felt he "had everything [he] wanted and knew [he] would never be so happy again."

But so intense was his delight in life and so powerful his conviction that you could dominate it if you only tried hard enough that he kept on for some years trying to absorb into his feelings about experience these new discoveries without surrendering his old convictions about the infinite possibilities of life. He kept dealing with the complications—the decline of ecstasy into habit, of spontaneity into the disorder of too many parties and too many "world-weary New Yorkers [who chose] to spend their week-ends at the Fitzgerald house in the country"—by making jokes of them, as if they were merely temporary distortions of the normal order of things. It was only very slowly and reluctantly that he began to see the possibility that habit was the usual state of things and ecstasy by its very nature temporary and almost always disappointed by its objects.

To reach this point was not, however, to reconcile himself to the life of habit or to believe it good. I am very far from wishing to suggest that Fitzgerald was able to state discursively all that is implied by *The Great Gatsby*; it is nonetheless revealing that he thought at the time he was writing it that "the whole burden of this novel" was "the loss of those illusions that give such color to the world so that you don't care whether things are true or false as long as they partake of the magical glory." It is precisely this loss which allows Gatsby to discover "what a grotesque thing a rose is and how raw the sunlight was upon the scarcely created grass." "No amount of fire or freshness can challenge what a man can store up in his ghostly heart." This is the attitude which dominates the second period of Fitzgerald's work and dictates the technique of the stories he wrote at this time: they are, as "Winter Dreams" is, characteristically committed to the pathos of the loss of illusion and they tend toward climaxes of rhetoric in which Fitzgerald tries to convey the horror of the loss and—sometimes—the hopelessness of it. This rhetoric has remarkable qualities; it is frequently dialogue or the kind of summary of a character's thoughts which is, rhetorically, very close to dialogue; and it exploits the characteristic qualities of American speech, especially the rhythms of American speech, very beautifully. ("I believe we could try. I'd try so hard.") Obvious examples of this kind of rhetorical climax are the conclusions of "Winter Dreams" (1922), of "'The Sensible Thing'" (1924), of "The Rich Boy" (1926). There is a good illustration of it in Nicole's closing words in "One Trip Abroad":

"It's just that we don't understand what's the matter," she said. "Why did we lose peace and love and health, one after the other? If we knew, if there was anybody to tell us, I believe we could try. I'd try so hard."

But the finest illustration of all is of course the last page of *The Great Gatsby*.

[9]

The stories which lead up to these climaxes are usually fairly long and their scenes fairly fully developed (Fitzgerald's first mature stories were designed for the *Post*). They are carefully plotted, but their essential object is to realize the qualities of a set of occasions and to show how these occasions modified—usually without his knowing when or how—the vital feelings of a central character. Thus, by the end of the story, the enchantment has gone for Dexter Green and George O'Kelly, responsibility and pride have become sterile for Anson Hunter, the discipline of what they believed was seriousness has lost its hold for Nicole and Nelson. Like Gatsby, they become sensible by somehow losing all they really care about, the "illusion" of a value felt.

In "One Hundred False Starts" Fitzgerald makes it clear that the essential thing for him as a writer was "an emotion—one that's close to me and that I can understand." He was always conscientious about realizing the emotion as action, and seems to have had a healthy instinctive distrust of the impulse to try to make fiction out of confession. But in the stories of this period the personally experienced emotion is the essential thing and is anterior to the plot. He loved good stories, but he lived, very deep in his sensibility, what he called emotions. His characteristic failures were "plots without emotions, emotions without plots," his characteristic successes the inventions of stories which would carry the emotion he cared about.

Very gradually, under the pressure of great personal suffering, out of the toughness of his Irish determination not to be beaten, with the help of the New England conscience he had developed in Minnesota, Fitzgerald achieved a kind of acceptance of this state of "lost illusion." It is impossible to say that he ever accepted it as necessary: he seems always to have felt that unnecessary personal failures were really responsible for it. But at least he learned how to live with it. Out of this attitude came the themes of his last stories with their marvelous and subtle balance between an unquestioned acceptance of what he and his world are and an acute awareness of what they might be and, indeed, in some respects at least once were.

Sometimes this balance expressed itself as comedy, a triumph of understanding which is genuinely amused over grim personal suffering, as it does in "Financing Finnegan" (1938), that generous and deserved tribute to Maxwell Perkins and Harold Ober. Occasionally

Fitzgerald invented a plot, in the old way, to embody this balance of feelings, or an aspect of it, as he does in " 'I Didn't Get Over' " (1936), or in "The Long Way Out" (1937), or in "Design in Plaster" (1939). But most characteristically he reduced plot in the usual sense to a minimum and made the tension of his feelings themselves the action. Something like this happens in "Afternoon of an Author" (1936), "The Lost Decade" (1939), and "News of Paris—Fifteen Years Ago" (1940). It is this balance of feelings also which gives the special quality they have to both the "Crack-Up" essays and *The Last Tycoon*.

In this way the lifelong character of his sensibility was able to realize itself fully again after the collapse of his health and his capacity to create in the mid-thirties, once more to find a place for the cool, detached observer in him and a place for the completely involved sufferer and to hold these two aspects of his understanding in a tension which is all the more alive because it is so quiet in tone and so casual, almost offhand, about its ironies.

It is possible to think of "Afternoon of an Author" as our final glimpse of the boy we first meet in "A Night at the Fair," and in a very real sense it is. But I think it is much more important to recognize that the complicated set of feelings embodied in "Afternoon of an Author" is the wisdom at which the gay and somewhat confused young man of "Who's Who—and Why" arrived, and that the power he can generate with a carefully placed noun and an adjective ("struck blind for a moment with the glow of his two thousand books") is the final refinement of style of the writer who had begun twenty-five years before with a lively but scattered account of the exact number of rejection slips that "were pinned in a frieze about my room."

It is possible, too, to think of "News of Paris—Fifteen Years Ago" as a kind of final vision of what the indirect knowledge of European culture and the direct experience of Europe itself had meant to Fitzgerald's generation and—since all generations of Americans must come to terms with these things—may in part mean to all Americans. It thus constitutes the final—and I think subtlest—version of what Fitzgerald had tried to grasp with his imagination in "Princeton," in "How to Live on Practically Nothing a Year," in "One Trip Abroad." The remarkable thing about "News of Paris—

Fifteen Years Ago" is the way it communicates, for all its clear and disenchanted judgment of its Americans in Paris, the enchantment of life which Fitzgerald could always understand and love, even if, like the hero of "Outside the Cabinet-Maker's," "he could never see or touch [it] any more himself."

PART I

A Night at the Fair

DURING 1928 Fitzgerald wrote nine stories about Basil Duke Lee. Eight of these were printed in *The Saturday Evening Post*. Fitzgerald published five of them in *Taps at Reveille*. This is the first in time of the other three that appeared in the *Post*, where it was printed July 21, 1928.

All the Basil stories are based very immediately on Fitzgerald's boyhood experience in St. Paul, on his career at Newman, and on his freshman life at Princeton. Their characters are modelled on Fitzgerald and his friends—in addition to Fitzgerald himself, who is of course the model for Basil, the important characters in this story are Cecil Reed, the model for Riply Buckner, and Reuben Warner, the model for Hubert Blair. The idea for this story is indicated by a note in Fitzgerald's Ledger under September, 1911: "Attended State fair and took chicken on roller-coaster."

But Fitzgerald remembered the experience of his boyhood with such minuteness because the experience was charged with feeling for him. This feeling, which constituted his sense of the value and significance of what had happened to him then, made these occasions memorable to him. The use of knowing the facts of his experience in which the idea for the story originated is that it allows us to see how his sense of their significance has transmuted actuality and made the personal experiences into the representative occasions of the young manhood of the American middle class.

THE TWO CITIES were separated only by a thin well-bridged river; their tails curling over the banks met and mingled, and at the juncture, under the jealous eye of each, lay, every fall, the State Fair. Because of this advantageous position, and because of the agricultural eminence of the state, the fair was one of the most magnificent in America. There were immense exhibits of grain, livestock and farming machinery; there were horse races and automobile races and, lately, aeroplanes that really left the ground; there was a tumultuous Midway with Coney Island thrillers to whirl you through space, and a whining, tinkling hoochie-coochie show. As a compromise between the serious and the trivial, a grand exhibition of fireworks, culminating in a representation of the Battle of Gettysburg, took place in the Grand Concourse every night.

At the late afternoon of a hot September day two boys of fifteen, somewhat replete with food and pop, and fatigued by eight hours of constant motion, issued from the Penny Arcade. The one with dark, handsome, eager eyes was, according to the cosmic inscription in his last year's Ancient History, "Basil Duke Lee, Holly Avenue, St. Paul, Minnesota, United States, North America, Western Hemisphere, the

World, the Universe." Though slightly shorter than his companion, he appeared taller, for he projected, so to speak, from short trousers, while Riply Buckner, Jr., had graduated into long ones the week before. This event, so simple and natural, was having a disrupting influence on the intimate friendship between them that had endured for several years.

During that time Basil, the imaginative member of the firm, had been the dominating partner, and the displacement effected by two feet of blue serge filled him with puzzled dismay—in fact, Riply Buckner had become noticeably indifferent to the pleasure of Basil's company in public. His own assumption of long trousers had seemed to promise a liberation from the restraints and inferiorities of boyhood, and the companionship of one who was, in token of his short pants, still a boy was an unwelcome reminder of how recent was his own metamorphosis. He scarcely admitted this to himself, but a certain shortness of temper with Basil, a certain tendency to belittle him with superior laughter, had been in evidence all afternoon. Basil felt the new difference keenly. In August a family conference had decided that even though he was going East to school, he was too small for long trousers. He had countered by growing an inch and a half in a fortnight, which added to his reputation for unreliability, but led him to hope that his mother might be persuaded, after all.

Coming out of the stuffy tent into the glow of sunset, the two boys hesitated, glancing up and down the crowded highway with expressions compounded of a certain ennui and a certain inarticulate yearning. They were unwilling to go home before it became necessary, yet they knew they had temporarily glutted their appetite for sights; they wanted a change in the tone, the motif, of the day. Near them was the parking space, as yet a modest yard; and as they lingered indecisively, their eyes were caught and held by a small car, red in color and slung at that proximity to the ground which indicated both speed of motion and speed of life. It was a Blatz Wildcat, and for the next five years it represented the ambition of several million American boys. Occupying it, in the posture of aloof exhaustion exacted by the sloping seat, was a blonde, gay, baby-faced girl.

The two boys stared. She bent upon them a single cool glance and then returned to her avocation of reclining in a Blatz Wildcat and looking haughtily at the sky. The two boys exchanged a glance, but made no move to go. They watched the girl—when they felt that their stares were noticeable they dropped their eyes and gazed at the car.

After several minutes a young man with a very pink face and pink hair, wearing a yellow suit and hat and drawing on yellow gloves, appeared and got into the car. There was a series of frightful explosions; then, with a measured tup-tup-tup from the open cut-out, insolent, percussive and thrilling as a drum, the car and the girl and the young man whom they had recognized as Speed Paxton slid smoothly away.

Basil and Riply turned and strolled back thoughtfully toward the Midway. They knew that Speed Paxton was dimly terrible—the wild and pampered son of a local brewer—but they envied him—to ride off into the sunset in such a chariot, into the very hush and mystery of night, beside him the mystery of that baby-faced girl. It was probably this envy that made them begin to shout when they perceived a tall youth of their own age issuing from a shooting gallery.

"Oh, El! Hey, El! Wait a minute!"

Elwood Leaming turned around and waited. He was the dissipated one among the nice boys of the town—he had drunk beer, he had learned from chauffeurs, he was already thin from too many cigarettes. As they greeted him eagerly, the hard, wise expression of a man of the world met them in his half-closed eyes.

"Hello, Rip. Put it there, Rip. Hello, Basil, old boy. Put it there."

"What you doing, El?" Riply asked.

"Nothing. What are you doing?"

"Nothing."

Elwood Leaming narrowed his eyes still further, seemed to give thought, and then made a decisive clicking sound with his teeth.

"Well, what do you say we pick something up?" he suggested. "I saw some pretty good stuff around here this afternoon."

Riply and Basil drew tense, secret breaths. A year before they had been shocked because Elwood went to the burlesque shows at the Star—now here he was holding the door open to his own speedy life.

The responsibility of his new maturity impelled Riply to appear most eager. "All right with me," he said heartily.

He looked at Basil.

"All right with me," mumbled Basil.

Riply laughed, more from nervousness than from derision. "Maybe you better grow up first, Basil." He looked at Elwood, seeking approval. "You better stick around till you get to be a man."

"Oh, dry up!" retorted Basil. "How long have you had yours? Just a week!"

But he realized that there was a gap separating him from these two, and it was with a sense of tagging them that he walked along beside.

Glancing from right to left with the expression of a keen and experienced frontiersman, Elwood Leaming led the way. Several pairs of strolling girls met his mature glance and smiled encouragingly, but he found them unsatisfactory—too fat, too plain or too hard. All at once their eyes fell upon two who sauntered along a little ahead of them, and they increased their pace, Elwood with confidence, Riply with its nervous counterfeit and Basil suddenly in the grip of wild excitement.

They were abreast of them. Basil's heart was in his throat. He looked away as he heard Elwood's voice.

"Hello, girls! How are you this evening?"

Would they call for the police? Would his mother and Riply's suddenly turn the corner?

"Hello, yourself, kiddo!"

"Where you going, girls?"

"Nowhere."

"Well, let's all go together."

Then all of them were standing in a group and Basil was relieved to find that they were only girls his own age, after all. They were pretty, with clear skins and red lips and maturely piled up hair. One he immediately liked better than the other—her voice was quieter and she was shy. Basil was glad when Elwood walked on with the bolder one, leaving him and Riply to follow with the other, behind.

The first lights of the evening were springing into pale existence; the afternoon crowd had thinned a little, and the lanes, empty of people, were heavy with the rich various smells of pop corn and peanuts, molasses and dust and cooking Wienerwurst and a not-unpleasant overtone of animals and hay. The Ferris wheel, pricked out now in lights, revolved leisurely through the dusk; a few empty cars of the roller coaster rattled overhead. The heat had blown off and there was the crisp stimulating excitement of Northern autumn in the air.

They walked. Basil felt that there was some way of talking to this girl, but he could manage nothing in the key of Elwood Leaming's intense and confidential manner to the girl ahead—as if he had inadvertently discovered a kinship of tastes and of hearts. So to save the progression from absolute silence—for Riply's contribution amounted only to an occasional burst of silly laughter—Basil pretended an interest in the sights they passed and kept up a sort of comment thereon.

"There's the six-legged calf. Have you seen it?"

"No, I haven't."

"There's where the man rides the motorcycle around. Did you go there?"

"No, I didn't."

"Look! They're beginning to fill the balloon. I wonder what time they start the fireworks."

"Have you been to the fireworks?"

"No, I'm going tomorrow night. Have you?"

"Yes, I been every night. My brother works there. He's one of them that helps set them off."

"Oh!"

He wondered if her brother cared that she had been picked up by strangers. He wondered even more if she felt as silly as he. It must be getting late, and he had promised to be home by half-past seven on pain of not being allowed out tomorrow night. He walked up beside Elwood.

"Hey, El," he asked, "where we going?"

Elwood turned to him and winked. "We're going around the Old Mill."

"Oh!"

Basil dropped back again—became aware that in his temporary absence Riply and the girl had linked arms. A twinge of jealousy went through him and he inspected the girl again and with more appreciation, finding her prettier than he had thought. Her eyes, dark and intimate, seemed to have wakened at the growing brilliance of the illumination overhead; there was the promise of excitement in them now, like the promise of the cooling night.

He considered taking her other arm, but it was too late; she and Riply were laughing together at something—rather, at nothing. She had asked him what he laughed at all the time and he had laughed again for an answer. Then they both laughed hilariously and sporadically together.

Basil looked disgustedly at Riply. "I never heard such a silly laugh in my life," he said indignantly.

"Didn't you?" chuckled Riply Buckner. "Didn't you, little boy?"

He bent double with laughter and the girl joined in. The words "little boy" had fallen on Basil like a jet of cold water. In his excitement he had forgotten something, as a cripple might forget his limp only to discover it when he began to run.

"You think you're so big!" he exclaimed. "Where'd you get the pants? Where'd you get the pants?" He tried to work this up with gusto and was about to add: "They're your father's pants," when he remembered that Riply's father, like his own, was dead.

The couple ahead reached the entrance to the Old Mill and waited for them. It was an off hour, and half a dozen scows bumped in the wooden offing, swayed by the mild tide of the artificial river. Elwood and his girl got into the front seat and he promptly put his arm around her. Basil helped the other girl into the rear seat, but, dispirited, he offered no resistance when Riply wedged in and sat down between.

They floated off, immediately entering upon a long echoing darkness. Somewhere far ahead a group in another boat were singing, their voices now remote and romantic, now nearer and yet more mysterious, as the canal doubled back and the boats passed close to each other with an invisible veil between.

The three boys yelled and called, Basil attempting by his vociferousness and variety to outdo Riply in the girl's eyes, but after a few moments there was no sound except his own voice and the continual bump-bump of the boat against the wooden sides, and he knew without looking that Riply had put his arm about the girl's shoulder.

They slid into a red glow—a stage set of hell, with grinning demons and lurid paper fires—he made out that Elwood and his girl sat cheek to cheek—then again into the darkness, with the gently lapping water and the passing of the singing boat now near, now far away. For a while Basil pretended that he was interested in this other boat, calling to them, commenting on their proximity. Then he discovered that the scow could be rocked and took to this poor amusement until Elwood Leaming turned around indignantly and cried:

"Hey! What are you trying to do?"

They came out finally to the entrance and the two couples broke apart. Basil jumped miserably ashore.

"Give us some more tickets," Riply cried. "We want to go around again."

"Not me," said Basil with elaborate indifference. "I have to go home."

Riply began to laugh in derision and triumph. The girl laughed too.

"Well, so long, little boy," Riply cried hilariously.

"Oh, shut up! So long, Elwood."

"So long, Basil."

The boat was already starting off; arms settled again about the girls' shoulders.

"So long, little boy!"

"So long, you big cow!" Basil cried. "Where'd you get the pants? Where'd you get the pants?"

But the boat had already disappeared into the dark mouth of the tunnel, leaving the echo of Riply's taunting laughter behind.

It is an ancient tradition that all boys are obsessed with the idea of being grown. This is because they occasionally give voice to their impatience with the restraints of youth, while those great stretches of time when they are more than content to be boys find expression in action and not in words. Sometimes Basil wanted to be just a little bit older, but no more. The question of long pants had not seemed vital to him—he wanted them, but as a costume they had no such romantic significance as, for example, a football suit or an officer's uniform, or even the silk hat and opera cape in which gentlemen burglars were wont to prowl the streets of New York by night.

But when he awoke next morning they were the most important necessity in his life. Without them he was cut off from his contemporaries, laughed at by a boy whom he had hitherto led. The actual fact that last night some chickens had preferred Riply to himself was of no importance in itself, but he was fiercely competitive and he resented being required to fight with one hand tied behind his back. He felt that parallel situations would occur at school, and that was unbearable. He approached his mother at breakfast in a state of wild excitement.

"Why, Basil," she protested in surprise, "I thought when we talked it over you didn't especially care."

"I've got to have them," he declared. "I'd rather be dead than go away to school without them."

"Well, there's no need of being silly."

"It's true—I'd rather be dead. If I can't have long trousers I don't see any use in my going away to school."

His emotion was such that the vision of his demise began actually to disturb his mother.

"Now stop that silly talk and come and eat your breakfast. You can go down and buy some at Barton Leigh's this morning."

Mollified, but still torn by the urgency of his desire, Basil strode up and down the room.

"A boy is simply helpless without them," he declared vehemently. The phrase pleased him and he amplified it. "A boy is simply and utterly helpless without them. I'd rather be dead than go away to school—"

"Basil, stop talking like that. Somebody has been teasing you about it."

"Nobody's been teasing me," he denied indignantly—"nobody at all."

After breakfast, the maid called him to the phone.

"This is Riply," said a tentative voice. Basil acknowledged the fact coldly. "You're not sore about last night, are you?" Riply asked.

"Me? No. Who said I was sore?"

"Nobody. Well, listen, you know about us going to the fireworks together tonight."

"Yes." Basil's voice was still cold.

"Well, one of those girls—the one Elwood had—has got a sister that's even nicer than she is, and she can come out tonight and you could have her. And we thought we could meet about eight, because the fireworks don't start till nine."

"What do?"

"Well, we could go on the Old Mill again. We went around three times more last night."

There was a moment's silence. Basil looked to see if his mother's door was closed.

"Did you kiss yours?" he demanded into the transmitter.

"Sure I did!" Over the wire came the ghost of a silly laugh. "Listen, El thinks he can get his auto. We could call for you at seven."

"All right," agreed Basil gruffly, and he added, "I'm going down and get some long pants this morning."

"Are you?" Again Basil detected ghostly laughter. "Well, you be ready at seven tonight."

Basil's uncle met him at Barton Leigh's clothing store at ten, and Basil felt a touch of guilt at having put his family to all this trouble and expense. On his uncle's advice, he decided finally on two suits— a heavy chocolate brown for every day and a dark blue for formal wear. There were certain alterations to be made but it was agreed that one of the suits was to be delivered without fail that afternoon.

His momentary contriteness at having been so expensive made him save carfare by walking home from downtown. Passing along Crest Avenue, he paused speculatively to vault the high hydrant in front of the Van Schellinger house, wondering if one did such things in long trousers and if he would ever do it again. He was impelled to leap it two or three times as a sort of ceremonial farewell, and was so engaged when the Van Schellinger limousine turned into the drive and stopped at the front door.

"Oh, Basil," a voice called.

A fresh delicate face, half buried under a mass of almost white curls, was turned toward him from the granite portico of the city's second largest mansion.

"Hello, Gladys."

"Come here a minute, Basil."

He obeyed. Gladys Van Schellinger was a year younger than Basil —a tranquil, carefully nurtured girl who, so local tradition had it, was being brought up to marry in the East. She had a governess and always played with a certain few girls at her house or theirs, and was not allowed the casual freedom of children in a Midwestern city. She was never present at such rendezvous as the Whartons' yard, where the others played games in the afternoons.

"Basil, I wanted to ask you something—are you going to the State Fair tonight?"

"Why, yes, I am."

"Well, wouldn't you like to come and sit in our box and watch the fireworks?"

Momentarily he considered the matter. He wanted to accept, but he was mysteriously impelled to refuse—to forgo a pleasure in order to pursue a quest that in cold logic did not interest him at all.

"I can't. I'm awfully sorry."

A shadow of discontent crossed Gladys' face. "Oh? Well, come and see me sometime soon, Basil. In a few weeks I'm going East to school."

He walked on up the street in a state of dissatisfaction. Gladys Van Schellinger had never been his girl, nor indeed anyone's girl, but the fact that they were starting away to school at the same time gave him a feeling of kinship for her—as if they had been selected for the glamorous adventure of the East, chosen together for a high destiny that transcended the fact that she was rich and he was only comfortable. He was sorry that he could not sit with her in her box tonight.

By three o'clock, Basil, reading the Crimson Sweater up in his room, began giving attentive ear to every ring at the bell. He would go to the head of the stairs, lean over and call, "Hilda, was that a package for me?" And at four, dissatisfied with her indifference, her lack of feeling for important things, her slowness in going to and returning from the door, he moved downstairs and began attending to it himself. But nothing came. He phoned Barton Leigh's and was told by a busy clerk: "You'll get that suit. I'll guarantee that you'll get that suit." But he did not believe in the clerk's honor and he moved out on the porch and watched for Barton Leigh's delivery wagon.

His mother came home at five. "There were probably more alterations than they thought," she suggested helpfully. "You'll probably get it tomorrow morning."

"Tomorrow morning!" he exclaimed incredulously. "I've got to have that suit tonight."

"Well, I wouldn't be too disappointed if I were you, Basil. The stores all close at half-past five."

Basil took one agitated look up and down Holly Avenue. Then he got his cap and started on a run for the street car at the corner. A moment later a cautious afterthought caused him to retrace his steps with equal rapidity.

"If they get here, keep them for me," he instructed his mother—a man who thought of everything.

"All right," she promised dryly, "I will."

It was later than he thought. He had to wait for a trolley, and when he reached Barton Leigh's he saw with horror that the doors were locked and the blinds drawn. He intercepted a last clerk coming out and explained vehemently that he had to have his suit to night. The clerk knew nothing about the matter. . . . Was Basil Mr. Schwartze?

No, Basil was not Mr. Schwartze. After a vague argument wherein he tried to convince the clerk that whoever promised him the suit should be fired, Basil went dispiritedly home.

He would not go to the fair without his suit—he would not go at all. He would sit at home and luckier boys would go adventuring along its Great White Way. Mysterious girls, young and reckless, would glide with them through the enchanted darkness of the Old Mill, but because of the stupidity, selfishness and dishonesty of a clerk in a clothing store he would not be there. In a day or so the fair would be over—forever—those girls, of all living girls the most intangible, the most desirable, that sister, said to be nicest of all— would be lost out of his life. They would ride off in Blatz Wildcats into the moonlight without Basil having kissed them. No, all his life—though he would lose the clerk his position: "You see now what your act did to me"—he would look back with infinite regret upon that irretrievable hour. Like most of us, he was unable to perceive that he would have any desires in the future equivalent to those that possessed him now.

He reached home; the package had not arrived. He moped dismally about the house, consenting at half-past six to sit silently at dinner with his mother, his elbows on the table.

"Haven't you any appetite, Basil?"

"No, thanks," he said absently, under the impression he had been offered something.

"You're not going away to school for two more weeks. Why should it matter—"

"Oh, that isn't the reason I can't eat. I had a sort of headache all afternoon."

Toward the end of the meal his eye focused abstractedly on some slices of angel cake; with the air of a somnambulist, he ate three.

At seven he heard the sounds that should have ushered in a night of romantic excitement.

The Leaming car stopped outside, and a moment later Riply Buckner rang the bell. Basil rose gloomily.

"I'll go," he said to Hilda. And then to his mother, with vague impersonal reproach, "Excuse me a minute. I just want to tell them I can't go to the fair tonight."

"But of course you can go, Basil. Don't be silly. Just because—"

He scarcely heard her. Opening the door, he faced Riply on the steps. Beyond was the Leaming limousine, an old high car, quivering in silhouette against the harvest moon.

Clop-clop-clop! Up the street came the Barton Leigh delivery wagon. Clop-clop! A man jumped out, dumped an iron anchor to the pavement, hurried along the street, turned away, turned back again, came toward them with a long square box in his hand.

"You'll have to wait a minute," Basil was calling wildly. "It can't make any difference. I'll dress in the library. Look here, if you're a friend of mine, you'll wait a minute." He stepped out on the porch. "Hey, El, I've just got my—got to change my clothes. You can wait a minute, can't you?"

The spark of a cigarette flushed in the darkness as El spoke to the chauffeur; the quivering car came to rest with a sigh and the skies filled suddenly with stars.

Once again the fair—but differing from the fair of the afternoon as a girl in the daytime differs from her radiant presentation of herself at night. The substance of the cardboard booths and plaster palaces was gone, the forms remained. Outlined in lights, these forms suggested things more mysterious and entrancing than themselves, and the people strolling along the network of little Broadways shared this quality, as their pale faces singly and in clusters broke the half darkness.

The boys hurried to their rendezvous, finding the girls in the deep shadow of the Temple of Wheat. Their forms had scarcely merged into a group when Basil became aware that something was wrong. In growing apprehension, he glanced from face to face and, as the introductions were made, he realized the appalling truth—the younger sister was, in point of fact, a fright, squat and dingy, with a bad complexion brooding behind a mask of cheap pink powder and a shapeless mouth that tried ceaselessly to torture itself into the mold of charm.

In a daze he heard Riply's girl say, "I don't know whether I ought to go with you. I had a sort of date with another fellow I met this afternoon."

Fidgeting, she looked up and down the street, while Riply, in astonishment and dismay, tried to take her arm.

"Come on," he urged. "Didn't I have a date with you first?"

"But I didn't know whether you'd come or not," she said perversely.

Elwood and the two sisters added their entreaties.

"Maybe I could go on the Ferris wheel," she said grudgingly, "but not the Old Mill. This fellow would be sore."

Riply's confidence reeled with the blow; his mouth fell ajar, his hand desperately pawed her arm. Basil stood glancing now with agonized politeness at his own girl, now at the others, with an expression of infinite reproach. Elwood alone was successful and content.

"Let's go on the Ferris wheel," he said impatiently. "We can't stand here all night."

At the ticket booth the recalcitrant Olive hesitated once more, frowning and glancing about as if she still hoped Riply's rival would appear.

But when the swooping cars came to rest she let herself be persuaded in, and the three couples, with their troubles, were hoisted slowly into the air.

As the car rose, following the imagined curve of the sky, it occurred to Basil how much he would have enjoyed it in other company, or even alone, the fair twinkling beneath him with new variety, the velvet quality of the darkness that is on the edge of light and is barely permeated by its last attenuations. But he was unable to hurt anyone whom he thought of as an inferior. After a minute he turned to the girl beside him.

"Do you live in St. Paul or Minneapolis?" he inquired formally.

"St. Paul. I go to Number 7 School." Suddenly she moved closer. "I bet you're not so slow," she encouraged him.

He put his arm around her shoulder and found it warm. Again they reached the top of the wheel and the sky stretched out overhead, again they lapsed down through gusts of music from remote calliopes. Keeping his eyes turned carefully away, Basil pressed her to him, and as they rose again into darkness, leaned and kissed her cheek.

The significance of the contact stirred him, but out of the corner of his eye he saw her face—he was thankful when a gong struck below and the machine settled slowly to rest.

The three couples were scarcely reunited outside when Olive uttered a yelp of excitement.

"There he is!" she cried. "That Bill Jones I met this afternoon—that I had the date with."

A youth of their own age was approaching, stepping like a circus pony and twirling, with the deftness of a drum major, a small rattan cane. Under the cautious alias, the three boys recognized a friend and contemporary—none other than the fascinating Hubert Blair.

He came nearer. He greeted them all with a friendly chuckle. He took off his cap, spun it, dropped it, caught it, set it jauntily on the side of his head.

"You're a nice one," he said to Olive. "I waited here fifteen minutes this evening."

He pretended to belabor her with the cane; she giggled with delight. Hubert Blair possessed the exact tone that all girls of fourteen, and a somewhat cruder type of grown women, find irresistible. He was a gymnastic virtuoso and his figure was in constant graceful motion; he had a jaunty piquant nose, a disarming laugh and a shrewd talent for flattery. When he took a piece of toffee from his pocket, placed it on his forehead, shook it off and caught it in his mouth, it was obvious to any disinterested observer that Riply was destined to see no more of Olive that night.

So fascinated were the group that they failed to see Basil's eyes brighten with a ray of hope, his feet take four quick steps backward with all the guile of a gentleman burglar, his torso writhe through the parting of a tent wall into the deserted premises of the Harvester and Tractor Show. Once safe, Basil's tensity relaxed, and as he considered Riply's unconsciousness of the responsibilities presently to devolve upon him, he bent double with hilarious laughter in the darkness.

Ten minutes later, in a remote part of the fairgrounds, a youth made his way briskly and cautiously toward the fireworks exhibit, swinging as he walked a recently purchased rattan cane. Several girls eyed him with interest, but he passed them haughtily; he was weary of people for a brief moment—a moment which he had almost mislaid in the bustle of life—he was enjoying his long pants.

He bought a bleacher seat and followed the crowd around the race track, seeking his section. A few Union troops were moving cannon about in preparation for the Battle of Gettysburg, and, stopping to watch them, he was hailed by Gladys Van Schellinger from the box behind.

"Oh, Basil, don't you want to come and sit with us?"

He turned about and was absorbed. Basil exchanged courtesies with Mr. and Mrs. Van Schellinger and he was affably introduced to several other people as "Alice Riley's boy," and a chair was placed for him beside Gladys in front.

"Oh, Basil," she whispered, glowing at him, "isn't this fun?"

Distinctly, it was. He felt a vast wave of virtue surge through him. How anyone could have preferred the society of those common girls was at this moment incomprehensible.

"Basil, won't it be fun to go East? Maybe we'll be on the same train."

"I can hardly wait," he agreed gravely. "I've got on long pants. I had to have them to go away to school."

One of the ladies in the box leaned toward him. "I know your mother very well," she said. "And I know another friend of yours. I'm Riply Buckner's aunt."

"Oh, yes!"

"Riply's such a nice boy," beamed Mrs. Van Schillinger.

And then, as if the mention of his name had evoked him, Riply Buckner came suddenly into sight. Along the now empty and brightly illuminated race track came a short but monstrous procession, a sort of Lilliputian burlesque of the wild gay life. At its head marched Hubert Blair and Olive, Hubert prancing and twirling his cane like a drum major to the accompaniment of her appreciative screams of laughter. Next followed Elwood Leaming and his young lady, leaning so close together that they walked with difficulty, apparently wrapped in each other's arms. And bringing up the rear without glory were Riply Buckner and Basil's late companion, rivaling Olive in exhibitionist sound.

Fascinated, Basil stared at Riply, the expression of whose face was curiously mixed. At moments he would join in the general tone of the parade with silly guffaw, at others a pained expression would flit across his face, as if he doubted that, after all, the evening was a success.

The procession was attracting considerable notice—so much that not even Riply was aware of the particular attention focused upon him from this box, though he passed by it four feet away. He was out of hearing when a curious rustling sigh passed over its inhabitants and a series of discreet whispers began.

"What funny girls," Gladys said. "Was that first boy Hubert Blair?"

"Yes." Basil was listening to a fragment of conversation behind: "His mother will certainly hear of this in the morning."

As long as Riply had been in sight, Basil had been in an agony of shame for him, but now a new wave of virtue, even stronger than the first, swept over him. His memory of the incident would have reached actual happiness, save for the fact that Riply's mother might not let him go away to school. And a few minutes later, even that seemed endurable. Yet Basil was not a mean boy. The natural cruelty of his species toward the doomed was not yet disguised by hypocrisy—that was all.

In a burst of glory, to the alternate strains of Dixie and The Star-Spangled Banner, the Battle of Gettysburg ended. Outside by the waiting cars, Basil, on a sudden impulse, went up to Riply's aunt.

"I think it would be sort of a—a mistake to tell Riply's mother. He didn't do any harm. He—"

Annoyed by the event of the evening, she turned on him cool, patronizing eyes.

"I shall do as I think best," she said briefly.

He frowned. Then he turned and got into the Van Schellinger limousine.

Sitting beside Gladys in the little seats, he loved her suddenly. His hand swung gently against hers from time to time and he felt the warm bond that they were both going away to school tightened around them and pulling them together.

"Can't you come and see me tomorrow?" she urged him. "Mother's going to be away and she says I can have anybody I like."

"All right."

As the car slowed up for Basil's house, she leaned toward him swiftly. "Basil—"

He waited. Her breath was warm on his cheek. He wanted her to hurry, or, when the engine stopped, her parents, dozing in back, might hear what she said. She seemed beautiful to him then; that vague unexciting quality about her was more than compensated for by her exquisite delicacy, the fine luxury of her life.

"Basil—Basil, when you come tomorrow, will you bring that Hubert Blair?"

The chauffeur opened the door and Mr. and Mrs. Van Schellinger woke up with a start. When the car had driven off, Basil stood looking after it thoughtfully until it turned the corner of the street.

Forging Ahead

THIS story was printed in *The Saturday Evening Post*, March 30, 1929. If we can trust to the facts of Fitzgerald's life to guide us, as we probably can, Basil is two years older than he was in "A Night at the Fair." Fitzgerald was fifteen when he went to Newman; he spent two years there and entered Princeton as a freshman in September, 1913; he became seventeen the twenty-fourth of that month. Basil will be seventeen in September, when he starts off for Yale; he was fifteen the summer of "A Night at the Fair," the summer before he entered St. Regis.

Like "A Night at the Fair," this story had as its starting point an actual experience which is described in Fitzgerald's Ledger; even so minor a detail as Basil's job at the Great Northern car shops is based on actual experience. Again, however, it is the movement of feelings, realistic and fantastic, and the way they are placed in the context of a society, that give the story its force. Among other things, the ethos of rugged individualism, as it was made into a myth by Horatio Alger and others, is being judged here—or, at least, placed, for the story does not really make the sale of the Third Street Block overtly ironic. At most it allows Eddie Parmelee to describe the way money is actually made and then leaves us to judge for ourselves the extent to which Basil has forged ahead by his own initiative.

With the appearance of Minnie Bibble the war of the sexes begins in earnest for Basil. It reaches its climax in "Basil and Cleopatra."

BASIL DUKE LEE and Riply Buckner, Jr., sat on the Lees' front steps in the regretful gold of a late summer afternoon. Inside the house the telephone sang out with mysterious promise.

"I thought you were going home," Basil said.

"I thought you were."

"I am."

"So am I."

"Well, why don't you go, then?"

"Why don't you, then?"

"I am."

They laughed, ending with yawning gurgles that were not laughed out but sucked in. As the telephone rang again, Basil got to his feet.

"I've got to study trig before dinner."

"Are you honestly going to Yale this fall?" demanded Riply skeptically.

"Yes."

"Everybody says you're foolish to go at sixteen."

"I'll be seventeen in September. So long. I'll call you up tonight."

Basil heard his mother at the upstairs telephone and he was immediately aware of distress in her voice.

"Yes. . . . Isn't that awful, Everett! . . . Yes. . . . Oh-h my!" After a minute he gathered that it was only the usual worry about business and went on into the kitchen for refreshments. Returning, he met his mother hurrying downstairs. She was blinking rapidly and her hat was on backward—characteristic testimony to her excitement.

"I've got to go over to your grandfather's."

"What's the matter, mother?"

"Uncle Everett thinks we've lost a lot of money."

"How much?" he asked, startled.

"Twenty-two thousand dollars apiece. But we're not sure."

She went out.

"Twenty-two thousand dollars!" he repeated in an awed whisper.

His ideas of money were vague and somewhat debonair, but he had noticed that at family dinners the immemorial discussion as to whether the Third Street block would be sold to the railroads had given place to anxious talk of Western Public Utilities. At half-past six his mother telephoned for him to have his dinner, and with growing uneasiness he sat alone at the table, undistracted by The Mississippi Bubble, open beside his plate. She came in at seven, distraught and miserable, and dropping down at the table, gave him his first exact information about finance—she and her father and her brother Everett had lost something more than eighty thousand dollars. She was in a panic and she looked wildly around the dining room as if money were slipping away even here, and she wanted to retrench at once.

"I've got to stop selling securities or we won't have anything," she declared. "This leaves us only three thousand a year—do you realize that, Basil? I don't see how I can possibly afford to send you to Yale."

His heart tumbled into his stomach; the future, always glowing like a comfortable beacon ahead of him, flared up in glory and went out. His mother shivered, and then emphatically shook her head.

"You'll just have to make up your mind to go to the state university."

"Gosh!" Basil said.

Sorry for his shocked, rigid face, she yet spoke somewhat sharply, as people will with a bitter refusal to convey.

"I feel terribly about it—your father wanted you to go to Yale. But everyone says that, with clothes and railroad fare, I can count on it costing two thousand a year. Your grandfather helped me to send you to St. Regis School, but he always thought you ought to finish at the state university."

After she went distractedly upstairs with a cup of tea, Basil sat thinking in the dark parlor. For the present the loss meant only one thing to him—he wasn't going to Yale after all. The sentence itself, divorced from its meaning, overwhelmed him, so many times had he announced casually, "I'm going to Yale," but gradually he realized how many friendly and familiar dreams had been swept away. Yale was the faraway East, that he had loved with a vast nostalgia since he had first read books about great cities. Beyond the dreary railroad stations of Chicago and the night fires of Pittsburgh, back in the old states, something went on that made his heart beat fast with excitement. He was attuned to the vast, breathless bustle of New York, to the metropolitan days and nights that were tense as singing wires. Nothing needed to be imagined there, for it was all the very stuff of romance—life was as vivid and satisfactory as in books and dreams.

But first, as a sort of gateway to that deeper, richer life, there was Yale. The name evoked the memory of a heroic team backed up against its own impassable goal in the crisp November twilight, and later, of half a dozen immaculate noblemen with opera hats and canes standing at the Manhattan Hotel bar. And tangled up with its triumphs and rewards, its struggles and glories, the vision of the inevitable, incomparable girl.

Well, then, why not work his way through Yale? In a moment the idea had become a reality. He began walking rapidly up and down the room, declaring half aloud, "Of course, that's the thing to do." Rushing upstairs, he knocked at his mother's door and announced in the inspired voice of a prophet: "Mother, I know what I'm going to do! I'm going to work my way through Yale."

He sat down on her bed and she considered uncertainly. The men in her family had not been resourceful for several generations, and the idea startled her.

"It doesn't seem to me you're a boy who likes to work," she said. "Besides, boys who work their way through college have scholarships and prizes, and you've never been much of a student."

He was annoyed. He was ready for Yale a year ahead of his age and her reproach seemed unfair.

"What would you work at?" she said.

"Take care of furnaces," said Basil promptly. "And shovel snow off sidewalks. I think they mostly do that—and tutor people. You could let me have as much money as it would take to go to the state university?"

"We'll have to think it over."

"Well, don't you worry about anything," he said emphatically, "because my earning my way through Yale will really make up for the money you've lost, almost."

"Why don't you start by finding something to do this summer?"

"I'll get a job tomorrow. Maybe I can pile up enough so you won't have to help me. Good night, Mother."

Up in his room he paused only to thunder grimly to the mirror that he was going to work his way through Yale, and going to his bookcase, took down half a dozen dusty volumes of Horatio Alger, unopened for years. Then, much as a postwar young man might consult the George Washington Condensed Business Course, he sat at his desk and slowly began to turn the pages of Bound to Rise.

Two days later, after being insulted by the doorkeepers, office boys and telephone girls of the Press, the Evening News, the Socialist Gazette and a green scandal sheet called the Courier, and assured that no one wanted a reporter practically seventeen, after enduring every ignominy prepared for a young man in a free country trying to work his way through Yale, Basil Duke Lee, too "stuck-up" to apply to the parents of his friends, got a position with the railroad, through Eddie Parmelee, who lived across the way.

At 6.30 the following morning, carrying his lunch, and a new suit of overalls that had cost four dollars, he strode self-consciously into the Great Northern car shops. It was like entering a new school, except that no one showed any interest in him or asked him if he was going out for the team. He punched a time clock, which affected him strangely, and without even an admonition from the foreman to "go in and win," was put to carrying boards for the top of a car.

Twelve o'clock arrived; nothing had happened. The sun was blazing hot and his hands and back were sore, but no real events had ruffled the dull surface of the morning. The president's little daughter had not come by, dragged by a runaway horse; not even a superintendent had walked through the yard and singled him out with an approving eye. Undismayed, he toiled on—you couldn't expect much the first morning.

He and Eddie Parmelee ate their lunches together. For several years Eddie had worked here in vacations; he was sending himself to the state university this fall. He shook his head doubtfully over the idea of Basil's earning his way through Yale.

"Here's what you ought to do," he said: "You borrow two thousand dollars from your mother and buy twenty shares in Ware Plow and Tractor. Then go to a bank and borrow two thousand more with those shares for collateral, and with that two thousand buy twenty more shares. Then you sit on your back for a year, and after that you won't have to think about earning your way through Yale."

"I don't think mother would give me two thousand dollars."

"Well, anyhow, that's what I'd do."

If the morning had been uneventful, the afternoon was distinguished by an incident of some unpleasantness. Basil had risen a little, having been requested to mount to the top of a freight car and help nail the boards he had carried in the morning. He found that nailing nails into a board was more highly technical than nailing tacks into a wall, but he considered that he was progressing satisfactorily when an angry voice hailed him from below:

"Hey, you! Get up!"

He looked down. A foreman stood there, unpleasantly red in the face.

"Yes, you in the new suit. Get up!"

Basil looked about to see if someone was lying down, but the two sullen hunyaks seemed to be hard at work and it grew on him that he was indeed being addressed.

"I beg your pardon, sir," he said.

"Get up on your knees or get out! What the h—— do you think this is?"

He had been sitting down as he nailed, and apparently the foreman thought that he was loafing. After another look at the foreman, he suppressed the explanation that he felt steadier sitting down and decided to just let it go. There were probably no railroad shops at Yale; yet, he remembered with a pang the ominous name, New York, New Haven and Hartford.

The third morning, just as he had become aware that his overalls were not where he had hung them in the shop, it was announced that all men of less than six months' service were to be laid off. Basil received four dollars and lost his overalls. Learning that nails are driven from a kneeling position had cost him only carfare.

In a large old-fashioned house in the old section of the city lived Basil's great-uncle, Benjamin Reilly, and there Basil presented himself that evening. It was a last resort—Benjamin Reilly and Basil's grandfather were brothers and they had not spoken for twenty years.

He was received in the living room by the small, dumpy old man whose inscrutable face was hidden behind a white poodle beard. Behind him stood a woman of forty, his wife of six months, and her daughter, a girl of fifteen. Basil's branch of the family had not been invited to the wedding, and he had never seen these two additions before.

"I thought I'd come down and see you, Uncle Ben," he said with some embarrassment.

There was a certain amount of silence.

"Your mother well?" asked the old man.

"Oh, yes, thank you."

Mr. Reilly waited. Mrs. Reilly spoke to her daughter, who threw a curious glance at Basil and reluctantly left the room. Her mother made the old man sit down.

Out of sheer embarrassment Basil came to the point. He wanted a summer job in the Reilly Wholesale Drug Company.

His uncle fidgeted for a minute and then replied that there were no positions open.

"Oh."

"It might be different if you wanted a permanent place, but you say you want to go to Yale." He said this with some irony of his own, and glanced at his wife.

"Why, yes," said Basil. "That's really why I want the job."

"Your mother can't afford to send you, eh?" The note of pleasure in his voice was unmistakable. "Spent all her money?"

"Oh, no," answered Basil quickly. "She's going to help me."

To his surprise, aid came from an unpromising quarter. Mrs. Reilly suddenly bent and whispered in her husband's ear, whereupon the old man nodded and said aloud:

"I'll think about it, Basil. You go in there."

And his wife repeated: "We'll think about it. You go in the library with Rhoda while Mr. Reilly looks up and sees."

The door of the library closed behind him and he was alone with Rhoda, a square-chinned, decided girl with fleshy white arms and a white dress that reminded Basil domestically of the lacy pants that blew among the laundry in the yard. Puzzled by his uncle's change of front, he eyed her abstractedly for a moment.

"I guess you're my cousin," said Rhoda, closing her book, which he saw was The Little Colonel, Maid of Honor.

"Yes," he admitted.

"I heard about you from somebody." The implication was that her information was not flattering.

"From who?"

"A girl named Elaine Washmer."

"Elaine Washmer!" His tone dismissed the name scornfully. "That girl!"

"She's my best friend." He made no reply. "She said you thought you were wonderful."

Young people do not perceive at once that the giver of wounds is the enemy and the quoted tattle merely the arrow. His heart smoldered with wrath at Elaine Washmer.

"I don't know many kids here," said the girl, in a less aggressive key. "We've only been here six months. I never saw such a stuck-up bunch."

"Oh, I don't think so," he protested. "Where did you live before?"

"Sioux City. All the kids have much more fun in Sioux City."

Mrs. Reilly opened the door and called Basil back into the living room. The old man was again on his feet.

"Come down tomorrow morning and I'll find you something," he said.

"And why don't you have dinner with us tomorrow night?" added Mrs. Reilly, with a cordiality wherein an adult might have detected disingenuous purpose.

"Why, thank you very much."

His heart, buoyant with gratitude, had scarcely carried him out the door before Mrs. Reilly laughed shortly and called in her daughter.

"Now we'll see if you don't get around a little more," she announced. "When was it you said they had those dances?"

"Thursdays at the College Club and Saturdays at the Lake Club," said Rhoda promptly.

"Well, if this young man wants to hold the position your father has given him, you'll go to them all the rest of the summer."

Arbitrary groups formed by the hazards of money or geography may be sufficiently quarrelsome and dull, but for sheer unpleasantness the condition of young people who have been thrust together by a common unpopularity can be compared only with that of prisoners herded in a cell. In Basil's eyes the guests at the little dinner the following night were a collection of cripples. Lewis and Hector Crum, dullard cousins who were tolerable only to each other; Sidney Rosen, rich but awful; ugly Mary Haupt, Elaine Washmer, and Betty Geer, who reminded Basil of a cruel parody they had once sung to the tune of Jungle Town:

> *Down below the hill*
> *There lives a pill*
> *That makes me ill,*
>   *And her name is Betty Geer.*
>   *We had better stop right here. . . .*
> *She's so fat,*
> *She looks just like a cat,*
> *And she's the queen of pills.*

Moreover, they resented Basil, who was presumed to be "stuck-up," and walking home afterward, he felt dreary and vaguely exploited. Of course, he was grateful to Mrs. Reilly for her kindness, yet he couldn't help wondering if a cleverer boy couldn't have got out of taking Rhoda to the Lake Club next Saturday night. The proposal had caught him unaware; but when he was similarly trapped the following week, and the week after that, he began to realize the situation. It was a part of his job, and he accepted it grimly, unable, nevertheless, to understand how such a bad dancer and so unsociable a person should want to go where she was obviously a burden. "Why doesn't she just sit at home and read a book," he thought disgustedly, "or go away somewhere—or sew?"

It was one Saturday afternoon while he watched a tennis tournament and felt the unwelcome duty of the evening creep up on him, that he found himself suddenly fascinated by a girl's face a few yards away. His heart leaped into his throat and the blood in his pulse beat with excitement; and then, when the crowd rose to go, he saw to his astonishment that he had been staring at a child ten years old. He looked away, oddly disappointed; after a moment he looked back again. The lovely, self-conscious face suggested a train of thought and sensation that he could not identify. As he passed on, forgoing a vague intention of discovering the child's identity, there was beauty suddenly all around him in the afternoon; he could hear its unmistakable whisper, its never-inadequate, never-failing promise of happiness. "Tomorrow—one day soon now—this fall—maybe tonight." Irresistibly compelled to express himself, he sat down and tried to write to a girl in New York. His words were stilted and the girl seemed cold and far away. The real image on his mind, the force that had propelled him into this state of yearning, was the face of the little girl seen that afternoon.

When he arrived with Rhoda Sinclair at the Lake Club that night, he immediately cast a quick look around to see what boys were present who were indebted to Rhoda or else within his own sphere of influence. This was just before cutting-in arrived, and ordinarily he was able to dispose of half a dozen dances in advance, but tonight an older crowd was in evidence and the situation was unpromising. However, as Rhoda emerged from the dressing room he saw Bill Kampf and thankfully bore down upon him.

"Hello, old boy," he said, exuding personal good will. "How about dancing once with Rhoda tonight?"

"Can't," Bill answered briskly. "We've got people visiting us. Didn't you know?"

"Well, why couldn't we swap a dance anyhow?"

Bill looked at him in surprise.

"I thought you knew," he exclaimed. "Erminie's here. She's been talking about you all afternoon."

"Erminie Bibble!"

"Yes. And her father and mother and her kid sister. Got here this morning."

Now, indeed, the emotion of two hours before bubbled up in Basil's blood, but this time he knew why. It was the little sister of Erminie Gilbert Labouisse Bibble whose strangely familiar face had so attracted him. As his mind swung sharply back to a long afternoon on the Kampfs' veranda at the lake, ages ago, a year ago, a real voice rang in his ear, "Basil!" and a sparkling little beauty of fifteen came up to him with a fine burst of hurry, taking his hand as though she was stepping into the circle of his arm.

"Basil, I'm so glad!" Her voice was husky with pleasure, though she was at the age when pleasure usually hides behind grins and mumbles. It was Basil who was awkward and embarrassed, despite the intention of his heart. He was a little relieved when Bill Kampf, more conscious of his lovely cousin than he had been a year ago, led her out on the floor.

"Who was that?" Rhoda demanded, as he returned in a daze. "I never saw her around."

"Just a girl." He scarcely knew what he was saying.

"Well, I know that. What's her name?"

"Minnie Bibble, from New Orleans."

"She certainly looks conceited. I never saw anybody so affected in my life."

"Hush!" Basil protested involuntarily. "Let's dance."

It was a long hour before Basil was relieved by Hector Crum, and then several dances passed before he could get possession of Minnie, who was now the center of a moving whirl. But she made it up to him by pressing his hand and drawing him out to a veranda which overhung the dark lake.

"It's about time," she whispered. With a sort of instinct she found the darkest corner. "I might have known you'd have another crush."

"I haven't," he insisted in horror. "That's a sort of a cousin of mine."

"I always knew you were fickle. But I didn't think you'd forget me so soon."

She had wriggled up until she was touching him. Her eyes, floating into his, said, What does it matter? We're alone.

In a curious panic he jumped to his feet. He couldn't possibly kiss her like this—right at once. It was all so different and older than a year ago. He was too excited to do more than walk up and down and say, "Gosh, I certainly am glad to see you," supplementing this unoriginal statement with an artificial laugh.

Already mature in poise, she tried to soothe him: "Basil, come and sit down!"

"I'll be all right," he gasped, as if he had just fainted. "I'm a little fussed, that's all."

Again he contributed what, even to his pounding ears, sounded like a silly laugh.

"I'll be here three weeks. Won't it be fun?" And she added, with warm emphasis: "Do you remember on Bill's veranda that afternoon?"

All he could find to answer was: "I work now in the afternoon."

"You can come out in the evenings, Basil. It's only half an hour in a car."

"I haven't got a car."

"I mean you can get your family's car."

"It's an electric."

She waited patiently. He was still romantic to her—handsome, incalculable, a little sad.

"I saw your sister," he blurted out. Beginning with that, he might bridge this perverse and intolerable reverence she inspired. "She certainly looks like you."

"Does she?"

"It was wonderful," he said. "Wonderful! Let me tell you—"

"Yes, do." She folded her hands expectantly in her lap.

"Well, this afternoon—"

The music had stopped and started several times. Now, in an intermission, there was the sound of determined footsteps on the veranda, and Basil looked up to find Rhoda and Hector Crum.

"I got to go home, Basil," squeaked Hector in his changing voice. "Here's Rhoda."

Take Rhoda out to the dock and push her in the lake. But only Basil's mind said this; his body stood up politely.

"I didn't know where you were, Basil," said Rhoda in an aggrieved tone. "Why didn't you come back?"

"I was just coming." His voice trembled a little as he turned to Minnie. "Shall I find your partner for you?"

"Oh, don't bother," said Minnie. She was not angry, but she was somewhat astonished. She could not be expected to guess that the young man walking away from her so submissively was at the moment employed in working his way through Yale.

From the first, Basil's grandfather, who had once been a regent at the state university, wanted him to give up the idea of Yale, and now his mother, picturing him hungry and ragged in a garret, adjoined her persuasions. The sum on which he could count from her was far below the necessary minimum, and although he stubbornly refused to consider defeat, he consented, "just in case anything happened," to register at the university for the coming year.

In the administration building he ran into Eddie Parmelee, who introduced his companion, a small, enthusiastic Japanese.

"Well, well," said Eddie. "So you've given up Yale!"

"I given up Yale," put in Mr. Utsonomia, surprisingly. "Oh, yes, long time I given up Yale." He broke into enthusiastic laughter. "Oh, sure. Oh, yes."

"Mr. Utsonomia's a Japanese," explained Eddie, winking. "He's a sub-freshman too."

"Yes, I given up Harvard, Princeton too," continued Mr. Utsonomia. "They give me choice back in my country. I choose here."

"You did?" said Basil, almost indignantly.

"Sure, more strong here. More peasants come, with strength and odor of ground."

Basil stared at him. "You like that?" he asked incredulously.

Utsonomia nodded. "Here I get to know real American peoples. Girls too. Yale got only boys."

"But they haven't got college spirit here," explained Basil patiently.

Utsonomia looked blankly at Eddie.

"Rah-rah!" elucidated Eddie, waving his arms. "Rah-rah-rah! You know."

"Besides, the girls here—" began Basil, and stopped.

"You know girls here?" grinned Utsonomia.

"No, I don't know them," said Basil firmly. "But I know they're not like the girls that you'd meet down at the Yale proms. I don't think they even have proms here. I don't mean the girls aren't all right, but they're just not like the ones at Yale. They're just coeds."

"I hear you got a crush on Rhoda Sinclair," said Eddie.

"Yes, I have!" said Basil ironically.

"They used to invite me to dinner sometimes last spring, but since you take her around to all the club dances—"

"Good-bye," said Basil hastily. He exchanged a jerky bow for Mr. Utsonomia's more formal dip, and departed.

From the moment of Minnie's arrival the question of Rhoda had begun to assume enormous proportions. At first he had been merely indifferent to her person and a little ashamed of her lacy, oddly reminiscent clothes, but now, as he saw how relentlessly his services were commandeered, he began to hate her. When she complained of a headache, his imagination would eagerly convert it into a long, lingering illness from which she would recover only after college opened in the fall. But the eight dollars a week which he received from his great-uncle would pay his fare to New Haven, and he knew that if he failed to hold this position his mother would refuse to let him go.

Not suspecting the truth, Minnie Bibble found the fact that he only danced with her once or twice at each hop, and was then strangely moody and silent, somehow intriguing. Temporarily, at least, she was fascinated by his indifference, and even a little unhappy. But her precociously emotional temperament would not long stand neglect, and it was agony for Basil to watch several rivals beginning to emerge. There were moments when it seemed too big a price to pay even for Yale.

All his hopes centered upon one event. That was a farewell party in her honor for which the Kampfs had engaged the College Club and to which Rhoda was not invited. Given the mood and the moment, he might speed her departure knowing that he had stamped himself indelibly on her heart.

Three days before the party he came home from work at six to find the Kampfs' car before his door and Minnie sitting alone on the front porch.

"Basil, I had to see you," she said. "You've been so funny and distant to me."

Intoxicated by her presence on his familiar porch, he found no words to answer.

"I'm meeting the family in town for dinner and I've got an hour. Can't we go somewhere? I've been frightened to death your mother would come home and think it was fresh for me to call on you." She spoke in a whisper, though there was no one close enough to hear. "I wish we didn't have the old chauffeur. He listens."

"Listens to what?" Basil asked, with a flash of jealousy.

"He just listens."

"I'll tell you," he proposed: "We'll have him drop us by grampa's house and I'll borrow the electric."

The hot wind blew the brown curls around her forehead as they glided along Crest Avenue.

That he contributed the car made him feel more triumphantly astride the moment. There was a place he had saved for such a time as this—a little pigtail of a road left from the excavations of Prospect Park, where Crest Avenue ran obliviously above them and the late sun glinted on the Mississippi flats a mile away.

The end of summer was in the afternoon; it had turned a corner, and what was left must be used while there was yet time.

Suddenly she was whispering in his arms, "You're first, Basil—nobody but you."

"You just admitted you were a flirt."

"I know, but that was years ago. I used to like to be called fast when I was thirteen or fourteen, because I didn't care what people said; but about a year ago I began to see there was something better in life—honestly, Basil—and I've tried to act properly. But I'm afraid I'll never be an angel."

The river flowed in a thin scarlet gleam between the public baths and the massed tracks upon the other side. Booming, whistling, far-away railroad sounds reached them from down there; the voices of children playing tennis in Prospect Park sailed frailly overhead.

"I really haven't got such a line as everybody thinks, Basil, for I mean a lot of what I say way down deep, and nobody believes me. You know how much alike we are, and in a boy it doesn't matter, but a girl has to control her feelings, and that's hard for me, because I'm emotional."

"Haven't you kissed anybody since you've been in St. Paul?"

"No."

He saw she was lying, but it was a brave lie. They talked from their hearts—with the half truths and evasions peculiar to that organ, which has never been famed as an instrument of precision. They pieced together all the shreds of romance they knew and made garments for each other no less warm than their childish passion, no less wonderful than their sense of wonder.

He held her away suddenly, looked at her, made a strained sound of delight. There it was, in her face touched by sun—that promise—in the curve of her mouth, the tilted shadow of her nose on her cheek, the point of dull fire in her eyes—the promise that she could lead him into a world in which he would always be happy.

"Say I love you," he whispered.

"I'm in love with you."

"Oh, no; that's not the same."

She hesitated. "I've never said the other to anybody."

"Please say it."

She blushed the color of the sunset.

"At my party," she whispered. "It'd be easier at night."

When she dropped him in front of his house she spoke from the window of the car:

"This is my excuse for coming to see you. My uncle couldn't get the club Thursday, so we're having the party at the regular dance Saturday night."

Basil walked thoughtfully into the house; Rhoda Sinclair was also giving a dinner at the College Club dance Saturday night.

It was put up to him frankly. Mrs. Reilly listened to his tentative excuses in silence and then said:

"Rhoda invited you first for Saturday night, and she already has one girl too many. Of course, if you choose to simply turn your back on your engagement and go to another party, I don't know how Rhoda will feel, but I know how I should feel."

And the next day his great-uncle, passing through the stock room, stopped and said: "What's all this trouble about parties?"

Basil started to explain, but Mr. Reilly cut him short. "I don't see the use of hurting a young girl's feelings. You better think it over."

Basil had thought it over; on Saturday afternoon he was still expected at both dinners and he had hit upon no solution at all.

Yale was only a month away now, but in four days Erminie Bibble would be gone, uncommitted, unsecured, grievously offended, lost forever. Not yet delivered from adolescence, Basil's moments of foresight alternated with those when the future was measured by a day. The glory that was Yale faded beside the promise of that incomparable hour.

On the other side loomed up the gaunt specter of the university, with phantoms flitting in and out its portals that presently disclosed themselves as peasants and girls. At five o'clock, in a burst of contempt for his weakness, he went to the phone and left word with a maid at the Kampfs' house that he was sick and couldn't come tonight. Nor would he sit with the dull left-overs of his generation—too sick for one party, he was too sick for the other. The Reillys could have no complaint as to that.

Rhoda answered the phone and Basil tried to reduce his voice to a weak murmur:

"Rhoda, I've been taken sick. I'm in bed now," he murmured feebly, and then added: "The phone's right next to the bed, you see; so I thought I'd call you up myself."

"You mean to say you can't come?" Dismay and anger were in her voice.

"I'm sick in bed," he repeated doggedly. "I've got chills and a pain and a cold."

"Well, can't you come anyhow?" she asked, with what to the invalid seemed a remarkable lack of consideration. "You've just got to. Otherwise there'll be two extra girls."

"I'll send someone to take my place," he said desperately. His glance, roving wildly out the window, fell on a house over the way. "I'll send Eddie Parmelee."

Rhoda considered. Then she asked with quick suspicion: "You're not going to that other party?"

"Oh, no; I told them I was sick too."

Again Rhoda considered. Eddie Parmelee was mad at her.

"I'll fix it up," Basil promised. "I know he'll come. He hasn't got anything to do tonight."

A few minutes later he dashed across the street. Eddie himself, tying a bow on his collar, came to the door. With certain reservations, Basil hastily outlined the situation. Would Eddie go in his place?

"Can't do it, old boy, even if I wanted to. Got a date with my real girl tonight."

"Eddie, I'd make it worth your while," he said recklessly. "I'd pay you for your time—say, five dollars."

Eddie considered, there was hesitation in his eyes, but he shook his head.

"It isn't worth it, Basil. You ought to see what I'm going out with tonight."

"You could see her afterward. They only want you—I mean me—because they've got more girls than men for dinner—and listen, Eddie, I'll make it ten dollars."

Eddie clapped him on the shoulder.

"All right, old boy, I'll do it for an old friend. Where's the pay?"

More than a week's salary melted into Eddie's palm, but another sort of emptiness accompanied Basil back across the street—the emptiness of the coming night. In an hour or so the Kampfs' limousine would draw up at the College Club and—time and time again his imagination halted miserably before that single picture, unable to endure any more.

In despair he wandered about the dark house. His mother had let the maid go out and was at his grandfather's for dinner, and momentarily Basil considered finding some rake like Elwood Leaming and going down to Carling's Restaurant to drink whiskey, wines and beer. Perhaps on her way back to the lake after the dance, Minnie, passing by, would see his face among the wildest of the revelers and understand.

"I'm going to Maxim's," he hummed to himself desperately; then he added impatiently: "Oh, to heck with Maxim's!"

He sat in the parlor and watched a pale moon come up over the Lindsays' fence at McKubben Street. Some young people came by, heading for the trolley that went to Como Park. He pitied their horrible dreariness—they were not going to dance with Minnie at the College Club tonight.

Eight-thirty—she was there now. Nine—they were dancing between courses to "Peg of My Heart" or doing the Castle Walk that Andy Lockheart brought home from Yale.

At ten o'clock he heard his mother come in, and almost immediately the phone rang. For a moment he listened without interest to her voice; then abruptly he sat up in his chair.

"Why, yes; how do you do, Mrs. Reilly. . . . Oh, I see. . . . Oh. . . . Are you sure it isn't Basil you want to speak to? . . . Well, frankly, Mrs. Reilly, I don't see that it's my affair."

Basil got up and took a step toward the door; his mother's voice was growing thin and annoyed: "I wasn't here at the time and I don't know who he promised to send."

Eddie Parmelee hadn't gone after all—well, that was the end.

". . . Of course not. It must be a mistake. I don't think Basil would possibly do that; I don't think he even knows any Japanese."

Basil's brain reeled. For a moment he was about to dash across the street after Eddie Parmelee. Then he heard a definitely angry note come into his mother's voice:

"Very well, Mrs. Reilly. I'll tell my son. But his going to Yale is scarcely a matter I care to discuss with you. In any case, he no longer needs anyone's assistance."

He had lost his position and his mother was trying to put a proud face on it. But her voice continued, soaring a little:

"Uncle Ben might be interested to know that this afternoon we sold the Third Street block to the Union Depot Company for four hundred thousand dollars."

Mr. Utsonomia was enjoying himself. In the whole six months in America he had never felt so caught up in its inner life before. At first it had been a little hard to make plain to the lady just whose place it was he was taking, but Eddie Parmelee had assured him that such substitutions were an American custom, and he was spending the evening collecting as much data upon American customs as possible.

He did not dance, so he sat with the elderly lady until both the ladies went home, early and apparently a little agitated, shortly after dinner. But Mr. Utsonomia stayed on. He watched and he wandered. He was not lonesome; he had grown accustomed to being alone.

About eleven he sat on the veranda pretending to be blowing the smoke of a cigarette—which he hated—out over the city, but really listening to a conversation which was taking place just behind. It had been going on for half an hour, and it puzzled him, for apparently it was a proposal, and it was not refused. Yet, if his eyes did not deceive him, the contracting parties were of an age that Americans did not associate with such serious affairs. Another thing puzzled him even more: obviously, if one substituted for an absent guest, the absent guest should not be among those present, and he was almost sure that the young man who had just engaged himself for marriage was Mr. Basil Lee. It would be bad manners to intrude now, but he would urbanely ask him about a solution of this puzzle when the state university opened in the fall.

Basil and Cleopatra

THIS story was printed in *The Saturday Evening Post*, April 27, 1929. It concludes the Basil series, because it brings Basil to the edge of manhood, to the point where he is forced to recognize, with grief and regret, what Henry Dell in "News of Paris—Fifteen Years Ago" will assert with grim familiarity a decade later in Fitzgerald's career, that "You couldn't be with women incessantly." The man's world, with its peculiar challenges and triumphs, is wholly separated from the world of women. If Basil, unlike Antony, has no real choice between these two worlds, he nonetheless triumphs by recognizing their separateness and keeping himself intact. Fitzgerald knows very well how comic this comparison between Minnie Bibble and Cleopatra is. Yet he is at bottom quite serious about it: because he remembers and recognizes his own feelings about Ginevra King, he knows that feelings are as deep at Basil's age as they ever are.

Fitzgerald is also depending on his own experience for Basil's discovery of the world of men. He too struggled with make-up examinations when he entered college. He too went out for freshman football filled with dreams of glory. He was cut from the freshman squad almost immediately, but he spent the rest of his life dreaming (he tells us exactly how in "Sleeping and Waking") of a football career like Basil's.

His feelings about the comedy and seriousness of Basil's recognition of life are beautifully focussed in the story's final image of Basil standing on the veranda of the Lawn Club, alert for that "high white note [of the wind's trumpeting] for which he always listened" and noting with the "practiced eye of the commander . . . that one star was no longer there." A decade later, the author of "Author's House" would stand in the cupola of his "house" listening for a moment to "a gale around the tower" and say, "I lived up here once. . . . just a little while when I was young."

WHEREVER she was, became a beautiful and enchanted place to Basil, but he did not think of it that way. He thought the fascination was inherent in the locality, and long afterward a commonplace street or the mere name of a city would exude a peculiar glow, a sustained sound, that struck his soul alert with delight. In her presence he was too absorbed to notice his surroundings; so that her absence never made them empty, but, rather, sent him seeking for her through haunted rooms and gardens that he had never really seen before.

This time, as usual, he saw only the expression of her face, the mouth that gave an attractive interpretation of any emotion she felt or pretended to feel—oh, invaluable mouth—and the rest of her, new as a peach and old as sixteen. He was almost unconscious that they stood in a railroad station and entirely unconscious that she had just glanced over his shoulder and fallen in love with another young man. Turning to walk with the rest to the car, she was already acting for the stranger; no less so because her voice was pitched for Basil and she clung to him, squeezing his arm.

Had Basil noticed this other young man that the train discharged he would merely have been sorry for him—as he had been sorry for the wretched people in the villages along the railroad and for his fellow travelers—they were not entering Yale in a fortnight nor were they about to spend three days in the same town with Miss Erminie Gilbert Labouisse Bibble. There was something dense, hopeless and a little contemptible about them all.

Basil had come to visit here because Erminie Bibble was visiting here. On the sad eve of her departure from his native Western city a month before, she had said, with all the promise one could ask in her urgent voice:

"If you know a boy in Mobile, why don't you make him invite you down when I'll be there?"

He had followed this suggestion. And now with the soft, unfamiliar Southern city actually flowing around him, his excitement led him to believe that Fat Gaspar's car floated off immediately they entered it. A voice from the curb came as a surprise:

"Hi, Bessie Belle. Hi, William. How you all?"

The newcomer was tall and lean and a year or so older than Basil. He wore a white linen suit and a panama hat, under which burned fierce, undefeated Southern eyes.

"Why, Littleboy Le Moyne!" exclaimed Miss Cheever. "When did you get home?"

"Jus' now, Bessie Belle. Saw you lookin' so fine and pretty, had to come and see closer."

He was introduced to Minnie and Basil.

"Drop you somewhere, Littleboy?" asked Fat—on his native heath, William.

"Why—" Le Moyne hesitated. "You're very kind, but the man ought to be here with the car."

"Jump in."

Le Moyne swung his bag on top of Basil's and with courteous formality got in the back seat beside them. Basil caught Minnie's eye and she smiled quickly back, as if to say, "This is too bad, but it'll soon be over."

"Do you happen to come from New Orleans, Miss Bibble?" asked Le Moyne.

"Sure do."

" 'Cause I just came from there and they told me one of their mos' celebrated heartbreakers was visiting up here, and meanwhile her suitors were shooting themselves all over the city. That's the truth. I used to help pick 'em up myself sometimes when they got littering the streets."

This must be Mobile Bay on the left, Basil thought; "Down Mobile," and the Dixie moonlight and darky stevedores singing. The houses on either side of the street were gently faded behind proud, protecting vines; there had been crinolines on these balconies, and guitars by night in these broken gardens.

It was so warm; the voices were so sure they had time to say everything—even Minnie's voice, answering the banter of the youth with the odd nickname, seemed slower and lazier—he had scarcely ever thought of her as a Southern girl before. They stopped at a large gate where flickers of a yellow house showed through luscious trees. Le Moyne got out.

"I certainly hope you both enjoy your visit here. If you'll permit me I'll call around and see if there's anything I can do to add to your pleasure." He swooped his panama. "I bid you good day."

As they started off, Bessie Belle turned around and smiled at Minnie.

"Didn't I tell you?" she demanded.

"I guessed it in the station, before he came up to the car," said Minnie. "Something told me that was him."

"Did you think he was good looking?"

"He was divine," Minnie said.

"Of course he's always gone with an older crowd."

To Basil, this prolonged discussion seemed a little out of place. After all, the young man was simply a local Southerner who lived here; add to that, that he went with an older crowd, and it seemed that his existence was being unnecessarily insisted upon.

But now Minnie turned to him, said, "Basil," wriggled invitingly and folded her hands in a humble, expectant way that invariably caused disturbances in his heart.

"I loved your letters," she said.

"You might have answered them."

"I haven't had a minute, Basil. I visited in Chicago and then in Nashville. I haven't even been home." She lowered her voice. "Father and mother are getting a divorce, Basil. Isn't that awful?"

He was startled; then, after a moment, he adjusted the idea to her and she became doubly poignant; because of its romantic connection with her, the thought of divorce would never shock him again.

"That's why I didn't write. But I've thought of you so much. You're the best friend I have, Basil. You always understand."

This was decidedly not the note upon which they had parted in St. Paul. A dreadful rumor that he hadn't intended to mention rose to his lips.

"Who is this fellow Bailey you met at Lake Forest?" he inquired lightly.

"Buzz Bailey!" Her big eyes opened in surprise. "He's very attractive and a divine dancer, but we're just friends." She frowned. "I bet Connie Davies has been telling tales in St. Paul. Honestly, I'm so sick of girls that, just out of jealousy or nothing better to do, sit around and criticize you if you have a good time."

He was convinced now that something had occurred in Lake Forest, but he concealed the momentary pang from Minnie.

"Anyhow, you're a fine one to talk." She smiled suddenly. "I guess everybody knows how fickle you are, Mr. Basil Duke Lee."

Generally such an implication is considered flattering, but the lightness, almost the indifference, with which she spoke increased his alarm—and then suddenly the bomb exploded.

"You needn't worry about Buzz Bailey. At present I'm absolutely heartwhole and fancy free."

Before he could even comprehend the enormity of what she had said, they stopped at Bessie Belle Cheever's door and the two girls ran up the steps, calling back, "We'll see you this afternoon."

Mechanically Basil climbed into the front seat beside his host.

"Going out for freshman football, Basil?" William asked.

"What? Oh, sure. If I can get off my two conditions." There was no if in his heart; it was the greatest ambition of his life.

"You'll probably make the freshman team easy. That fellow Littleboy Le Moyne you just met is going to Princeton this fall. He played end at V. M. I."

"Where'd he get that crazy name?"

"Why, his family always called him that and everybody picked it up." After a moment he added, "He asked them to the country-club dance with him tonight."

"When did he?" Basil demanded in surprise.

"Right then. That's what they were talking about. I meant to ask them and I was just leading up to it gradually, but he stepped in before I could get a chance." He sighed, blaming himself. "Well, anyhow, we'll see them there."

"Sure; it doesn't matter," said Basil. But was it Fat's mistake? Couldn't Minnie have said right out: "But Basil came all this way to see me and I ought to go with him on his first night here."

What had happened? One month ago, in the dim, thunderous Union Station at St. Paul, they had gone behind a baggage truck and he had kissed her, and her eyes had said: Again. Up to the very end, when she disappeared in a swirl of vapor at the car window, she had been his—those weren't things you thought; they were things you knew. He was bewildered. It wasn't like Minnie, who, for all her glittering popularity, was invariably kind. He tried to think of something in his letters that might have offended her, and searched himself for new shortcomings. Perhaps she didn't like him the way he was in the morning. The joyous mood in which he had arrived was vanishing into air.

She was her familiar self when they played tennis that afternoon; she admired his strokes and once, when they were close at the net, she suddenly patted his hand. But later, as they drank lemonade on the Cheevers' wide, shady porch, he couldn't seem to be alone with her even for a minute. Was it by accident that, coming back from the courts, she had sat in front with Fat? Last summer she had made opportunities to be alone with him—made them out of nothing. It was in a state that seemed to border on some terrible realization that he dressed for the country-club dance.

The club lay in a little valley, almost roofed over by willows, and down through their black silhouettes, in irregular blobs and patches, dripped the light of a huge harvest moon. As they parked the car, Basil's tune of tunes, Chinatown, drifted from the windows and dissolved into its notes which thronged like elves through the glade.

His heart quickened, suffocating him; the throbbing tropical darkness held a promise of such romance as he had dreamed of; but
faced with it, he felt himself too small and impotent to seize the
felicity he desired. When he danced with Minnie he was ashamed
of inflicting his merely mortal presence on her in this fairyland
whose unfamiliar figures reached towering proportions of magnificence and beauty. To make him king here, she would have to
reach forth and draw him close to her with soft words; but she only
said, "Isn't it wonderful, Basil? Did you ever have a better time?"

Talking for a moment with Le Moyne in the stag line, Basil was
hesitantly jealous and oddly shy. He resented the tall form that
stooped down so fiercely over Minnie as they danced, but he found
it impossible to dislike him or not to be amused by the line of sober-
faced banter he kept up with passing girls. He and William Gaspar
were the youngest boys here, as Bessie Belle and Minnie were the
youngest girls, and for the first time in his life he wanted passionately
to be older, less impressionable, less impressed. Quivering at every
scent, sigh or tune, he wanted to be blasé and calm. Wretchedly he
felt the whole world of beauty pour down upon him like moonlight, pressing on him, making his breath now sighing, now short,
as he wallowed helplessly in a superabundance of youth for which a
hundred adults present would have given years of life.

Next day, meeting her in a world that had shrunk back to reality,
things were more natural, but something was gone and he could not
bring himself to be amusing and gay. It would be like being brave
after the battle. He should have been all that the night before. They
went downtown in an unpaired foursome and called at a photog-
rapher's for some pictures of Minnie. Basil liked one proof that no
one else liked—somehow, it reminded him of her as she had been
in St. Paul—so he ordered two—one for her to keep and one to send
after him to Yale. All afternoon she was distracted and vaguely
singing, but back at the Cheevers' she sprang up the steps at the
sound of the phone inside. Ten minutes later she appeared, sulky
and lowering, and Basil heard a quick exchange between the two
girls:

"He can't get out of it."

"—a pity."

"—back Friday."

It could only be Le Moyne who had gone away, and to Minnie

it mattered. Presently, unable to endure her disappointment, he got up wretchedly and suggested to William that they go home. To his surprise, Minnie's hand on his arm arrested him.

"Don't go, Basil. It doesn't seem as if I've seen you a minute since you've been here."

He laughed unhappily.

"As if it mattered to you."

"Basil, don't be silly." She bit her lip as if she were hurt. "Let's go out to the swing."

He was suddenly radiant with hope and happiness. Her tender smile, which seemed to come from the heart of freshness, soothed him and he drank down her lies in grateful gulps like cool water. The last sunshine touched her cheeks with the unearthly radiance he had seen there before, as she told him how she hadn't wanted to accept Le Moyne's invitation, and how surprised and hurt she had been when he hadn't come near her last night.

"Then do one thing, Minnie," he pleaded: "Won't you let me kiss you just once?"

"But not here," she exclaimed, "you silly!"

"Let's go in the summerhouse, for just a minute."

"Basil, I can't. Bessie Belle and William are on the porch. Maybe some other time."

He looked at her distraught, unable to believe or disbelieve in her, and she changed the subject quickly:

"I'm going to Miss Beecher's school, Basil. It's only a few hours from New Haven. You can come up and see me this fall. The only thing is, they say you have to sit in glass parlors. Isn't that terrible?"

"Awful," he agreed fervently.

William and Bessie Belle had left the veranda and were out in front, talking to some people in a car.

"Minnie, come into the summerhouse now—for just a minute. They're so far away."

Her face set unwillingly.

"I can't, Basil. Don't you see I can't?"

"Why not? I've got to leave tomorrow."

"Oh, no."

"I have to. I only have four days to get ready for my exams. Minnie—"

He took her hand. It rested calmly enough in his, but when he tried to pull her to her feet she plucked it sharply away. The swing moved with the little struggle and Basil put out his foot and made it stop. It was terrible to swing when one was at a disadvantage.

She laid the recovered hand on his knee.

"I've stopped kissing people, Basil. Really. I'm too old; I'll be seventeen next May."

"I'll bet you kissed Le Moyne," he said bitterly.

"Well, you're pretty fresh—"

Basil got out of the swing.

"I think I'll go."

Looking up, she judged him dispassionately, as she never had before—his sturdy, graceful figure; the high, warm color through his tanned skin; his black, shining hair that she had once thought so romantic. She felt, too—as even those who disliked him felt— that there was something else in his face—a mark, a hint of destiny, a persistence that was more than will, that was rather a necessity of pressing its own pattern on the world, of having its way. That he would most probably succeed at Yale, that it would be nice to go there this year as his girl, meant nothing to her. She had never needed to be calculating. Hesitating, she alternatingly drew him toward her in her mind and let him go. There were so many men and they wanted her so much. If Le Moyne had been here at hand she wouldn't have hesitated, for nothing must interfere with the mysterious opening glory of that affair; but he was gone for three days and she couldn't decide quite yet to let Basil go.

"Stay over till Wednesday and I'll—I'll do what you want," she said.

"But I can't. I've got these exams to study for. I ought to have left this afternoon."

"Study on the train."

She wriggled, dropped her hands in her lap and smiled at him. Taking her hand suddenly, he pulled her to her feet and toward the summerhouse and the cool darkness behind its vines.

The following Friday Basil arrived in New Haven and set about crowding five days' work into two. He had done no studying on the train; instead he sat in a trance and concentrated upon Minnie, wondering what was happening now that Le Moyne was there. She had kept her promise to him, but only literally—kissed him once in the playhouse, once, grudgingly, the second evening; but the day of his departure there had been a telegram from Le Moyne, and in front of Bessie Belle she had not even dared to kiss him good-bye. As a sort of amend she had given him permission to call on the first day permitted by Miss Beecher's school.

The opening of college found him rooming with Brick Wales and George Dorsey in a suite of two bedrooms and a study in Wright Hall. Until the result of his trigonometry examination was published he was ineligible to play football, but watching the freshmen practice on Yale field, he saw that the quarterback position lay between Cullum, last year's Andover captain, and a man named Danziger from a New Bedford high school. There was a rumor that Cullum would be moved to halfback. The other quarterbacks did not appear formidable and Basil felt a great impatience to be out there with a team in his hands to move over the springy turf. He was sure he could at least get in some of the games.

Behind everything, as a light showing through, was the image of Minnie; he would see her in a week, three days, tomorrow. On the eve of the occasion he ran into Fat Gaspar, who was in Sheff, in the oval by Haughton Hall. In the first busy weeks they had scarcely met; now they walked along for a little way together.

"We all came North together," Fat said. "You ought to have been along. We had some excitement. Minnie got in a jam with Littleboy Le Moyne."

Basil's blood ran cold.

"It was funny afterward, but she was pretty scared for a while," continued Fat. "She had a compartment with Bessie Belle, but she and Littleboy wanted to be alone; so in the afternoon Bessie Belle came and played cards in ours. Well, after about two hours Bessie Belle and I went back, and there were Minnie and Littleboy standing in the vestibule arguing with the conductor; Minnie white as a sheet. Seems they locked the door and pulled down the blinds, and I guess there was a little petting going on. When he came along after the tickets and knocked on the door, they thought it was us kidding them, and wouldn't let him in at first, and when they did, he was pretty upset. He asked Littleboy if that was his compartment, and whether he and Minnie were married that they locked the door, and Littleboy lost his temper trying to explain that there was nothing wrong. He said the conductor had insulted Minnie and he wanted

him to fight. But that conductor could have made trouble, and believe me, I had an awful time smoothing it all over."

With every detail imagined, with every refinement of jealousy
beating in his mind, including even envy for their community of
misfortune as they stood together in the vestibule, Basil went up to
Miss Beecher's next day. Radiant and glowing, more mysteriously
desirable than ever, wearing her very sins like stars, she came down
to him in her plain white uniform dress, and his heart turned over
at the kindness of her eyes.

"You were wonderful to come up, Basil. I'm so excited having a
beau so soon. Everybody's jealous of me."

The glass doors hinged like French windows, shutting them in
on all sides. It was hot. Down through three more compartments he
could see another couple—a girl and her brother, Minnie said—and
from time to time they moved and gestured soundlessly, as unreal
in these tiny human conservatories as the vase of paper flowers on
the table. Basil walked up and down nervously.

"Minnie, I want to be a great man some day and I want to do
everything for you. I understand you're tired of me now. I don't
know how it happened, but somebody else came along—it doesn't
matter. There isn't any hurry. But I just want you to—oh, remember
me in some different way—try to think of me as you used to, not as
if I was just another one you threw over. Maybe you'd better not
see me for a while—I mean at the dance this fall. Wait till I've
accomplished some big scene or deed, you know, and I can show it
to you and say I did that all for you."

It was very futile and young and sad. Once, carried away by the
tragedy of it all, he was on the verge of tears, but he controlled himself to that extent. There was sweat on his forehead. He sat across
the room from her, and Minnie sat on the couch, looking at the floor,
and said several times: "Can't we be friends, Basil? I always think of
you as one of my best friends."

Toward the end she rose patiently.

"Don't you want to see the chapel?"

They walked upstairs and he glanced dismally into a small dark
space, with her living, sweet-smelling presence half a yard from his
shoulder. He was almost glad when the funereal business was over
and he walked out of the school into the fresh autumn air.

Back in New Haven he found two pieces of mail on his desk. One was a notice from the registrar telling him that he had failed his trigonometry examination and would be ineligible for football. The second was a photograph of Minnie—the picture that he had liked and ordered two of in Mobile. At first the inscription puzzled him: "L. L. from E. G. L. B. Trains are bad for the heart." Then suddenly he realized what had happened, and threw himself on his bed, shaken with wild laughter.

Three weeks later, having requested and passed a special examination in trigonometry, Basil began to look around him gloomily to see if there was anything left in life. Not since his miserable first year at school had he passed through such a period of misery; only now did he begin for the first time to be aware of Yale. The quality of romantic speculation reawoke, and, listlessly at first, then with growing determination, he set about merging himself into this spirit which had fed his dreams so long.

I want to be chairman of the News or the Record, thought his old self one October morning, and I want to get my letter in football, and I want to be in Skull and Bones.

Whenever the vision of Minnie and Le Moyne on the train occurred to him, he repeated this phrase like an incantation. Already he thought with shame of having stayed over in Mobile, and there began to be long strings of hours when he scarcely brooded about her at all.

He had missed half of the freshman football season, and it was with scant hope that he joined the squad on Yale field. Dressed in his black and white St. Regis jersey, amid the motley of forty schools, he looked enviously at the proud two dozen in Yale blue. At the end of four days he was reconciling himself to obscurity for the rest of the season when the voice of Carson, assistant coach, singled him suddenly out of a crowd of scrub backs.

"Who was throwing those passes just now?"

"I was, sir."

"I haven't seen you before, have I?"

"I just got eligible."

"Know the signals?"

"Yes, sir."

"Well, you take this team down the field—ends, Krutch and Bispam; tackles—"

A moment later he heard his own voice snapping out on the crisp air: "Thirty-two, sixty-five, sixty-seven, twenty-two—"

There was a ripple of laughter.

"Wait a minute! Where'd you learn to call signals like that?" said Carson.

"Why, we had a Harvard coach, sir."

"Well, just drop the Haughton emphasis. You'll get everybody too excited."

After a few minutes they were called in and told to put on head-gears.

"Where's Waite?" Carson asked. "Test, eh? Well, you then—what's your name?—in the black and white sweater?"

"Lee."

"You call signals. And let's see you get some life into this outfit. Some of you guards and tackles are big enough for the varsity. Keep them on their toes, you—what's your name?"

"Lee."

They lined up with possession of the ball on the freshmen's twenty-yard line. They were allowed unlimited downs, but when, after a dozen plays, they were in approximately that same place, the ball was given to the first team.

That's that! thought Basil. That finishes me.

But an hour later, as they got out of the bus, Carson spoke to him: "Did you weigh this afternoon?"

"Yes. Hundred and fifty-eight."

"Let me give you a tip—you're still playing prep-school football. You're still satisfied with stopping them. The idea here is that if you lay them down hard enough you wear them out. Can you kick?"

"No, sir."

"Well, it's too bad you didn't get out sooner."

A week later his name was read out as one of those to go to Andover. Two quarterbacks ranked ahead of him, Danziger and a little hard rubber ball of a man, named Appleton, and Basil watched the game from the sidelines, but when, the following Tuesday, Danziger splintered his arm in practice, Basil was ordered to report to training table.

On the eve of the game with the Princeton freshmen, the egress of the student body to Princeton for the Varsity encounter left the campus almost deserted. Deep autumn had set in, with a crackling wind from the west, and walking back to his room after final skull practice, Basil felt the old lust for glory sweep over him. Le Moyne was playing end on the Princeton freshmen and it was probable that Minnie would be in the stands, but now, as he ran along the springy grass in front of Osborne, swaying to elude imaginary tacklers, the fact seemed of less importance than the game. Like most Americans, he was seldom able really to grasp the moment, to say: "This, for me, is the great equation by which everything else will be measured; this is the golden time," but for once the present was sufficient. He was going to spend two hours in a country where life ran at the pace he demanded of it.

The day was fair and cool; an unimpassioned crowd, mostly townsmen, was scattered through the stands. The Princeton freshmen looked sturdy and solid in their diagonal stripes, and Basil picked out Le Moyne, noting coldly that he was exceptionally fast, and bigger than he had seemed in his clothes. On an impulse Basil turned and searched for Minnie in the crowd, but he could not find her. A minute later the whistle blew; sitting at the coach's side, he concentrated all his faculties on the play.

The first half was played between the thirty-yard lines. The main principles of Yale's offense seemed to Basil too simple; less effective than the fragments of the Haughton system he had learned at school, while the Princeton tactics, still evolved in Sam White's long shadow, were built around a punter and the hope of a break. When the break came, it was Yale's. At the start of the second half Princeton fumbled and Appleton sent over a drop kick from the thirty-yard line.

It was his last act of the day. He was hurt on the next kick-off and, to a burst of freshmen cheering, assisted from the game.

With his heart in a riot, Basil sprinted out on the field. He felt an overpowering strangeness, and it was someone else in his skin who called the first signals and sent an unsuccessful play through the line. As he forced his eyes to take in the field slowly, they met Le Moyne's, and Le Moyne grinned at him. Basil called for a short pass over the line, throwing it himself for a gain of seven yards. He sent Cullum off tackle for three more and a first down. At the forty, with more latitude, his mind began to function smoothly and surely. His short passes worried the Princeton fullback, and, in consequence, the running gains through the line were averaging four yards instead of two.

At the Princeton forty he dropped back to kick formation and tried Le Moyne's end, but Le Moyne went under the interfering halfback and caught Basil by a foot. Savagely Basil tugged himself free, but too late—the halfback bowled him over. Again Le Moyne's face grinned at him, and Basil hated it. He called the same end and, with Cullum carrying the ball, they rolled over Le Moyne six yards, to Princeton's thirty-two. He was slowing down, was he? Then run him ragged! System counseled a pass, but he heard himself calling the end again. He ran parallel to the line, saw his interference melt away and Le Moyne, his jaw set, coming for him. Instead of cutting in, Basil turned full about and tried to reverse his field. When he was trapped he had lost fifteen yards.

A few minutes later the ball changed hands and he ran back to the safety position thinking: They'd yank me if they had anybody to put in my place.

The Princeton team suddenly woke up. A long pass gained thirty yards. A fast new back dazzled his way through the line for another first down. Yale was on the defensive, but even before they had realized the fact, the disaster had happened. Basil was drawn on an apparently developed play; too late he saw the ball shoot out of scrimmage to a loose end; saw, as he was neatly blocked, that the Princeton substitutes were jumping around wildly, waving their blankets. They had scored.

He got up with his heart black, but his brain cool. Blunders could be atoned for—if they only wouldn't take him out. The whistle blew for the quarter, and squatting on the turf with the exhausted team, he made himself believe that he hadn't lost their confidence, kept his face intent and rigid, refusing no man's eye. He had made his errors for today.

On the kick-off he ran the ball back to the thirty-five, and a steady rolling progress began. The short passes, a weak spot inside tackle, Le Moyne's end. Le Moyne was tired now. His face was drawn and dogged as he smashed blindly into the interference; the ball carrier eluded him—Basil or another.

Thirty more to go—twenty—over Le Moyne again. Disentangling himself from the pile, Basil met the Southerner's weary glance and insulted him in a crisp voice:

"You've quit, Littleboy. They better take you out."

He started the next play at him and, as Le Moyne charged in

furiously, tossed a pass over his head for the score. Yale 10, Princeton 7. Up and down the field again, with Basil fresher every minute and another score in sight, and suddenly the game was over.

Trudging off the field, Basil's eye ranged over the stands, but he could not see her.

I wonder if she knows I was pretty bad, he thought, and then bitterly: If I don't, he'll tell her.

He could hear him telling her in that soft Southern voice—the voice that had wooed her so persuasively that afternoon on the train. As he emerged from the dressing room an hour later he ran into Le Moyne coming out of the visitors' quarters next door. He looked at Basil with an expression at once uncertain and angry.

"Hello, Lee." After a momentary hesitation he added: "Good work."

"Hello, Le Moyne," said Basil, clipping his words.

Le Moyne turned away, turned back again.

"What's the matter?" he demanded. "Do you want to carry this any further?"

Basil didn't answer. The bruised face and the bandaged hand assuaged his hatred a little, but he couldn't bring himself to speak. The game was over, and now Le Moyne would meet Minnie somewhere, make the defeat negligible in the victory of the night.

"If it's about Minnie, you're wasting your time being sore," Le Moyne exploded suddenly. "I asked her to the game, but she didn't come."

"Didn't she?" Basil was startled.

"That was it, eh? I wasn't sure. I thought you were just trying to get my goat in there." His eyes narrowed. "The young lady kicked me about a month ago."

"Kicked you?"

"Threw me over. Got a little weary of me. She runs through things quickly."

Basil perceived that his face was miserable.

"Who is it now?" he asked in more civil tone.

"It seems to be a classmate of yours named Jubal—and a mighty sad bird, if you ask me. She met him in New York the day before her school opened, and I hear it's pretty heavy. She'll be at the Lawn Club Dance tonight."

Basil had dinner at the Taft with Jobena Dorsey and her brother George. The Varsity had won at Princeton and the college was jubilant and enthusiastic; as they came in, a table of freshmen by the door gave Basil a hand.

"You're getting very important," Jobena said.

A year ago Basil had thought for a few weeks that he was in love with Jobena; when they next met he knew immediately that he was not.

"And why was that?" he asked her now, as they danced. "Why did it all go so quick?"

"Do you really want to know?"

"Yes."

"Because I let it go."

"You let it go?" he repeated. "I like that!"

"I decided you were too young."

"Didn't I have anything to do with it?"

She shook her head.

"That's what Bernard Shaw says," Basil admitted thoughtfully. "But I thought it was just about older people. So you go after the men."

"Well, I should say not!" Her body stiffened indignantly in his arms. "The men are usually there, and the girl blinks at them or something. It's just instinct."

"Can't a man make a girl fall for him?"

"Some men can—the ones who really don't care."

He pondered this awful fact for a moment and stowed it away for future examination. On the way to the Lawn Club he brought forth more questions. If a girl who had been "crazy about a boy" became suddenly infatuated with another, what ought the first boy to do?

"Let her go," said Jobena.

"Supposing he wasn't willing to do that. What ought he to do?"

"There isn't anything to do."

"Well, what's the best thing?"

Laughing, Jobena laid her head on his shoulder.

"Poor Basil," she said, "I'll be Laura Jean Libbey and you tell me the whole story."

He summarized the affair. "You see," he concluded, "if she was just anybody I could get over it, no matter how much I loved her.

But she isn't—she's the most popular, most beautiful girl I've ever seen. I mean she's like Messalina and Cleopatra and Salome and all that."

"Louder," requested George from the front seat.

"She's sort of an immortal woman," continued Basil in a lower voice. "You know, like Madame du Barry and all that sort of thing. She's not just—"

"Not just like me."

"No. That is, you're sort of like her—all the girls I've cared about are sort of the same. Oh, Jobena, you know what I mean."

As the lights of the New Haven Lawn Club loomed up she became obligingly serious:

"There's nothing to do. I can see that. She's more sophisticated than you. She staged the whole thing from the beginning, even when you thought it was you. I don't know why she got tired, but evidently she is, and she couldn't create it again, even if she wanted to, and you couldn't because you're—"

"Go on. What?"

"You're too much in love. All that's left for you to do is to show her you don't care. Any girl hates to lose an old beau; so she may even smile at you—but don't go back. It's all over."

In the dressing room Basil stood thoughtfully brushing his hair. It was all over. Jobena's words had taken away his last faint hope, and after the strain of the afternoon the realization brought tears to his eyes. Hurriedly filling the bowl, he washed his face. Someone came in and slapped him on the back.

"You played a nice game, Lee."

"Thanks, but I was rotten."

"You were great. That last quarter—"

He went into the dance. Immediately he saw her, and in the same breath he was dizzy and confused with excitement. A little dribble of stags pursued her wherever she went, and she looked up at each one of them with the bright-eyed, passionate smile he knew so well. Presently he located her escort and indignantly discovered it was a flip, blatant boy from Hill School he had already noticed and set down as impossible. What quality lurked behind those watery eyes that drew her? How could that raw temperament appreciate that she was one of the immortal sirens of the world?

Having examined Mr. Jubal desperately and in vain for the answers to these questions, he cut in and danced all of twenty feet with her, smiling with cynical melancholy when she said:

"I'm so proud to know you, Basil. Everybody says you were wonderful this afternoon."

But the phrase was precious to him and he stood against the wall repeating it over to himself, separating it into its component parts and trying to suck out any lurking meaning. If enough people praised him it might influence her. "I'm proud to know you, Basil. Everybody says you were wonderful this afternoon."

There was a commotion near the door and someone said, "By golly, they got in after all!"

"Who?" another asked.

"Some Princeton freshmen. Their football season's over and three or four of them broke training at the Hofbrau."

And now suddenly the curious specter of a young man burst out of the commotion, as a back breaks through a line, and neatly straight-arming a member of the dance committee, rushed unsteadily onto the floor. He wore no collar with his dinner coat, his shirt front had long expelled its studs, his hair and eyes were wild. For a moment he glanced around as if blinded by the lights; then his glance fell on Minnie Bibble and an unmistakable love light came into his face. Even before he reached her he began to call her name aloud in a strained, poignant Southern voice.

Basil sprang forward, but others were before him, and Littleboy Le Moyne, fighting hard, disappeared into the coatroom in a flurry of legs and arms, many of which were not his own. Standing in the doorway, Basil found his disgust tempered with a monstrous sympathy; for Le Moyne, each time his head emerged from under the faucet, spoke desperately of his rejected love.

But when Basil danced with Minnie again, he found her frightened and angry; so much so that she seemed to appeal to Basil for support, made him sit down.

"Wasn't he a fool?" she cried feelingly. "That sort of thing gives a girl a terrible reputation. They ought to have put him in jail."

"He didn't know what he was doing. He played a hard game and he's all in, that's all."

But her eyes filled with tears.

"Oh, Basil," she pleaded, "am I just perfectly terrible? I never want to be mean to anybody; things just happen."

He wanted to put his arm around her and tell her she was the most romantic person in the world, but he saw in her eyes that she scarcely perceived him; he was a lay figure—she might have been talking to another girl. He remembered what Jobena had said—there was nothing left except to escape with his pride.

"You've got more sense." Her soft voice flowed around him like an enchanted river. "You know that when two people aren't—aren't crazy about each other any more, the thing is to be sensible."

"Of course," he said, and forced himself to add lightly: "When a thing's over, it's over."

"Oh, Basil, you're so satisfactory. You always understand." And now suddenly, for the first time in months, she was actually thinking of him. He would be an invaluable person in any girl's life, she thought, if that brain of his, which was so annoying sometimes, was really used "to sort of understand."

He was watching Jobena dance, and Minnie followed his eyes. "You brought a girl, didn't you? She's awfully pretty."

"Not as pretty as you."

"Basil."

Resolutely he refused to look at her, guessing that she had wriggled slightly and folded her hands in her lap. And as he held on to himself an extraordinary thing happened—the world around, outside of her, brightened a little. Presently more freshmen would approach him to congratulate him on the game, and he would like it—the words and the tribute in their eyes. There was a good chance he would start against Harvard next week.

"Basil!"

His heart made a dizzy tour of his chest. Around the corner of his eyes he felt her eyes waiting. Was she really sorry? Should he seize the opportunity to turn to her and say: "Minnie, tell this crazy nut to go jump in the river, and come back to me." He wavered, but a thought that had helped him this afternoon returned: He had made all his mistakes for this time. Deep inside of him the plea expired slowly.

Jubal the impossible came up with an air of possession, and Basil's heart went bobbing off around the ballroom in a pink silk dress. Lost again in a fog of indecision, he walked out on the veranda. There was a flurry of premature snow in the air and the stars looked cold. Staring up at them he saw that they were his stars as always—

symbols of ambition, struggle and glory. The wind blew through them, trumpeting that high white note for which he always listened, and the thin-blown clouds, stripped for battle, passed in review. The scene was of an unparalleled brightness and magnificence, and only the practiced eye of the commander saw that one star was no longer there.

Princeton

This essay on Princeton was originally written for a series on American colleges printed in *College Humor*. Fitzgerald's essay appeared there in December, 1927; it was reprinted in 1929 in a volume called *Ten Years of Princeton '17*. It was Fitzgerald's humor to place the events of any fiction he wrote about undergraduate life at Yale. But the real source of Basil Duke Lee's inner experience at Yale was Scott Fitzgerald's experience at Princeton, and this essay shows us what Princeton was for Fitzgerald's imagination, in a more responsible way, in some respects, than does *This Side of Paradise*, where, as he here points out, he was influenced by a desire to romanticize Princeton in a way he no longer thought possible when he came to write this essay.

Not that this essay is not romantic in another sense; in fact, it is a particularly good example of the way Fitzgerald could summon up before the court of memory the exact imaginative force of an earlier experience and another occasion. It puts us back in a time when the great middle-western universities hardly existed for the American understanding, when Dexter Green of "Winter Dreams" would make immense sacrifices to go to an eastern university and the University of Minnesota was largely populated—one thought—by farce characters like Mr. Utsonomia of "Forging Ahead"; it was a time when one dreaded the effect of the "insatiable millions" on the bloody-bandaged glory of Big-Three football players—when, in short, one could seriously consider the possibility of a survival in American society of a world of responsible and cultivated aristocrats, "a meadow lark among the smoke stacks." Fitzgerald does not criticize Princeton for being undemocratic, but for being snobbish instead of aristocratic. This is a very precise representation of the attitude of a time and a place, and perhaps of the attitude of later times and other places with different names.

In preparatory school and up to the middle of sophomore year in college, it worried me that I wasn't going and hadn't gone to Yale. Was I missing a great American secret? There was a gloss upon Yale that Princeton lacked; Princeton's flannels hadn't been pressed for a week, its hair always blew a little in the wind. Nothing was ever carried through at Princeton with the same perfection as the Yale Junior Prom or the elections to their senior societies. From the ragged squabble of club elections with its scars of snobbishness and adolescent heartbreak, to the enigma that faced you at the end of senior year as to what Princeton *was* and what, bunk and cant aside, it really stood for, it never presented itself with Yale's hard, neat, fascinating brightness. Only when you tried to tear part of your past out of your heart, as I once did, were you aware of its power of arousing a deep and imperishable love.

Princeton men take Princeton for granted and resent any attempt at analysis. As early as 1899 Jesse Lynch Williams was anathematized for reporting that Princeton wine helped to make the nineties golden. If the Princetonian had wanted to assert in sturdy chorus that his college was the true flower of American democracy, was deliberately and passionately America's norm in ideals of conduct and success, he would have gone to Yale. His brother and many of the men from his school went there. Contrariwise he chooses Princeton because at seventeen the furies that whip on American youth have become too coercive for his taste. He wants something quieter, mellower and less exigent. He sees himself being caught up into a wild competition that will lead him headlong into New Haven and dump him pell-mell out into the world. The series of badges which reward the winner of each sprint are no doubt desirable, but he seeks the taste of pleasant pastures and a moment to breathe deep and ruminate before he goes into the clamorous struggle of American life. He finds at Princeton other men like himself and thus is begotten Princeton's scoffing and mildly ironic attitude toward Yale.

Harvard has never existed as a conception at Princeton. Harvard men were "Bostonians with affected accents," or they were "That Isaacs fellow who got the high school scholarship out home." Lee Higginson & Company hired their athletes for them but no matter how much one did for Harvard one couldn't belong to "Fly" or "Porcellian" without going to Groton or St. Mark's. Such ideas were satisfying if inaccurate, for Cambridge, in more senses than one, was many miles away. Harvard was a series of sporadic relationships, sometimes pleasant, sometimes hostile—that was all.

Princeton is in the flat midlands of New Jersey, rising, a green Phoenix, out of the ugliest country in the world. Sordid Trenton sweats and festers a few miles south; northward are Elizabeth and the Erie Railroad and the suburban slums of New York; westward the dreary upper purlieus of the Delaware River. But around Princeton, shielding her, is a ring of silence—certified milk dairies, great estates with peacocks and deer parks, pleasant farms and woodlands which we paced off and mapped down in the spring of 1917 in preparation for the war. The busy East has already dropped away when the branch train rattles familiarly from the junction. Two tall spires and then suddenly all around you spreads out the loveliest riot of Gothic architecture in America, battlement linked on to battlement, hall to hall, arch-broken, vine-covered—luxuriant and lovely over two square miles of green grass. Here is no monotony, no feeling that it was all built yesterday at the whim of last week's millionaire; Nassau Hall was already thirty years old when Hessian bullets pierced its sides.

Alfred Noyes has compared Princeton to Oxford. To me the two are sharply different. Princeton is thinner and fresher, at once less profound and more elusive. For all its past, Nassau Hall stands there hollow and barren, not like a mother who has borne sons and wears the scars of her travail but like a patient old nurse, skeptical and affectionate with these foster children who, as Americans, can belong to no place under the sun.

In my romantic days I tried to conjure up the Princeton of Aaron Burr, Philip Freneau, James Madison and Light Horse Harry Lee, to tie on, so to speak, to the eighteenth century, to the history of man. But the chain parted at the Civil War, always the broken link in the continuity of American life. Colonial Princeton was, after all, a small denominational college. The Princeton I knew and belonged to grew from President McCosh's great shadow in the seventies, grew with the great *post bellum* fortunes of New York and Philadelphia to include coaching parties and keg parties and the later American conscience and Booth Tarkington's Triangle Club and Wilson's cloistered plans for an educational utopia. Bound up with it somewhere was the rise of American football.

For at Princeton, as at Yale, football became, back in the nineties, a sort of symbol. Symbol of what? Of the eternal violence of American life? Of the eternal immaturity of the race? The failure of a culture within the walls? Who knows? It became something at first satisfactory, then essential and beautiful. It became, long before the insatiable millions took it, with Gertrude Ederle and Mrs. Snyder, to its heart, the most intense and dramatic spectacle since the Olympic games. The death of Johnny Poe with the Black Watch in Flanders starts the cymbals crashing for me, plucks the strings of nervous violins as no adventure of the mind that Princeton ever offered. A year ago in the Champs Elysées I passed a slender dark-haired young man with an indolent characteristic walk. Something stopped inside me; I turned and looked after him. It was the romantic Buzz Law whom I had last seen one cold fall twilight in 1915, kicking from behind his goal line with a bloody bandage round his head.

After the beauty of its towers and the drama of its arenas, the widely known feature of Princeton is its "clientele."

A large proportion of such gilded youth as will absorb an education drifts to Princeton. Goulds, Rockefellers, Harrimans, Morgans, Fricks, Firestones, Perkinses, Pynes, McCormicks, Wanamakers, Cudahys and Du Ponts light there for a season, well or less well regarded. The names of Pell, Biddle, Van Rensselaer, Stuyvesant, Schuyler and Cooke titillate second generation mammas and papas with a social row to hoe in Philadelphia or New York. An average class is composed of three dozen boys from such Midas academies as St. Paul's, St. Mark's, St. George's, Pomfret and Groton, a hundred and fifty more from Lawrenceville, Hotchkiss, Exeter, Andover and Hill, and perhaps another two hundred from less widely known preparatory schools. The remaining twenty per cent enter from the high schools and these last furnish a large proportion of the eventual leaders. For them the business of getting to Princeton has been more arduous, financially as well as scholastically. They are trained and eager for the fray.

In my time, a decade ago, the mid-winter examinations in freshman year meant a great winnowing. The duller athletes, the rich boys of thicker skulls than their forbears, fell in droves by the wayside. Often they had attained the gates at twenty or twenty-one and with the aid of a tutoring school only to find the first test too hard. They were usually a pleasant fifty or sixty, those first flunk-outs. They left many regrets behind.

Nowadays only a few boys of that caliber ever enter. Under the new system of admissions they are spotted by their early scholastic writhings and balkings and informed that Princeton has space only for those whose brains are of normal weight. This is because a few years ago the necessity arose of limiting the enrollment. The war prosperity made college possible for many boys and by 1921 the number of candidates, who each year satisfied the minimum scholastic requirements for Princeton, was far beyond the university's capacity.

So, in addition to the college board examinations, the candidate must present his scholastic record, the good word of his schools, of two Princeton alumni, and must take a psychological test for general intelligence. The six hundred or so who with these credentials make the most favorable impression on the admissions committee are admitted. A man who is deficient in one scholastic subject may succeed in some cases over a man who has passed them all. A boy with a really excellent record, in, say science and mathematics, and a poor one in English, is admitted in preference to a boy with a fair general average and no special aptitude. The plan has raised the standard of scholarships and kept out such men as A, who in my time turned up in four different classes as a sort of perennial insult to the intelligence.

Whether the proverbially narrow judgments of head masters upon adolescents will serve to keep out the Goldsmiths, the Byrons, the Whitmans and the O'Neills it is too early to tell.

I can't help hoping that a few disreputable characters will slip in to salt the salt of the earth. Priggishness sits ill on Princeton. It was typified in my day by the Polity Club. This was a group that once a fortnight sat gravely at the feet of Mr. Schwab or Judge Gary or some other pard-like spirit imported for the occasion. Had these inspired plutocrats disclosed trade secrets or even remained on the key of brisk business cynicism the occasion might have retained dignity, but the Polity Club were treated to the warmed over straw soup of the house organ and the production picnic, with a few hot sops thrown in about "future leaders of men." Looking through a copy of the latest year book I do not find the Polity Club at all. Perhaps it now serves worthier purposes.

President Hibben is a mixture of "normalcy" and discernment, of staunch allegiance to the *status quo* and of a fine tolerance amounting almost to intellectual curiosity. I have heard him in a speech mask with rhetoric statements of incredible shallowness; yet I have never known him to take a mean, narrow or short-sighted stand within Princeton's walls. He fell heir to the throne in 1912 during the reaction to the Wilson idealism, and I believe that, learning vicariously, he has pushed out his horizon amazingly since then. His situation was not unlike Harding's ten years later, but, surrounding himself with such men as Gauss, Heermance and Alexander Smith, he has abjured the merely passive and conducted a progressive and often brilliant administration.

Under him functions a fine philosophy department, an excellent department of classics, fathered by the venerable Dean West, a scientific faculty starred by such names as Oswald Veblen and Conklin; and a surprisingly pallid English department, top-heavy, undistinguished and with an uncanny knack of making literature distasteful to young men. Dr. Spaeth, one of several exceptions, coached the crew in the afternoon and in the morning aroused interest and even enthusiasm for the romantic poets, an interest later killed in the preceptorial rooms where mildly poetic gentlemen resented any warmth of discussion and called the prominent men of the class by their first names.

The *Nassau Literary Magazine* is the oldest college publication in America. In its files you can find the original Craig Kennedy story, as well as prose or poetry by Woodrow Wilson, John Grier Hibben, Henry van Dyke, David Graham Phillips, Stephen French Whitman, Booth Tarkington, Struthers Burt, Jesse Lynch Williams— almost every Princeton writer save Eugene O'Neill. To Princeton's misfortune, O'Neill's career terminated by request three years too soon. The *Princetonian*, the daily, is a conventional enough affair, though its editorial policy occasionally embodies coherent ideas, notably under James Bruce, Forrestal and John Martin, now of *Time*. The *Tiger*, the comic, is generally speaking, inferior to the *Lampoon*, the *Record* and the *Widow*. When it was late to press, John Biggs and I used to write whole issues in the interval between darkness and dawn.

The Triangle Club (acting, singing and dancing) is Princeton's most characteristic organization. Founded by Booth Tarkington with the production of his libretto, *The Honorable Julius Cæsar*, it blooms in a dozen cities every Christmastide. On the whole it represents a remarkable effort and under the wing of Donald Clive Stuart, it has become, unlike the Mask and Wig Club of Pennsylvania, entirely an intramural affair. Its best years have been due to the residence of such talented improvisers as Tarkington, Roy Durstine, Walker Ellis, Ken Clark, or Erdman Harris. In my day it had a rowdy side but now the inebriated comedians and the all-night rehearsals are no more. It furnishes a stamping ground for the multiplying virtuosos of jazz, and the competition for places in the cast and chorus testifies to its popularity and power.

Princeton's sacred tradition is the honor system, a method of pledging that to the amazement of outsiders actually works, with consequent elimination of suspicion and supervision. It is handed over as something humanly precious to the freshmen within a week of their entrance. Personally I have never seen or heard of a Princeton man cheating in an examination, though I am told a few such cases have been mercilessly and summarily dealt with. I can think of a dozen times when a page of notes glanced at in a wash room would have made the difference between failure and success for me, but I can't recall any moral struggles in the matter. It simply doesn't occur to you, any more than it would occur to you to rifle your roommate's pocketbook. Perhaps the thing that struck deepest in the last autumn's unfortunate *Lampoon* was the mention of the honor system with an insinuation and a sneer.

No freshmen allowed on Prospect Street; these are the eighteen upper class clubs. I first heard of them in an article by, I think, Owen Johnson, in the *Saturday Evening Post* nearly twenty years ago. Pictures of Ivy, Cottage, Tiger Inn, and Cap and Gown smiled from the page not like the tombs of robber barons on the Rhine but like friendly and distinguished havens where juniors and seniors might eat three semiprivate meals a day. Later I remember Prospect Street as the red torchlight of the freshman parade flickered over the imposing façades of the houses and the white shirt fronts of the upper classmen, and gleamed in the champagne goblets raised to toast the already prominent members of my class.

There are no fraternities at Princeton; toward the end of each year the eighteen clubs take in an average of about twenty-five sophomores each, seventy-five per cent of the class. The remaining twenty-five per cent continue to eat in the university dining halls and this situation has been the cause of revolutions, protests, petitions, and innumerable editorials in the *Alumni Weekly*. But the clubs represent an alumni investment of two million dollars—the clubs remain.

The Ivy Club was founded in 1879 and four years out of every five it is the most coveted club in Princeton. Its prestige is such that, broadly speaking, it can invite twenty boys out of every class and get fifteen of them. Not infrequently it has its debacles. Cottage, Tiger Inn or Cap and Gown—these three with Ivy have long been known as the "big" clubs—will take ten or fifteen of the boys that Ivy wants and Ivy will be left with a skeleton section of a dozen and considerable bitterness toward its successful rival. The University Cottage Club, feared and hated politically, has made several such raids. Architecturally the most sumptuous of the clubs, Cottage was founded in 1887. It has a large Southern following, particularly in St. Louis and Baltimore. Unlike these two, Tiger Inn cultivates a bluff simplicity. Its membership is largely athletic and while it pretends to disdain social qualifications it has a sharp exclusiveness of its own. The fourth big club, Cap and Gown, began as an organization of earnest and somewhat religious young men, but during the last ten years social and political successes have overshadowed its original purpose. As late as 1916 its president could still sway a wavering crowd of sophomores with the happy slogan of "Join Cap and Gown and Meet God."

Of the others Colonial, an old club with a history of ups and downs, Charter, a comparative newcomer, and Quadrangle, the only club with a distinctly intellectual flavor, are the most influential. One club vanished in the confusion of the war. Two have been founded since, both of them in a little old building which has seen the birth of many. The special characteristics of the clubs vary so that it is hazardous to describe them. One whose members in my day were indefatigable patrons of the Nassau Inn Bar, is now, I am told, a sort of restaurant for the Philadelphian Society.

The Philadelphian Society is Princeton's Y.M.C.A., and in more sagacious moments it is content to function as such. Occasionally, though, it becomes inspired with a Messianic urge to evangelize the university. In my day for example, it imported for the purpose a noted rabble rouser, one Dr. X, who brought along in all seriousness a reformed Bad Example. Such students as out of piety or curiosity could be assembled were herded into Alexander Hall and there ensued one of the most grotesque orgies ever held in the shadow of a great educational institution. When Dr. X's sermon had risen to an inspirational chant, several dozen boys rose, staunch as colored gentlemen, and went forward to be saved. Among them was a popular free thinker and wine bibber whose sincerity we later probed but never determined. The climax of the occasion was the Bad Example's account of his past excesses, culminating in his descent into an actual stone gutter, his conversion and his rise to the position of Bad Example for Dr. X's traveling circus.

By this time the tenderer spirits in the audience had become uncomfortable, the tougher ones riotous; a few left the hall. The unctuousness of the proceedings was too much even for those more timorous days, and later there were protests on the grounds of sheer good taste. Last year "Buchmanism," a milder form of the same melodrama, came in for some outspoken and impatient criticism in the university press.

There is so much of Princeton that I have omitted to touch. Perhaps to be specific for a moment will be a method of being most general. Vivid lights played on the whole colorful picture during the winter and early spring of 1917, just before the war.

Never had the forces which compose the university been so strong and so in evidence. Four score sophomores had democratically refused to join clubs, under the leadership of David Bruce (a son of Senator Bruce), Richard Cleveland (a son of President Cleveland), and Henry Hyacinth Strater of Louisville, Kentucky. Not content with this, the latter, the first man in his class to make the *Princetonian* and an ardent devotee of Tolstoy and Edward Carpenter, came out as a pacifist. He was brilliant and deeply popular; he was much patronized, somewhat disapproved of but never in the slightest degree persecuted. He made a few converts who joined the Quakers and remained pacifists to the end.

The *Nassau Literary Magazine* under John Peale Bishop made a sudden successful bid for popular attention. Jack Newlin, later killed in France, drew Beardsley-like pictures for frontispieces; I wrote stories about current prom girls, stories that were later incorporated into a novel; John Biggs imagined the war with sufficient virtuosity to deceive veterans; and John Bishop made a last metrical effort to link up the current crusade with the revolution—while we all, waiting to go to training camps, found time heartily to despise the bombast and rhetoric of the day. We published a satirical number, a parody on the *Cosmopolitan Magazine*, which infuriated the less nimble-witted members of the English department. We—this time the board of the *Tiger*—issued an irreverent number which burlesqued the faculty, the anticlub movement and then the clubs themselves, by their real names. Everything around us seemed to be breaking up. These were the great days; battle was on the horizon; nothing was ever going to be the same again and nothing mattered. And for the next two years nothing did matter. Five per cent of my class, twenty-one boys, were killed in the war.

That spring I remember late nights at the Nassau Inn with Bill

Coan, the proctor, waiting outside to hale selected specimens before the dean next morning. I remember the long afternoons of military drill on the soccer fields, side by side perhaps with an instructor of the morning. We used to snicker at Professor Wardlaw Miles' attempts to reconcile the snap of the drill manual with his own precise and pedantic English. There were no snickers two years later when he returned from France with a leg missing and his breast bright with decorations. A thousand boys cheered him to his home. I remember the last June night when, with two-thirds of us in uniform, our class sang its final song on the steps of Nassau Hall and some of us wept because we knew we'd never be quite so young any more as we had been here. And I seem to remember a host of more intimate things that are now as blurred and dim as our cigarette smoke or the ivy on Nassau Hall that last night.

Princeton is itself. Williams College is not "what Princeton used to be." Williams is for guided boys whose female relatives want them protected from reality. Princeton is of the world; it is somehow on the "grand scale"; and for sixty years it has been approximately the same. There is less singing and more dancing. The keg parties are over but the stags line up for a hundred yards to cut in on young Lois Moran. There is no Elizabethan Club as at Yale to make a taste for poetry respectable, sometimes too respectable; exceptional talent must create its own public at Princeton, as it must in life. In spite of all persuasions the varsity man conservatively wears his P on the inside of his sweater, but so far no Attorney General Palmers or Judge Thayers have bobbed up among the alumni. President Hibben sometimes disagrees aloud with Secretary Mellon and only ninety-two members of the senior class proclaimed themselves dry last year.

Looking back over a decade one sees the ideal of a university become a myth, a vision, a meadow lark among the smoke stacks. Yet perhaps it is there at Princeton, only more elusive than under the skies of the Prussian Rhineland or Oxfordshire; or perhaps some men come upon it suddenly and possess it, while others wander forever outside. Even these seek in vain through middle age for any corner of the republic that preserves so much of what is fair, gracious, charming and honorable in American life.

PART II

Who's Who—and Why

THIS brief autobiographical essay was written for *The Saturday Evening Post*; it was printed there September 18, 1920. It gives us a glimpse of Fitzgerald in the mood which was characteristic of him in the first flush of his success, six months after the publication of *This Side of Paradise* and his marriage. It shows very clearly why Edmund Wilson said that *This Side of Paradise* was "immaturely imagined" and why he felt it was about the worst book "*of any merit* ever published." (The italics are mine.) Fitzgerald is still inclined to throw his hat in the air and shout. He cannot resist telling us how many stories he has sold, how fast he wrote them, how promptly *This Side of Paradise* was accepted. He is full of high-spirited exaggerations—of how obsessed he was in school by musical comedy, of how many courses he flunked in his freshman year. He is still capable of boyishly bad jokes such as the one with which he ends this essay. It is all very young and happy, and dazed with success, and—if you like to make that kind of judgment—in slightly bad taste.

All these things are the startlingly direct expression of his immediate involvement in his own experience. But even here, dazed and delighted as he is, a part of him is uninvolved, is free to judge his personal experience and the social attitudes of his time. "I went to my regiment happy. I had written a novel. The war could now go on." "I had only three months to live—in those days all infantry officers thought they had only three months to live."

THE HISTORY of my life is the history of the struggle between an overwhelming urge to write and a combination of circumstances bent on keeping me from it.

When I lived in St. Paul and was about twelve I wrote all through every class in school in the back of my geography book and first year Latin and on the margins of themes and declensions and mathematics problems. Two years later a family congress decided that the only way to force me to study was to send me to boarding school. This was a mistake. It took my mind off my writing. I decided to play football, to smoke, to go to college, to do all sorts of irrelevant things that had nothing to do with the real business of life, which, of course, was the proper mixture of description and dialogue in the short story.

But in school I went off on a new tack. I saw a musical comedy called The Quaker Girl, and from that day forth my desk bulged with Gilbert & Sullivan librettos and dozens of notebooks containing the germs of dozens of musical comedies.

Near the end of my last year at school I came across a new musical-comedy score lying on top of the piano. It was a show called His Honor the Sultan, and the title furnished the information that it had been presented by the Triangle Club of Princeton University.

That was enough for me. From then on the university question was settled. I was bound for Princeton.

I spent my entire Freshman year writing an operetta for the Triangle Club. To do this I failed in algebra, trigonometry, coördinate geometry and hygiene. But the Triangle Club accepted my show, and by tutoring all through a stuffy August I managed to come back a Sophomore and act in it as a chorus girl. A little after this came a hiatus. My health broke down and I left college one December to spend the rest of the year recuperating in the West. Almost my final memory before I left was of writing a last lyric on that year's Triangle production while in bed in the infirmary with a high fever.

The next year, 1916-17, found me back in college, but by this time I had decided that poetry was the only thing worth while, so with my head ringing with the meters of Swinburne and the matters of Rupert Brooke I spent the spring doing sonnets, ballads and rondels into the small hours. I had read somewhere that every great poet had written great poetry before he was twenty-one. I had only a year and, besides, war was impending. I must publish a book of startling verse before I was engulfed.

By autumn I was in an infantry officers' training camp at Fort Leavenworth, with poetry in the discard and a brand-new ambition— I was writing an immortal novel. Every evening, concealing my pad behind Small Problems for Infantry, I wrote paragraph after paragraph on a somewhat edited history of me and my imagination. The outline of twenty-two chapters, four of them in verse, was made, two chapters were completed; and then I was detected and the game was up. I could write no more during study period.

This was a distinct complication. I had only three months to live— in those days all infantry officers thought they had only three months to live—and I had left no mark on the world. But such consuming ambition was not to be thwarted by a mere war. Every Saturday at one o'clock when the week's work was over I hurried to the Officers' Club, and there, in a corner of a roomful of smoke, conversation and rattling newspapers, I wrote a one-hundred-and-twenty-thousand-word novel on the consecutive week-ends of three months. There was no revising; there was no time for it. As I finished each chapter I sent it to a typist in Princeton.

Meanwhile I lived in its smeary pencil pages. The drills, marches and Small Problems for Infantry were a shadowy dream. My whole heart was concentrated upon my book.

I went to my regiment happy. I had written a novel. The war could now go on. I forgot paragraphs and pentameters, similes and syllogisms. I got to be a first lieutenant, got my orders overseas— and then the publishers wrote me that though The Romantic Egotist was the most original manuscript they had received for years they couldn't publish it. It was crude and reached no conclusion.

It was six months after this that I arrived in New York and presented my card to the office boys of seven city editors asking to be taken on as a reporter. I had just turned twenty-two, the war was over, and I was going to trail murderers by day and do short stories by night. But the newspapers didn't need me. They sent their office boys out to tell me they didn't need me. They decided definitely and irrevocably by the sound of my name on a calling card that I was absolutely unfitted to be a reporter.

Instead I became an advertising man at ninety dollars a month, writing the slogans that while away the weary hours in rural trolley cars. After hours I wrote stories—from March to June. There were nineteen altogether; the quickest written in an hour and a half, the slowest in three days. No one bought them, no one sent personal letters. I had one hundred and twenty-two rejection slips pinned in a frieze about my room. I wrote movies. I wrote song lyrics. I wrote complicated advertising schemes. I wrote poems. I wrote sketches. I wrote jokes. Near the end of June I sold one story for thirty dollars.

On the Fourth of July, utterly disgusted with myself and all the editors, I went home to St. Paul and informed family and friends that I had given up my position and had come home to write a novel. They nodded politely, changed the subject and spoke of me very gently. But this time I knew what I was doing. I had a novel to write at last, and all through two hot months I wrote and revised and compiled and boiled down. On September fifteenth This Side of Paradise was accepted by special delivery.

In the next two months I wrote eight stories and sold nine. The ninth was accepted by the same magazine that had rejected it four months before. Then, in November, I sold my first story to the editors of *The Saturday Evening Post*. By February I had sold them half a dozen. Then my novel came out. Then I got married. Now I spend my time wondering how it all happened.

In the words of the immortal Julius Cæsar: "That's all there is; there isn't any more."

How to Live on $36,000 a Year

THIS essay was written for *The Saturday Evening Post*, where it was printed April 5, 1924. As it at least lightly suggests, it had its source in the six months of driving work between November, 1923, and April, 1924, during which Fitzgerald produced eleven short stories and earned something over $17,000 to pay off the debts that had accumulated during the previous year, especially during the production of *The Vegetable*. "I really worked hard as hell last winter," he said of this period in a letter to Edmund Wilson "—but it was all trash and it nearly broke my heart as well as my iron constitution." This comment is an exaggerated expression of Fitzgerald's lifelong desire to be a serious writer and an orderly man. This essay's amused sense of his helplessness as one of the "newly rich" is about equally exaggerated, partly, no doubt, because that tone was the right one for the *Post*, but mainly, I think, because his characteristic sense of the representative nature of his own case and his acute insight into the attitudes of the group he represented demanded this kind of irony.

Few writers have put the comic helplessness of the newly rich in our fluid and—for that very reason—etiquette-ridden society so well. How clearly he understands the seduction of success ("Why, it was impossible that I should be poor! I was living at the best hotel in New York!"), how well he knows that most of the newly rich are "mild, slightly used young men" with perfectly good manners, how clearly he sees the absurdity of budgets which allow you "to get the Sunday paper once a month or to subscribe for an almanac." This is the real history of a group (it can hardly be called a class in a society in which no group is stable long enough to acquire continuity) to which at one time or another nearly every one in American society has belonged, though usually in a less spectacular and therefore less classically complete way than Fitzgerald.

You ought to start saving money," The Young Man With a Future assured me just the other day. "You think it's smart to live up to your income. Some day you'll land in the poorhouse."

I was bored, but I knew he was going to tell me anyhow, so I asked him what I'd better do.

"It's very simple," he answered impatiently; "only you establish a trust fund where you can't get your money if you try."

I had heard this before. It is System Number 999. I tried System Number 1 at the very beginning of my literary career four years ago. A month before I was married I went to a broker and asked his advice about investing some money.

"It's only a thousand," I admitted, "but I feel I ought to begin to save right now."

He considered.

"You don't want Liberty Bonds," he said. "They're too easy to turn into cash. You want a good, sound, conservative investment, but also you want it where you can't get at it every five minutes."

He finally selected a bond for me that paid 7 per cent and wasn't listed on the market. I turned over my thousand dollars, and my career of amassing capital began that day.

On that day, also, it ended.

The Heirloom No One Would Buy

My wife and I were married in New York in the spring of 1920, when prices were higher than they had been within the memory of man. In the light of after events it seems fitting that our career should have started at that precise point in time. I had just received a large check from the movies and I felt a little patronizing toward the millionaires riding down Fifth Avenue in their limousines—because my income had a way of doubling every month. This was actually the case. It had done so for several months—I had made only thirty-five dollars the previous August, while here in April I was making three thousand—and it seemed as if it was going to do so forever. At the end of the year it must reach half a million. Of course with such a state of affairs, economy seemed a waste of time. So we went to live at the most expensive hotel in New York, intending to wait there until enough money accumulated for a trip abroad.

To make a long story short, after we had been married for three months I found one day to my horror that I didn't have a dollar in the world, and the weekly hotel bill for two hundred dollars would be due next day.

I remember the mixed feelings with which I issued from the bank on hearing the news.

"What's the matter?" demanded my wife anxiously, as I joined her on the sidewalk. "You look depressed."

"I'm not depressed," I answered cheerfully; "I'm just surprised. We haven't got any money."

"Haven't got any money," she repeated calmly, and we began to walk up the Avenue in a sort of trance. "Well, let's go to the movies," she suggested jovially.

It all seemed so tranquil that I was not a bit cast down. The cashier had not even scowled at me. I had walked in and said to him, "How much money have I got?" And he had looked in a big book and answered, "None."

That was all. There were no harsh words, no blows. And I knew that there was nothing to worry about. I was now a successful author, and when successful authors ran out of money all they had to do was to sign checks. I wasn't poor—they couldn't fool me. Poverty meant being depressed and living in a small remote room and eating at a *rôtisserie* on the corner, while I—why, it was impossible that I should be poor! I was living at the best hotel in New York!

My first step was to try to sell my only possession—my $1000 bond. It was the first of many times I made the attempt; in all financial crises I dig it out and with it go hopefully to the bank, supposing that, as it never fails to pay the proper interest, it has at last assumed a tangible value. But as I have never been able to sell it, it has gradually acquired the sacredness of a family heirloom. It is always referred to by my wife as "your bond," and it was once turned in at the Subway offices after I left it by accident on a car seat!

This particular crisis passed next morning when the discovery that publishers sometimes advance royalties sent me hurriedly to mine. So the only lesson I learned from it was that my money usually turns up somewhere in time of need, and that at the worst you can always borrow—a lesson that would make Benjamin Franklin turn over in his grave.

For the first three years of our marriage our income averaged a little more than $20,000 a year. We indulged in such luxuries as a baby and a trip to Europe, and always money seemed to come easier and easier with less and less effort, until we felt that with just a little more margin to come and go on, we could begin to save.

Plans

We left the Middle West and moved East to a town about fifteen miles from New York, where we rented a house for $300 a month. We hired a nurse for $90 a month; a man and his wife—they acted as butler, chauffeur, yard man, cook, parlor maid and chambermaid—for $160 a month; and a laundress, who came twice a week, for $36 a month. This year of 1923, we told each other, was to be our saving year. We were going to earn $24,000, and live on $18,000, thus giving us a surplus of $6,000 with which to buy safety and security for our old age. We were going to do better at last.

Now as everyone knows, when you want to do better you first buy a book and print your name in the front of it in capital letters. So my wife bought a book, and every bill that came to the house was carefully entered in it, so that we could watch living expenses and cut them away to almost nothing—or at least to $1,500 a month.

We had, however, reckoned without our town. It is one of those little towns springing up on all sides of New York which are built especially for those who have made money suddenly but have never had money before.

My wife and I are, of course, members of this newly rich class. That is to say, five years ago we had no money at all, and what we now do away with would have seemed like inestimable riches to us then. I have at times suspected that we are the only newly rich people in America, that in fact we are the very couple at whom all the articles about the newly rich were aimed.

Now when you say "newly rich" you picture a middle-aged and corpulent man who has a tendency to remove his collar at formal dinners and is in perpetual hot water with his ambitious wife and her titled friends. As a member of the newly rich class, I assure you that this picture is entirely libelous. I myself, for example, am a mild, slightly used young man of twenty-seven, and what corpulence I may have developed is for the present a strictly confidential matter between my tailor and me. We once dined with a bona fide nobleman, but we were both far too frightened to take off our collars or even to demand corned beef and cabbage. Nevertheless we live in a town prepared for keeping money in circulation.

When we came here, a year ago, there were, all together, seven merchants engaged in the purveyance of food—three grocers, three butchers and a fisherman. But when the word went around in food-purveying circles that the town was filling up with the recently enriched as fast as houses could be built for them, the rush of butchers, grocers, fishmen and delicatessen men became enormous. Trainloads of them arrived daily with signs and scales in hand to stake out a claim and sprinkle sawdust upon it. It was like the gold rush of '49, or a big bonanza of the 70's. Older and larger cities were denuded of their stores. Inside of a year eighteen food dealers had set up shop in our main street and might be seen any day waiting in their doorways with alluring and deceitful smiles.

Having long been somewhat overcharged by the seven previous food purveyors we all naturally rushed to the new men, who made it known by large numerical signs in their windows that they intended practically to give food away. But once we were snared, the prices began to rise alarmingly, until all of us scurried like frightened mice from one new man to another, seeking only justice, and seeking it in vain.

Great Expectations

What had happened, of course, was that there were too many food purveyors for the population. It was absolutely impossible for eighteen of them to subsist on the town and at the same time charge moderate prices. So each was waiting for some of the others to give up and move away; meanwhile the only way the rest of them could carry their loans from the bank was by selling things at two or three times the prices in the city fifteen miles away. And that is how our town became the most expensive one in the world.

Now in magazine articles people always get together and found community stores, but none of us would consider such a step. It would absolutely ruin us with our neighbors, who would suspect that we actually cared about our money. When I suggested one day to a local lady of wealth—whose husband, by the way, is reputed to have made his money by vending illicit liquids—that I start a community store known as "F. Scott Fitzgerald—Fresh Meats," she was horrified. So the idea was abandoned.

But in spite of the groceries, we began the year in high hopes. My first play was to be presented in the autumn, and even if living in the East forced our expenses a little over $1,500 a month, the play would easily make up for the difference. We knew what colossal sums were earned on play royalties, and just to be sure, we asked several playwrights what was the maximum that could be earned on a year's run. I never allowed myself to be rash. I took a sum halfway between the maximum and the minimum, and put that down as what we could fairly count on its earning. I think my figures came to about $100,000.

It was a pleasant year; we always had this delightful event of the play to look forward to. When the play succeeded we could buy a house, and saving money would be so easy that we could do it blindfolded with both hands tied behind our backs.

As if in happy anticipation we had a small windfall in March from an unexpected source—a moving picture—and for almost the first time in our lives we had enough surplus to buy some bonds. Of course we had "my" bond, and every six months I clipped the little coupon and cashed it, but we were so used to it that we never counted it as money. It was simply a warning never to tie up cash where we couldn't get at it in time of need.

No, the thing to buy was Liberty Bonds, and we bought four of them. It was a very exciting business. I descended to a shining and impressive room downstairs, and under the chaperonage of a guard deposited my $4,000 in Liberty Bonds, together with "my" bond, in a little tin box to which I alone had the key.

Less Cash Than Company

I left the bank, feeling decidedly solid. I had at last accumulated a capital. I hadn't exactly accumulated it, but there it was anyhow, and if I had died next day it would have yielded my wife $212 a year for life—or for just as long as she cared to live on that amount.

"That," I said to myself with some satisfaction, "is what is called providing for the wife and children. Now all I have to do is to deposit the $100,000 from my play and then we're through with worry forever."

I found that from this time on I had less tendency to worry about current expenses. What if we did spend a few hundred too much now and then? What if our grocery bills did vary mysteriously from $85 to $165 a month, according as to how closely we watched the kitchen? Didn't I have bonds in the bank? Trying to keep under $1,500 a month the way things were going was merely niggardly. We were going to save on a scale that would make such petty economies seem like counting pennies.

The coupons on "my" bond are always sent to an office on lower Broadway. Where Liberty Bond coupons are sent I never had a chance to find out, as I didn't have the pleasure of clipping any. Two of them I was unfortunately compelled to dispose of just one month after I first locked them up. I had begun a new novel, you see, and it occurred to me it would be much better business in the end to keep at the novel and live on the Liberty Bonds while I was writing it. Unfortunately the novel progressed slowly, while the Liberty Bonds went at an alarming rate of speed. The novel was interrupted whenever there was any sound above a whisper in the house, while the Liberty Bonds were never interrupted at all.

And the summer drifted too. It was an exquisite summer and it became a habit with many world-weary New Yorkers to pass their week-ends at the Fitzgerald house in the country. Along near the end of a balmy and insidious August I realized with a shock that only three chapters of my novel were done—and in the little tin safety-deposit vault, only "my" bond remained. There it lay—paying storage on itself and a few dollars more. But never mind; in a little while the box would be bursting with savings. I'd have to hire a twin box next door.

But the play was going into rehearsal in two months. To tide over the interval there were two courses open to me—I could sit down and write some short stories or I could continue to work on the novel and borrow the money to live on. Lulled into a sense of security by our sanguine anticipations I decided on the latter course, and my publishers lent me enough to pay our bills until the opening night.

So I went back to my novel, and the months and money melted away; but one morning in October I sat in the cold interior of a New York theater and heard the cast read through the first act of my play. It was magnificent; my estimate had been too low. I could almost hear the people scrambling for seats, hear the ghostly voices of the movie magnates as they bid against one another for the picture rights. The novel was now laid aside; my days were spent at the theater and my nights in revising and improving the two or three little weak spots in what was to be the success of the year.

The time approached and life became a breathless affair. The November bills came in, were glanced at, and punched onto a bill file on the bookcase. More important questions were in the air. A disgusted letter arrived from an editor telling me I had written only two short stories during the entire year. But what did that matter? The main thing was that our second comedian got the wrong intonation in his first-act exit line.

The play opened in Atlantic City in November. It was a colossal frost. People left their seats and walked out, people rustled their programs and talked audibly in bored impatient whispers. After the second act I wanted to stop the show and say it was all a mistake but the actors struggled heroically on.

There was a fruitless week of patching and revising, and then we gave up and came home. To my profound astonishment the year, the great year, was almost over. I was $5,000 in debt, and my one idea was to get in touch with a reliable poorhouse where we could hire a room and bath for nothing a week. But one satisfaction nobody could take from us. We had spent $36,000, and purchased for one year the right to be members of the newly rich class. What more can money buy?

Taking Account of Stock

The first move, of course, was to get out "my" bond, take it to the bank and offer it for sale. A very nice old man at a shining table was firm as to its value as security, but he promised that if I became overdrawn he would call me up on the phone and give me a chance to make good. No, he never went to lunch with depositors. He considered writers a shiftless class, he said, and assured me that the whole bank was absolutely burglarproof from cellar to roof.

Too discouraged even to put the bond back in the now yawning deposit box, I tucked it gloomily into my pocket and went home. There was no help for it—I must go to work. I had exhausted my resources and there was nothing else to do. In the train I listed all our possessions on which, if it came to that, we could possibly raise money. Here is the list:

1 Oil stove, damaged.
9 Electric lamps, all varieties.
2 Bookcases with books to match.
1 Cigarette humidor, made by a convict.
2 Framed crayon portraits of my wife and me.
1 Medium-priced automobile, 1921 model.
1 Bond, par value $1,000; actual value unknown.

"Let's cut down expenses right away," began my wife when I reached home. "There's a new grocery in town where you pay cash and everything costs only half what it does anywhere else. I can take the car every morning and—"

"Cash!" I began to laugh at this. "Cash!"

The one thing it was impossible for us to do now was to pay cash. It was too late to pay cash. We had no cash to pay. We should rather have gone down on our knees and thanked the butcher and grocer for letting us charge. An enormous economic fact became clear to me at that moment—the rarity of cash, the latitude of choice that cash allows.

"Well," she remarked thoughtfully, "that's too bad. But at least we don't need three servants. We'll get a Japanese to do general housework, and I'll be nurse for a while until you get us out of danger."

"Let them go?" I demanded incredulously. "But we can't let them go! We'd have to pay them an extra two weeks each. Why, to get them out of the house would cost us $125—in cash! Besides, it's nice to have the butler; if we have an awful smash we can send him up to New York to hold us a place in the bread line."

"Well, then, how can we economize?"

"We can't. We're too poor to economize. Economy is a luxury. We could have economized last summer—but now our only salvation is in extravagance."

"How about a smaller house?"

"Impossible! Moving is the most expensive thing in the world; and besides, I couldn't work during the confusion. No," I went on, "I'll just have to get out of this mess the only way I know how, by making more money. Then when we've got something in the bank we can decide what we'd better do."

Over our garage is a large bare room whither I now retired with pencil, paper and the oil stove, emerging the next afternoon at five o'clock with a 7,000-word story. That was something; it would pay the rent and last month's overdue bills. It took twelve hours a day for five weeks to rise from abject poverty back into the middle class, but within that time we had paid our debts, and the cause for immediate worry was over.

But I was far from satisfied with the whole affair. A young man can work at excessive speed with no ill effects, but youth is unfortunately not a permanent condition of life.

I wanted to find out where the $36,000 had gone. Thirty-six thousand is not very wealthy—not yacht-and-Palm-Beach wealthy—but it sounds to me as though it should buy a roomy house full of furniture, a trip to Europe once a year, and a bond or two besides. But our $36,000 had bought nothing at all.

So I dug up my miscellaneous account books, and my wife dug up her complete household record for the year 1923, and we made out the monthly average. Here it is:

HOUSEHOLD EXPENSES	*Apportioned per Month*
Income tax	$ 198.00
Food	202.00
Rent	300.00
Coal, wood, ice, gas, light, phone and water	114.50
Servants	295.00
Golf clubs	105.50
Clothes—three people	158.00
Doctor and dentist	42.50
Drugs and cigarettes	32.50
Automobile	25.00
Books	14.50
All other household expenses	112.50
Total	$1,600.00

"Well, that's not bad," we thought when we had got thus far. "Some of the items are pretty high, especially food and servants. But there's about everything accounted for, and it's only a little more than half our income."

Then we worked out the average monthly expenditures that could be included under pleasure.

Hotel bills—this meant spending the night or charging meals in New York	$ 51.00
Trips—only two, but apportioned per month	43.00
Theater tickets	55.00
Barber and hairdresser	25.00
Charity and loans	15.00
Taxis	15.00
Gambling—this dark heading covers bridge, craps and football bets	33.00
Restaurant parties	70.00
Entertaining	70.00
Miscellaneous	23.00
Total	$400.00

Some of these items were pretty high. They will seem higher to a Westerner than to a New Yorker. Fifty-five dollars for theater tickets means between three and five shows a month, depending on the type of show and how long it's been running. Football games are also included in this, as well as ringside seats to the Dempsey-Firpo fight. As for the amount marked "restaurant parties"—$70 would perhaps take three couples to a popular after-theater cabaret—but it would be a close shave.

We added the items marked "pleasure" to the items marked "household expenses," and obtained a monthly total.

"Fine," I said. "Just $3,000. Now at least we'll know where to cut down, because we know where it goes."

She frowned; then a puzzled, awed expression passed over her face.

"What's the matter?" I demanded. "Isn't it all right? Are some of the items wrong?"

"It isn't the items," she said staggeringly; "it's the total. This only adds up to $2,000 a month."

I was incredulous, but she nodded.

"But listen," I protested; "my bank statements show that we've spent $3,000 a month. You don't mean to say that every month we lose $1,000 dollars?"

"This only adds up to $2,000," she protested, "so we must have."

"Give me the pencil."

For an hour I worked over the accounts in silence, but to no avail.

"Why, this is impossible!" I insisted. "People don't lose $12,000 in a year. It's just—it's just missing."

There was a ring at the doorbell and I walked over to answer it, still dazed by these figures. It was the Banklands, our neighbors from over the way.

"Good heavens!" I announced. "We've just lost $12,000!"

Bankland stepped back alertly.

"Burglars?" he inquired.

"Ghosts," answered my wife.

Mrs. Bankland looked nervously around.

"Really?"

We explained the situation, the mysterious third of our income that had vanished into thin air.

"Well, what we do," said Mrs. Bankland, "is, we have a budget."

"We have a budget," agreed Bankland, "and we stick absolutely to it. If the skies fall we don't go over any item of that budget. That's the only way to live sensibly and save money."

"That's what we ought to do," I agreed.

Mrs. Bankland nodded enthusiastically.

"It's a wonderful scheme," she went on. "We make a certain deposit every month, and all I save on it I can have for myself to do anything I want with."

I could see that my own wife was visibly excited.

"That's what I want to do," she broke out suddenly. "Have a budget. Everybody does it that has any sense."

"I pity anyone that doesn't use that system," said Bankland solemnly. "Think of the inducement to economy—the extra money my wife'll have for clothes."

"How much have you saved so far?" my wife inquired eagerly of Mrs. Bankland.

"So far?" repeated Mrs. Bankland. "Oh, I haven't had a chance so far. You see we only began the system yesterday."

"Yesterday!" we cried.

"Just yesterday," agreed Bankland darkly. "But I wish to heaven I'd started it a year ago. I've been working over our accounts all week, and do you know, Fitzgerald, every month there's $2,000 I can't account for to save my soul."

Headed Toward Easy Street

Our financial troubles are now over. We have permanently left the newly rich class and installed the budget system. It is simple and sensible, and I can explain it to you in a few words. You consider your income as an enormous pie all cut up into slices, each slice representing one class of expenses. Somebody has worked it all out; so you know just what proportion of your income you can spend on each slice. There is even a slice for founding universities, if you go in for that.

For instance, the amount you spend on the theater should be half your drug-store bill. This will enable us to see one play every five and a half months, or two and a half plays a year. We have already picked out the first one, but if it isn't running five and a half months from now we shall be that much ahead. Our allowance for news-papers should be only a quarter of what we spend on self-improvement, so we are considering whether to get the Sunday paper once a month or to subscribe for an almanac.

According to the budget we will be allowed only three-quarters of a servant, so we are on the lookout for a one-legged cook who can come six days a week. And apparently the author of the budget book lives in a town where you can still go to the movies for a nickel and get a shave for a dime. But we are going to give up the expenditure called "Foreign missions, etc.," and apply it to the life of crime instead. Altogether, outside of the fact that there is no slice allowed for "missing" it seems to be a very complete book, and according to the testimonials in the back, if we make $36,000 again this year, the chances are that we'll save at least $35,000.

"But we can't get any of that first $36,000 back," I complained around the house. "If we just had something to show for it I wouldn't feel so absurd."

My wife thought a long while.

"The only thing you can do," she said finally, "is to write a magazine article and call it How to Live on $36,000 a Year."

"What a silly suggestion!" I replied coldly.

How to Live on Practically Nothing a Year

THIS essay was printed in *The Saturday Evening Post*, September 20, 1924. Presumably the success of "How to Live on $36,000 a Year" encouraged Fitzgerald to produce this sequel to it. About six months later he wrote a third essay for the series called "The High Cost of Macaroni" which dealt with the Fitzgeralds' experiences during the next winter in Italy. The *Post* must have rejected it; at least it was not printed during Fitzgerald's lifetime. Like most sequels, this one is not quite so good as its predecessor. When Fitzgerald is at his very best, as he is in "How to Live on $36,000 a Year," he not only makes his personal experience representative—he does that here, too—but gives the representative case the full life of his personal experience. Good as some of the details are here, I think Fitzgerald's personal experience of these places had not yet gone deep enough to allow him to do for the Riviera what he had done for Great Neck in "How to Live on $36,000 a Year."

But the process has begun, and the first signs of the new quality his experience was to acquire on the Riviera are here, especially in the melancholy charm, the almost déja-vu feeling at the end of the essay for the quiet moment when he sits in the garden with René and Bobbé (they were both very real people: René was to play a very important part in his life that summer) and the "liquid dark comes down." This facet of his sensibility had hitherto expressed itself either as humorous helplessness or as exaggerated despair, neither of which involves real commitment; the new mode it begins to show here reached its full development in *Tender Is the Night*, where the liquid dark is all around him.

A LL RIGHT," I said hopefully, "what did it come to for the month?" "Two thousand three hundred and twenty dollars and eighty-two cents." It was the fifth of five long months during which we had tried by every device we knew of to bring the figure of our expenditures safely below the figure of our income. We had succeeded in buying less clothes, less food and fewer luxuries; in fact we had succeeded in everything except in saving money.

"Let's give up," said my wife gloomily. "Look, here's another bill I haven't even opened."

"It isn't a bill; it's got a French stamp."

It was a letter. I read it aloud, and when I finished we looked at each other in a wild, expectant way.

"I don't see why everybody doesn't come over here," it said. "I am now writing from a little inn in France where I just had a meal fit for a king, washed down with champagne, for the absurd sum of sixty-one cents. It costs about one-tenth as much to live over here. From where I sit I can see the smoky peaks of the Alps rising behind a town that was old before Alexander the Great was born. . . ."

By the time we had read the letter for the third time we were in our car bound for New York. As we rushed into the steamship office half an hour later, overturning a rolltop desk and bumping an office boy up against the wall, the agent looked up with mild surprise.

Off to the Riviera to Economize

"Don't utter a word," he said. "You're the twelfth this morning and I understand. You've just got a letter from a friend in Europe telling you how cheap everything is and you want to sail right away. How many?"

"One child," we told him breathlessly.

"Good!" he exclaimed, spreading out a deck of cards on his flat table. "The suits read that you are going on a long, unexpected journey, that you have illness ahead of you and that you will soon meet a number of dark men and women who mean you no good."

As we threw him heavily from the window his voice floated up to us from somewhere between the sixteenth story and the street:

"You sail one week from tomorrow."

Now when a family goes abroad to economize, they don't go to the Wembley exhibition or the Olympic games; in fact they don't go to London and Paris at all, but hasten to the Riviera, which is the southern coast of France and which is reputed to be the cheapest as well as the most beautiful locality in the world. Moreover we were going to the Riviera out of season, which is something like going to Palm Beach for July.

When the Riviera season finishes in late spring, all the wealthy British and Americans move up to Deauville and Trouville, and all the gambling houses and fashionable milliners and jewelers and second-story men close up their establishments and follow their quarry north. Immediately prices fall. The native Rivierans, who have been living on rice and fish all winter, come out of their caves and buy a bottle of red wine and splash about for a bit in their own blue sea.

For two reformed spendthrifts, the Riviera in summer had exactly the right sound. So we put our house in the hands of six real-estate agents and steamed off to France amid the deafening applause of a crowd of friends on the pier—both of whom waved wildly until we were out of sight.

We felt that we had escaped from extravagance and clamor and from all the wild extremes among which we had dwelt for five hectic years, from the tradesman who laid for us and the nurse who bullied us and the couple who kept our house for us and knew us all too well. We were going to the Old World to find a new rhythm for our lives, with a true conviction that we had left our old selves behind forever—and with a capital of just over seven thousand dollars.

The sun coming through high French windows woke us one week later. Outside we could hear the high, clear honk of strange auto horns and we remembered that we were in Paris.

The baby was already sitting up in her cot, ringing the bells which summoned the different *fonctionnaires* of the hotel as though she had determined to start the day immediately. It was indeed her day, for we were in Paris for no other reason than to get her a nurse.

"Entrez!" we shouted together as there was a knock at the door.

The Governess We Did Not Engage

A handsome waiter opened it and stepped inside, whereupon our child ceased her harmonizing upon the bells and regarded him with marked disfavor.

"Iss a mademoiselle who waited out in the street," he remarked.

"Speak French," I said sternly. "We're all French here."

He spoke French for some time.

"All right," I interrupted after a moment. "Now say that again very slowly in English; I didn't quite understand."

"His name's Entrez," remarked the baby helpfully.

"Be that as it may," I flared up, "his French strikes me as very bad."

We discovered finally that an English governess was outside to answer our advertisement in the paper.

"Tell her to come in."

After an interval, a tall, languid person in a Rue de la Paix hat strolled into the room and we tried to look as dignified as is possible when sitting up in bed.

"You're Americans?" she said, seating herself with scornful care.

"Yes."

"I understand you want a nurse. Is this the child?"

"Yes, ma'am."

Here is some high-born lady of the English court, we thought, in temporarily reduced circumstances.

"I've had a great deal of experience," she said, advancing upon our child and attempting unsuccessfully to take her hand. "I'm practically a trained nurse; I'm a lady born and I never complain."

"Complain of what?" demanded my wife.

The applicant waved her hand vaguely.

"Oh, the food, for example."

"Look here," I asked suspiciously, "before we go any farther, let me ask what salary you've been getting."

"For you," she hesitated, "one hundred dollars a month."

"Oh, you wouldn't have to do the cooking too," we assured her; "it's just to take care of one child."

She arose and adjusted her feather boa with fine scorn.

"You'd better get a French nurse," she said, "if you're that kind of people. She won't open the windows at night and your baby will never learn the French word for 'tub,' but you'll only have to pay her ten dollars a month."

"Good-by," we said together.

"I'll come for fifty."

"Good-by," we repeated.

"For forty—and I'll do the baby's washing."

"We wouldn't take you for your board."

The hotel trembled slightly as she closed the door.

"Where's the lady gone?" asked our child.

"She's hunting Americans," we said. "She looked in the hotel register and thought she saw Chicago written after our names."

We are always witty like that with the baby. She considers us the most amusing couple she has ever known.

The Hot, Sweet South of France

After breakfast I went to the Paris branch of our American bank to get money; but I had no sooner entered it than I wished myself at the hotel, or at least that I had gone in by the back way, for I had evidently been recognized and an enormous crowd began to gather outside. The crowd grew, and I considered going to the window and making them a speech; but I thought that might only increase the disturbance, so I looked around intending to ask someone's advice. I recognized no one, however, except one of the bank officials and a Mr. and Mrs. Douglas Fairbanks from America, who were buying francs at a counter in the rear. So I decided not to show myself; and by the time I had cashed my check the crowd had given up and melted away.

I think now that we did well to get away from Paris in nine days, which, after all, was only a week more than we had intended. Every morning a new boatload of Americans poured into the boulevards, and every afternoon our room at the hotel was filled with familiar faces until—except that there was no faint taste of wood alcohol in the refreshments—we might have been in New York. But at last, with six thousand five hundred dollars remaining, and with an English nurse whom we engaged for twenty-six dollars a month, we boarded the train for the Riviera, the hot, sweet South of France.

When your eyes first fall upon the Mediterranean you know at once why it was here that man first stood erect and stretched out his arms toward the sun. It is a blue sea; or rather it is too blue for that hackneyed phrase which has described every muddy pool from pole to pole. It is the fairy blue of Maxfield Parrish's pictures; blue like blue books, blue oil, blue eyes, and in the shadow of the mountains a green belt of land runs along the coast for a hundred miles and makes a playground for the world. The Riviera! The names of its resorts, Cannes, Nice, Monte Carlo, call up the memory of a hundred kings and princes who have lost their thrones and come here to die, of mysterious rajahs and beys flinging blue diamonds to English dancing girls, of Russian millionaires tossing away fortunes at roulette in the lost caviar days before the war.

From Charles Dickens to Catherine de' Medici, from Prince Edward of Wales in the height of his popularity, to Oscar Wilde in the depth of his disgrace, the whole world has come here to forget or to rejoice, to hide its face or have its fling, to build white palaces out of the spoils of oppression or to write the books which sometimes batter those palaces down. Under striped awnings beside the sea grand dukes and gamblers and diplomats and noble courtesans and Balkan czars smoked their slow cigarettes while 1913 drifted into 1914 without a quiver of the calendar, and the fury gathered in the north that was to sweep three-fourths of them away.

Floundering in Flawless French

We reached Hyères, the town of our destination, in the blazing noon, aware immediately of the tropic's breath as it oozed out of the massed pines. A cabby with a large egg-shaped carbuncle in the center of his forehead struggled with a uniformed hotel porter for the possession of our grips.

"Je suis a stranger here," I said in flawless French. "Je veux aller to le best hotel dans le town."

The porter pointed to an imposing auto-bus in the station drive.

"Which is the best?" I asked.

For answer, he picked up our heaviest grip, balanced it a moment in his hand, hit the cabby a crashing blow on the forehead—I immediately understood the gradual growth of the carbuncle—and then pressed us firmly toward the car. I tossed several nickels—or rather francs—upon the prostrate carbuncular man.

"Isn't it hot," remarked the nurse.

"I like it very much indeed," I responded, mopping my forehead and attempting a cool smile. I felt that the moral responsibility was with me. I had picked out Hyères for no more reason than that a friend had once spent a winter there. Besides, we hadn't come here to keep cool; we had come here to economize, to live on practically nothing a year.

"Nevertheless, it's hot," said my wife, and a moment later the child shouted, "Coat off!" in no uncertain voice.

"He must think we want to see the town," I said when, after driving for a mile along a palm-lined road, we stopped in an ancient Mexican-looking square. "Hold on!"

This last was in alarm, for he was hurriedly disembarking our baggage in front of a dilapidated quick-lunch emporium.

"Is this a joke?" I demanded. "Did I tell you to go to the best hotel in town?"

"Here it is," he said.

"No, it isn't. This is the worst hotel I ever saw."

"I am the proprietor," he said.

"I'm sorry, but we've got a baby here"—the nurse obligingly held up the baby—"and we want a more modern hotel, with a bath."

"We have a bath."

"I mean a private bath."

"We will not use while you are here. All the big hotels have shut up themselves for during the summer."

"I don't believe him for a minute," said my wife.

I looked around helplessly. Two scanty, hungry women had come out of the door and were looking voraciously at our baggage. Suddenly I heard the sound of slow hoofs, and glancing up I beheld the carbuncular man driving disconsolately up the dusty street.

"What's le best hotel dans le town?" I shouted at him.

"Non, non, non, non!" he cried, waving his reins excitedly. "Jardin Hôtel open!"

As the proprietor dropped my grip and started toward the cabby at a run, I turned to the hungry women accusingly.

"What do you mean by having a bus like this?" I demanded.

I felt very American and superior; I intimated that if the morals of the French people were in this decadent state I regretted that we had ever entered the war.

"Daddy's hot too," remarked the baby irrelevantly.

"I am not hot!"

"Daddy had better stop talking and find us a hotel," remarked the English nurse, "before we all melt away."

It was the work of but an hour to pay off the proprietor, to add damages for his wounded feelings and to install ourselves in the Hôtel du Jardin, on the edge of town.

"Hyères," says my guidebook, "is the very oldest and warmest of the Riviera winter resorts and is now frequented almost exclusively by the English."

But when we arrived there late in May, even the English, except the very oldest and warmest, had moved away. At dinner, only a superannuated dozen, a slowly decaying dozen, a solemn and dispirited dozen remained. But we were to be there merely while we searched for a villa, and it had the advantage of being amazingly cheap for a first-class hotel. The rate for four of us, including meals, was one hundred and fifty francs—less than eight dollars a day.

The real-estate agent, an energetic young gentleman with his pants buttoned snugly around his chest, called on us next morning.

"Dozens of villas," he said enthusiastically. "We will take the horse and buggy and go see."

It was a simmering morning, but the streets already swarmed with the faces of Southern France—dark faces, for there is an Arab streak along the Riviera, left from turbulent, forgotten centuries. Once the Moors harried the coast for gain, and later, as they swept up through Spain in mad glory, they threw out frontier towns along the shores as outposts for their conquest of the world. They were not the first people, or the last, that have tried to overrun France. All that remains now for proud Moslem hopes is an occasional Moorish tower and the tragic glint of black Eastern eyes.

"Now this villa rents for thirty dollars a month," said the real-estate agent as we stopped at a small house on the edge of town.

"What's the matter with it?" asked my wife suspiciously.

"Nothing at all. It is superb. It has six rooms and a well."

"A well?"

"A fine well."

"Do you mean it has no bathroom?"

"Not what you would call an actual bathroom."

"Drive on," we said.

It was obvious by noon that there were no villas to be let in Hyères. Those we saw were all too hot, too small, too dirty or too *triste*, an expressive word which implies that the mad marquis still walks through the halls in his shroud.

"Yes, we have no villas today," remarked the agent, smiling.

"That's a very old played-out joke," I said, "and I am too hot to laugh."

Extracting Information

Our clothes were hanging on us like wet towels, but when I had established our identity by a scar on my left hand we were admitted to the hotel. I decided to ask one of the lingering Englishmen if there was perhaps another quiet town near by.

Now, asking something of an American or a Frenchman is a definite thing: the only difference is that you can understand the American's reply. But getting an answer from an Englishman is about as complicated as borrowing a match from the Secretary of State. The first one I approached dropped his paper, looked at me in horror and bolted precipitately from the room. This disconcerted me for a moment, but luckily my eyes fell on a man whom I had seen being wheeled in to dinner.

"Good morning," I said. "Could you tell me—" He jerked spasmodically, but to my relief, he was unable to leave his seat. "I wonder if you know a town where I could get a villa for the summer."

"Don't know any at all," he said coldly. "And I wouldn't tell you if I did."

He didn't exactly pronounce the last sentence, but I could read the words as they issued from his eyes.

"I suppose you're a newcomer too," I suggested.

"I've been here every winter for sixteen years."

Pretending to detect an invitation in this, I drew up my chair.

"Then you must know some town," I assured him.

"Cannes, Nice, Monte Carlo."

"But they're too expensive. I want a quiet place to do a lot of work."

"Cannes, Nice, Monte Carlo. All quiet in summer. Don't know any others. Wouldn't tell you if I did. Good day."

Upstairs, the nurse was counting the mosquito bites on the baby, all received during the night, and my wife was adding them up in a big book.

"Cannes, Nice, Monte Carlo," I said.

"I'm glad we're going to leave this broiling town," remarked the nurse.

"I think we'd better try Cannes."

"I think so too," said my wife eagerly. "I hear it's very gay—I mean, it's no economy to stay where you can't work, and I don't believe we can get a villa here after all."

"Let's go on the big boat," said the baby suddenly.

"Silence! We've come to the Riviera and we're here to stay."

The Villa of Our Dreams

So we decided to leave the nurse and baby in Hyères and run up to Cannes, which is a more fashionable town in a more northerly situation along the shore. Now when you run up to somewhere you have to have an automobile, so we bought the only new one in town next day. It had the power of six horses—the age of the horses was not stated—and it was so small that we loomed out of it like giants; so small that you could run it under the veranda for the night. It had no lock, no speedometer, no gauge, and its cost, including the parcel-post charge, was seven hundred and fifty dollars. We started for Cannes in it, and except for the warm exhaust when other cars drove over us, we found the trip comparatively cool.

All the celebrities of Europe have spent a season in Cannes; even the Man with the Iron Mask whiled away twelve years on an island off its shore. Its gorgeous villas are built of stone so soft that it is sawed instead of hewed. We looked at four of them next morning. They were small, neat and clean; you could have matched them in any suburb of Los Angeles. They rented at sixty-five dollars a month.

"I like them," said my wife firmly. "Let's rent one. They look awfully easy to run."

"We didn't come abroad to find a house that was easy to run," I objected. "How could I write looking out on a"—I glanced out the window and my eyes met a splendid view of the sea—"where I'd hear every whisper in the house."

So we moved on to the fourth villa, the wonderful fourth villa the memory of which still causes me to lie awake and hope that some bright day will find me there. It rose in white marble out of a great hill, like a château, like a castle of old. The very taxicab that took us there had romance in its front seat.

"Did you notice our driver?" said the agent, leaning toward me. "He used to be a Russian millionaire."

We peered through the glass at him—a thin dispirited man who ordered the gears about with a lordly air.

"The town is full of them," said the agent. "They're glad to get jobs as chauffeurs, butlers or waiters. The women work as *femmes de chambre* in the hotels."

"Why don't they open tea rooms like Americans do?"

"Many of them aren't fit for anything. We're awfully sorry for them, but—" He leaned forward and tapped on the glass. "Would you mind driving a little faster? We haven't got all day."

"Look," he said when we reached the château on the hill. "There's the Grand Duke Michael's villa next door."

"You mean he's the butler there?"

"Oh, no; he's got money. He's gone north for the summer."

When we had entered through scrolled brass gates that creaked massively as gates should for a king, and when the blinds had been drawn, we were in a high central hall hung with ancestral portraits of knights in armor and courtiers in satin and brocade. It was like a movie set. Flights of marble stairs rose in solid dignity to form a grand gallery into which light dropped through blue figured glass upon a mosaic floor. It was modern, too, with huge clean beds and a model kitchen and three bathrooms and a solemn, silent study overlooking the sea.

"It belonged to a Russian general," said the agent; "killed in Silesia during the war."

"How much is it?"

"For the summer, one hundred and ten dollars a month."

"Done!" I said. "Fix up the lease right away. My wife will go to Hyères immediately to get the—"

"Just a minute," she said, frowning. "How many servants will it take to run this house?"

"Why, I should say,"—the agent glanced at us sharply and hesitated—"about five."

"I should say about eight." She turned to me. "Let's go to Newport and rent the Vanderbilt house instead."

"Remember," said the agent, "you've got the Grand Duke Michael on your left."

"Will he come to see us?" I inquired.

"He would, of course," explained the agent, "only, you see, he's gone away."

We held debate upon the mosaic floor. My theory was that I couldn't work in the little houses and that this would be a real investment because of its romantic inspiration. My wife's theory was that eight servants eat a lot of food and that it simply wouldn't do. We apologized to the agent, shook hands respectfully with the millionaire taxi driver and gave him five francs, and in a state of great dejection returned to Hyères.

"Here's the hotel bill," said my wife as we went despondently in to dinner.

"Thank heaven, it's only fifty-five dollars."

I opened it. To my amazement, tax after tax had been added beneath the bill—government tax, city tax, a ten per cent tax to retip the servants.

I looked gloomily at a nameless piece of meat soaked in a lifeless gravy which reclined on my plate.

"I think it's goat's meat," said the nurse, following my eyes. She turned to my wife. "Did you ever taste goat's meat, Mrs. Fitzgerald?"

But Mrs. Fitzgerald had never tasted goat's meat and Mrs. Fitzgerald had fled.

Hunting His Majesty

As I wandered dismally about the hotel next day, hoping that our house on Long Island hadn't been rented so that we could go home for the summer, I noticed that the halls were even more deserted than usual. There seemed to be more old copies of the Illustrated London News about, and more empty chairs. At dinner we had the goat again. As I looked around the empty dining room I suddenly realized that the last Englishman had taken his cane and his conscience and fled to London. The management was keeping open a two-hundred-room hotel for us alone!

Hyères grew warmer and we rested there in a helpless daze. We knew now why Catherine de' Medici had chosen it for her favorite resort. A month of it in the summer and she must have returned to Paris with a dozen St. Bartholomew's sizzling in her head. In vain we took trips to Nice, to Antibes, to St.-Maximin—we were worried now; a fourth of our seven thousand had slipped away. Then one morning just five weeks after we had left New York we got off the train at a little town that we had never considered before. It was a red little town built close to the sea, with gay red-roofed houses and an air of repressed carnival about it; carnival that would venture forth into the streets before night. We knew that we would love to live in it and we asked a citizen the whereabouts of the real-estate agency.

"Ah, for that you had far better ask the king," he exclaimed.

A principality! A second Monaco! We had not known there were two of them along the French shore.

"And a bank that will cash a letter of credit?"

"For that, too, you must ask the king."

He pointed the way toward the palace down a long shady street, and my wife hurriedly produced a mirror and began powdering her face.

"But our dusty clothes," I said modestly. "Do you think the king will—"

He considered.

"I'm not sure about clothes," he answered. "But I think—yes, I think the king will attend to that for you too."

I hadn't meant that, but we thanked him and with much inward trepidation proceeded toward the imperial domain. After half an hour, when royal turrets had failed to rise against the sky, I stopped another man.

"Can you tell us the way to the imperial palace?"

"The what?"

"We want to get an interview with his majesty—his majesty the king."

The word "king" caught his attention. His mouth opened understandingly and he pointed to a sign over our heads:

"W. F. King," I read, "Anglo-American Bank, Real-Estate Agency, Railroad Tickets, Insurance, Tours and Excursions, Circulating Library."

Where Things are So Cheap

The potentate turned out to be a brisk, efficient Englishman of middle age who had gradually acquired the little town to himself over a period of twenty years.

"We are Americans come to Europe to economize," I told him. "We've combed the Riviera from Nice to Hyères and haven't been able to find a villa. Meanwhile our money is leaking gradually away."

He leaned back and pressed a button and almost immediately a lean, gaunt woman appeared in the door.

"This is Marthe," he said, "your cook."

We could hardly believe our ears.

"Do you mean you have a villa for us?"

"I have already selected one," he said. "My agents saw you getting off the train."

He pressed another button and a second woman stood respectfully beside the first.

"This is Jeanne, your *femme de chambre*. She does the mending, too, and waits on the table. You pay her thirteen dollars a month and you pay Marthe sixteen dollars. Marthe does the marketing, however, and expects to make a little on the side for herself."

"But the villa?"

"The lease is being made out now. The price is seventy-nine dollars a month and your check is good with me. We move you in tomorrow."

Within an hour we had seen our home, a clean cool villa set in a large garden on a hill above town. It was what we had been looking for all along. There was a summerhouse and a sand pile and two bathrooms and roses for breakfast and a gardener who called me milord. When we had paid the rent, only thirty-five hundred dollars, half our original capital, remained. But we felt that at last we could begin to live on practically nothing a year.

In the late afternoon of September 1, 1924, a distinguished-looking young man, accompanied by a young lady might have been seen lounging on a sandy beach in France. Both of them were burned to a deep chocolate brown, so that at first they seemed to be of Egyptian origin; but closer inspection showed that their faces had an Aryan cast and that their voices, when they spoke, had a faintly nasal, North American ring. Near them played a small black child with cotton-white hair who from time to time beat a tin spoon upon a pail and shouted, "*Regardez-moi!*" in no uncertain voice.

Out of the casino near by drifted weird rococo music—a song dealing with the non-possession of a specific yellow fruit in a certain otherwise well-stocked store. Waiters, both Senegalese and European, rushed around among the bathers with many-colored drinks, pausing now and then to chase away the children of the poor, who were dressing and undressing with neither modesty nor self-consciousness, upon the sand.

"Hasn't it been a good summer!" said the young man lazily. "We've become absolutely French."

"And the French are such an æsthetic people," said the young lady, listening for a moment to the banana music. "They know how to live. Think of all the nice things they have to eat!"

"Delicious things! Heavenly things!" exclaimed the young man, spreading some American deviled ham on some biscuits marked Springfield, Illinois. "But then they've studied the food question for two thousand years."

"And things are so cheap here!" cried the young lady enthusiastically. "Think of perfume! Perfume that would cost fifteen dollars in New York, you can get here for five."

The young man struck a Swedish match and lit an American cigarette.

"The trouble with most Americans in France," he remarked sonorously, "is that they won't lead a real French life. They hang around the big hotels and exchange opinions fresh from the States."

"I know," she agreed. "That's exactly what it said in the New York Times this morning."

The American music ended and the English nurse arose, imply-ing that it was time the child went home to supper. With a sigh, the young man arose, too, and shook himself violently, scattering a great quantity of sand.

"We've got to stop on the way and get some Arizon-oil gasoline," he said. "That last stuff was awful."

"The check, suh," said a Senegalese waiter with an accent from well below the Mason-Dixon Line. "That'll be ten francs fo' two glasses of beer."

The young man handed him the equivalent of seventy cents in the gold-colored hat checks of France. Beer was perhaps a little higher than in America, but then he had had the privilege of hear-ing the historic banana song on a real, or almost real, jazz band. And waiting for him at home was a regular French supper—baked beans from the quaint old Norman town of Akron, Ohio, an omelet fragrant with la Chicago bacon and a cup of English tea.

But perhaps you have already recognized in these two cultured Europeans the same barbaric Americans who had left America just five months before; and perhaps you wonder that the change could have come about so quickly. The secret is that they had entered fully into the life of the Old World. Instead of patronizing tourist hotels they had made excursions to quaint little out-of-the-way res-taurants, with the real French atmosphere, where supper for two rarely came to more than ten or fifteen dollars. Not for them the glittering capitals—Paris, Brussels, Rome. They were content with short trips to beautiful historic old towns, such as Monte Carlo, where they once left their automobile with a kindly garage man who paid their hotel bill and bought them tickets home.

The High Cost of Economizing

Yes, our summer had been a complete success. And we had lived on practically nothing—that is, on practically nothing except our original seven thousand dollars. It was all gone.

The trouble is that we had come to the Riviera out of season— that is, out of one season, but in the middle of another. For in sum-mer the people who are trying to economize come South, and the shrewd French know that this class is the very easiest game of all, as people who are trying to get something for nothing are very liable to be.

Exactly where the money went we don't know—we never do. There were the servants, for example. I was very fond of Marthe and Jeanne—and afterwards of their sisters Eugénie and Serpolette, who came in to help—but on my own initiative it would never have occurred to me to insure them all. Yet that was the law. If Jeanne suffocated in her mosquito netting, if Marthe tripped over a bone and broke her thumb, I was responsible. I wouldn't have minded so much except that the little on the side that Marthe made in doing our marketing amounted, as I figure, to about forty-five per cent.

Our weekly bills at the grocer's and the butcher's averaged sixty-five dollars, or higher than they had ever been in an expensive Long Island town. Whatever the meat actually cost, it was almost invariably inedible; while as for the milk, every drop of it had to be boiled, because the cows were tubercular in France. For fresh vegetables we had tomatoes and a little asparagus; that was all—the only garlic that can be put over on us must be administered in sleep. I wondered often how the Riviera middle class—the bank clerk, say, who supports a family on from forty to seventy dollars a month—manages to keep alive.

"It's even worse in winter," a little French girl told us on the beach. "The English and Americans drive the prices up until we can't buy and we don't know what to do. My sister had to go to Marseilles and find work, and she's only fourteen. Next winter I'll go too."

No Money and No Regrets

There simply isn't enough to go around; and the Americans who, because of their own high standard of material comfort, want the best obtainable, naturally have to pay. And in addition, the sharp French tradesmen are always ready to take advantage of a careless American eye.

"I don't like this bill," I said to the food-and-ice deliverer. "I arranged to pay you five francs and not eight francs a day."

He became unintelligible for a moment to gain time.

"My wife added it up," he said.

Those valuable Riviera wives! Always they are adding up their husbands' accounts, and the dear ladies simply don't know one figure from another. Such a talent in the wife of a railroad president would be an asset worth many million dollars.

It is twilight as I write this, and out of my window darkening banks of trees, set one clump behind another in many greens, slope down to the evening sea. The flaming sun has collapsed behind the peaks of the Estérels and the moon already hovers over the Roman aqueducts of Fréjus, five miles away. In half an hour René and Bobbé, officers of aviation, are coming to dinner in their white ducks; and René, who is only twenty-three and has never recovered from having missed the war, will tell us romantically how he wants to smoke opium in Peking and how he writes a few things "for myself alone." Afterwards, in the garden, their white uniforms will grow dimmer as the more liquid dark comes down, until they, like the heavy roses and the nightingales in the pines, will seem to take an essential and indivisible part in the beauty of this proud gay land.

And though we have saved nothing, we have danced the *carmagnole*; and, except for the day when my wife took the mosquito lotion for a mouth wash, and the time when I tried to smoke a French cigarette, and, as Ring Lardner would say, swooned, we haven't yet been sorry that we came.

The dark-brown child is knocking at the door to bid me good night.

"Going on the big boat, daddy?" she says in broken English.

"No."

"Why?"

"Because we're going to try it for another year, and besides—think of perfume!"

We are always like that with the baby. She considers us the wittiest couple she has ever known.

How to Waste Material: A Note on My Generation

THIS essay—or review—was printed in *The Bookman* in May, 1926. It was Fitzgerald's contribution to a campaign he was waging to get wide recognition for the work of Hemingway, whom he had recently got to know in Paris; the campaign is amusingly described by Glenway Wescott in "The Moral of Scott Fitzgerald" and there are some tangential references to it in *The Torrents of Spring*. The essay is a rare illustration of how acute Fitzgerald's adult literary insight was: in the thirty years since these notes on "The Doctor and the Doctor's Wife," "The End of Something," and "Soldier's Home" were written, they have seldom been improved on; and the judgments of such different writers as Sherwood Anderson and Waldo Frank are equally penetrating.

The vigor of Fitzgerald's attack on the fashionable concern at that time for books about American life may seem excess to modern readers, but it was not. It shows, moreover, how conscious Fitzgerald was by this time of what had been, to begin with, only an instinct with him, the crucial need to imagine fully whatever material one uses. What he is really attacking here is the failure of imagination in most of the people who were writing the fashionable books about the American peasants, and what he is asserting is the imagination's triumphant emergence in a book which is thoroughly American in another and better sense. It is typical of him that he thought of the unimagined book as a waste of material, as if the material of literature could be exhausted, like an oil well or a bank account. It is important that this realization of a then nearly unknown writer's achievement shows us how his sense of responsibility and—in a roundabout way—his guilt at not satisfying it were increasing.

EVER since Irving's preoccupation with the necessity for an American background, for some square miles of cleared territory on which colorful variants might presently arise, the question of material has hampered the American writer. For one Dreiser who made a single minded and irreproachable choice there have been a dozen like Henry James who have stupid-got with worry over the matter, and yet another dozen who, blinded by the fading tail of Walt Whitman's comet, have botched their books by the insincere compulsion to write "significantly" about America.

Insincere because it is not a compulsion found in themselves—it is "literary" in the most belittling sense. During the past seven years we have had at least half a dozen treatments of the American farmer, ranging from New England to Nebraska; at least a dozen canny books about youth, some of them with surveys of the American universities for background; more than a dozen novels reflecting various aspects of New York, Chicago, Washington, Detroit, Indianapolis, Wilmington, and Richmond; innumerable novels dealing with American politics, business, society, science, racial problems, art, literature, and moving pictures, and with Americans abroad at peace or in war; finally several novels of change and growth, tracing the swift decades for their own sweet lavender or protesting vaguely and ineffectually against the industrialization of our beautiful old American life. We have had an Arnold Bennett for every five towns—surely by this time the foundations have been laid! Are we competent only to toil forever upon a never completed first floor whose specifications change from year to year?

In any case we are running through our material like spendthrifts—just as we have done before. In the Nineties there began a feverish search for any period of American history that hadn't been "used," and once found it was immediately debauched into a pretty and romantic story. These past seven years have seen the same sort of literary gold rush; and for all our boasted sincerity and sophistication, the material is being turned out raw and undigested in much the same way. One author goes to a midland farm for three months to obtain the material for an epic of the American husbandmen! Another sets off on a like errand to the Blue Ridge Mountains, a third departs with a Corona for the West Indies—one is justified in the belief that what they get hold of will weigh no more than the journalistic loot brought back by Richard Harding Davis and John Fox, Jr., twenty years ago.

Worse, the result will be doctored up to give it a literary flavor. The farm story will be sprayed with a faint dilution of ideas and sensory impressions from Thomas Hardy; the novel of the Jewish tenement block will be festooned with wreaths from "Ulysses" and the later Gertrude Stein; the document of dreamy youth will be prevented from fluttering entirely away by means of great and half great names—Marx, Spencer, Wells, Edward Fitzgerald—dropped like paper weights here and there upon the pages. Finally the novel of business will be cudgeled into being satire by the questionable but constantly reiterated implication that the author and his readers don't partake of the American commercial instinct and aren't a little jealous.

And most of it—the literary beginnings of what was to have been a golden age—is as dead as if it had never been written. Scarcely one of those who put so much effort and enthusiasm, even intelligence, into it, got hold of any material at all.

To a limited extent this was the fault of two men—one of whom, H. L. Mencken, has yet done more for American letters than any man alive. What Mencken felt the absence of, what he wanted, and justly, back in 1920, got away from him, got twisted in his hand. Not because the "literary revolution" went beyond him but because his idea had always been ethical rather than æsthetic. In the history of culture no pure æsthetic idea has ever served as an offensive weapon. Mencken's invective, sharp as Swift's, made its point by the use of the most forceful prose style now written in English. Immediately, instead of committing himself to an infinite series of pronouncements upon the American novel, he should have modulated his tone to the more urbane, more critical one of his early essay on Dreiser.

But perhaps it was already too late. Already he had begotten a family of hammer and tongs men—insensitive, suspicious of glamour, preoccupied exclusively with the external, the contemptible, the "national" and the drab, whose style was a debasement of his least effective manner and who, like glib children, played continually with his themes in his maternal shadow. These were the men who manufactured enthusiasm when each new mass of raw data was dumped on the literary platform—mistaking incoherence for vitality, chaos for vitality. It was the "new poetry movement" over again, only that this time its victims were worth the saving. Every week some new novel gave its author membership in "that little band who are producing a worthy American literature." As one of the charter members of that little band I am proud to state that it has now swollen to seventy or eighty members.

And through a curious misconception of his work, Sherwood Anderson must take part of the blame for this enthusiastic march up a blind alley in the dark. To this day reviewers solemnly speak of him as an inarticulate, fumbling man, bursting with ideas—when, on the contrary, he is the possessor of a brilliant and almost inimitable prose style, and of scarcely any ideas at all. Just as the prose of Joyce in the hands of, say, Waldo Frank becomes insignificant and idiotic, so the Anderson admirers set up Hergesheimer as an anti-Christ and then proceed to imitate Anderson's lapses from that difficult simplicity they are unable to understand. And here again critics support them by discovering merits in the very disorganization that is to bring their books to a timely and unregretted doom.

Now the business is over. "Wolf" has been cried too often. The public, weary of being fooled, has gone back to its Englishmen, its memoirs and its prophets. Some of the late brilliant boys are on lecture tours (a circular informs me that most of them are to speak upon "the literary revolution!"), some are writing pot boilers, a few have definitely abandoned the literary life—they were never sufficiently aware that material, however closely observed, is as elusive as the moment in which it has its existence unless it is purified by an incorruptible style and by the catharsis of a passionate emotion.

Of all the work by the young men who have sprung up since 1920 one book survives—"The Enormous Room" by E. E. Cummings. It is scarcely a novel; it doesn't deal with the American scene; it was swamped in the mediocre downpour, isolated—forgotten. But it lives on, because those few who cause books to live have not been able to endure the thought of its mortality. Two other books, both about the war, complete the possible salvage from the work of the younger generation—"Through the Wheat" and "Three Soldiers," but the former despite its fine last chapters doesn't stand up as well as "Les Croix de Bois" and "The Red Badge of Courage," while the latter is marred by its pervasive flavor of contemporary indignation. But as an augury that someone has profited by this dismal record of high hope and stale failure comes the first work of Ernest Hemingway.

II

"In Our Time" consists of fourteen stories, short and long, with fifteen vivid miniatures interpolated between them. When I try to think of any contemporary American short stories as good as "Big Two-Hearted River," the last one in the book, only Gertrude Stein's "Melanctha," Anderson's "The Egg," and Lardner's "Golden Honeymoon" come to mind. It is the account of a boy on a fishing trip—he hikes, pitches his tent, cooks dinner, sleeps, and next morning casts for trout. Nothing more—but I read it with the most breathless unwilling interest I have experienced since Conrad first bent my reluctant eyes upon the sea.

The hero, Nick, runs through nearly all the stories, until the book takes on almost an autobiographical tint—in fact "My Old Man," one of the two in which this element seems entirely absent, is the least successful of all. Some of the stories show influences but they are invariably absorbed and transmuted, while in "My Old Man" there is an echo of Anderson's way of thinking in those sentimental "horse stories," which inaugurated his respectability and also his decline four years ago.

But with "The Doctor and the Doctor's Wife," "The End of Something," "The Three Day Blow," "Mr. and Mrs. Elliot," and "Soldier's Home" you are immediately aware of something temperamentally new. In the first of these a man is backed down by a half breed Indian after committing himself to a fight. The quality of humiliation in the story is so intense that it immediately calls up every such incident in the reader's past. Without the aid of a comment or a pointing finger one knows exactly the sharp emotion of young Nick who watches the scene.

The next two stories describe an experience at the last edge of adolescence. You are constantly aware of the continual snapping of ties that is going on around Nick. In the half stewed, immature conversation before the fire you watch the awakening of that vast unrest that descends upon the emotional type at about eighteen. Again there is not a single recourse to exposition. As in "Big Two-Hearted River," a picture—sharp, nostalgic, tense—develops before your eyes. When the picture is complete a light seems to snap out, the story is over. There is no tail, no sudden change of pace at the end to throw into relief what has gone before.

Nick leaves home penniless; you have a glimpse of him lying wounded in the street of a battered Italian town, and later of a love affair with a nurse on a hospital roof in Milan. Then in one of the best of the stories he is home again. The last glimpse of him is when his mother asks him, with all the bitter world in his heart, to kneel down beside her in the dining room in Puritan prayer.

Anyone who first looks through the short interpolated sketches will hardly fail to read the stories themselves. "The Garden at Mons" and "The Barricade" are profound essays upon the English officer, written on a postage stamp. "The King of Greece's Tea Party," "The Shooting of the Cabinet Ministers," and "The Cigar-store Robbery" particularly fascinated me, as they did when Edmund Wilson first showed them to me in an earlier pamphlet, over two years ago.

Disregard the rather ill considered blurbs upon the cover. It is sufficient that here is no raw food served up by the railroad restaurants of California and Wisconsin. In the best of these dishes there is not a bit to spare. And many of us who have grown weary of admonitions to "watch this man or that" have felt a sort of renewal of excitement at these stories wherein Ernest Hemingway turns a corner into the street.

PART III

Ten Years in the Advertising Business

THIS brief dialogue was printed in *The Princeton Alumni Weekly* for February 22, 1929, an issue which was devoted—on the whole quite seriously—to Princeton in advertising. It is the work of a Fitzgerald who, without losing them, has grown beyond both his experience in 1919 of writing car-card advertisements for Barron Collier for ninety dollars a month and his experience, ten years later, of appearing along with John Barrymore and several other great names as the judges for an advertising contest—for fifteen hundred dollars.

A good many of the important criticisms of America's business society are implicit here; the standard criticism of the advertising business is overt. Yet this is not simply a satirical attack. Fitzgerald was too honest to turn what he had lived, in all its richness and confusion, into a simple didactic condemnation. Like Gatsby, he knows that in itself the money is not important. But he knows, too, that what it does to people, the world it makes inside and outside them and that they have to live in, is important, that "only the names were the same ten years ago" and that he is puzzled but fascinated by "that gold building." He does not know quite how these things happened or what they mean. He does know that the advertising world is a nightmare reductio ad absurdum of the amusement-park world that he, like the priest of "Absolution," has lived in and been fascinated by for a decade. What he does not know is whether this decade has been wholly lost.

WELL, Mr. Fitzgerald, what can I do for you today?" It was in a high office with a view of that gold building.

"I want a raise, Mr. Cakebook," I said.

"Why?"

"I'm about to get married. You're only paying me Ninety-Five Dollars a month and, of course, with a family to support I've got to think of money."

Into his grey eyes came a faraway look.

"Ninety-Five Dollars is a pretty good salary. By the way, let me see that laundry slogan as it stands now."

"Here it is," I said, with eager pride. "Listen: 'We keep you clean in Muskateen.' How's that? Good, isn't it. 'We keep—'"

"Wait a minute," he interrupted. "Look here, Mr. Fitzgerald. You're too temperamental. Your ideas are too fancy, too imaginative. You ought to keep your feet on the ground. Now let me see that layout."

He worked over it for a moment, his large brain bulging a little from time to time, his lips moving as to melody.

"Now listen to this," he said, "I've got something good: 'Muskateen Laundry—we clean and press.' Listen Miss Schwartz, take that down right away. 'Muskateen Laundry—we clean and press.'"

Obsequiously I congratulated him—when he began to beam I returned to my thesis.

"Well, how about money?"

... "I don't know," he mused. "Of course we try to be fair. How much do you want?"

I thought for a moment.

"Suppose you name an amount."

"I'll tell you, Mr. Fitzgerald," he said, "we don't like to argue about money with anybody. You let us use your picture and your name as one of the judges in this contest and we'll call it a thousand dollars."

"But it'll take a couple of hours," I objected, "and, of course, with a family to support I've got to think of money."

"I realize that. We'll call it fifteen hundred."

"And it's understood that I'm in no sense to endorse this product."

"Perfectly. You merely pick the prettiest girl."

We stood up and I looked out the window at that gold building.

"Did I understand you to say you're about to get married?" he asked.

"Oh, no, I've been married ten years. That was back before those little dots."

"It must have been some other couple."

"It was," I assured him. "Only the names were the same. The tissues change every decade. Good-bye, Mr. Cakebook."

"Good-bye, Mr. Fitzgerald."

One Hundred False Starts

THIS essay was printed in *The Saturday Evening Post*, March 4, 1933. No doubt it makes Fitzgerald's life—or any author's—sound easier and pleasanter than it was, though the evidence of how hard it was is here, if you look, in such things as "I am alone in the privacy of my faded blue room with my sick cat, the bare February branches waving at the window, an ironic paper weight that says Business is Good, a New England conscience—developed in Minnesota—and my greatest problem." That is a very exact description of Fitzgerald in his study at La Paix in the dark thirties, when he headed a letter to Edmund Wilson "La Paix (My God!)."

The writer of this essay is the Fitzgerald who no longer could feel that life might be a thing of sustained joy. He was beginning to tell himself, as he does here, that he must be a tough professional, an attitude toward his work which he never in fact succeeded in establishing completely, though he was going to insist on it more and more, until the insistence reached a climax in "Pasting It Together." But the very irony with which "Afternoon of an Author" reasserts this idea shows the extent to which, even at the end, he had failed to commit himself to it completely. Because he was a writer who had to "start with an emotion—one that's close to me and that I can understand," personal emotional involvement in the experience he wrote about was as important to his work as was his objectivity. The deceptive simplicity with which this essay involves us in his personal struggles as a writer is a modest illustration of what that involvement meant for his work.

"CRACK!" goes the pistol and off starts this entry. Sometimes he has caught it just right; more often he has jumped the gun. On these occasions, if he is lucky, he runs only a dozen yards, looks around and jogs sheepishly back to the starting place. But too frequently he makes the entire circuit of the track under the impression that he is leading the field, and reaches the finish to find he has no following. The race must be run all over again.

A little more training, take a long walk, cut out that nightcap, no meat at dinner, and stop worrying about politics—

So runs an interview with one of the champion false starters of the writing profession—myself. Opening a leather-bound wastebasket which I fatuously refer to as my "notebook," I pick out at random a small, triangular piece of wrapping paper with a canceled stamp on one side. On the other side is written:

Boopsie Dee was cute.

Nothing more. No cue as to what was intended to follow that pre-posterous statement. Boopsie Dee, indeed, confronting me with this single dogmatic fact about herself. Never will I know what happened to her, where and when she picked up her revolting name, and whether her cuteness got her into much trouble.

I pick out another scrap:

Article: Unattractive Things Girls Do, to pair with counter article by woman: Unattractive Things Men Do.
No. 1. Remove glass eye at dinner table.

That's all there is on that scrap. Evidently, an idea that had dissolved into hilarity before it had fairly got under way. I try to revive it seriously. What unattractive things do girls do—I mean universally nowadays—or what unattractive things do a great majority of them do, or a strong minority? I have a few feeble ideas, but no, the notion is dead. I can only think of an article I read somewhere about a woman who divorced her husband because of the way he stalked a chop, and wondering at the time why she didn't try him out on a chop before she married him. No, that all belongs to a gilded age when people could afford to have nervous breakdowns because of the squeak in daddy's shoes.

Lines to an Old Favorite

There are hundreds of these hunches. Not all of them have to do with literature. Some are hunches about importing a troupe of Ouled Naïl dancers from Africa, about bringing the Grand-Guignol from Paris to New York, about resuscitating football at Princeton—I have two scoring plays that will make a coach's reputation in one season—and there is a faded note to "explain to D. W. Griffith why costume plays are sure to come back." Also my plan for a film version of H. G. Wells' History of the World.

These little flurries caused me no travail—they were opium eater's illusions, vanishing with the smoke of the pipe, or you know what I mean. The pleasure of thinking about them was the exact equivalent of having accomplished them. It is the six-page, ten-page, thirty-page globs of paper that grieve me professionally, like unsuccessful oil shafts; they represent my false starts.

There is, for example, one false start which I have made at least a dozen times. It is—or rather has tried to take shape as—a short story. At one time or another, I have written as many words on it as would make a presentable novel, yet the present version is only about twenty-five hundred words long and hasn't been touched for two years. Its present name—it has gone under various aliases—is The Barnaby Family.

From childhood I have had a daydream—what a word for one whose entire life is spent noting them down—about starting at scratch on a desert island and building a comparatively high state of civilization out of the materials at hand. I always felt that Robinson Crusoe cheated when he rescued the tools from the wreck, and this applies equally to the Swiss Family Robinson, the Two Little Savages, and the balloon castaways of The Mysterious Island. In my story, not only would no convenient grain of wheat, repeating rifle, 4000 H. P. Diesel engine or technocratic butler be washed ashore but even my characters would be helpless city dwellers with no more wood lore than a cuckoo out of a clock.

The creation of such characters was easy, and it was easy washing them ashore:

For three long hours they were prostrated on the beach. Then Donald sat up.

"Well, here we are," he said with sleepy vagueness.

"Where?" his wife demanded eagerly.

"It couldn't be America and it couldn't be the Philippines," he said, "because we started from one and haven't got to the other."

"I'm thirsty," said the child.

Donald's eyes went quickly to the shore.

"Where's the raft?" He looked rather accusingly at Vivian. "Where's the raft?"

"It was gone when I woke up."

"It would be," he exclaimed bitterly. "Somebody might have thought of bringing the jug of water ashore. If I don't do it, nothing is done in this house—I mean this family."

All right, go on from there. Anybody—you back there in the tenth row—step up! Don't be afraid. Just go on with the story. If you get stuck, you can look up tropical fauna and flora in the encyclopedia, or call up a neighbor who has been shipwrecked.

Anyhow, that's the exact point where my story—and I still think it's a great plot—begins to creak and groan with unreality. I turn around after a while with a sense of uneasiness—how could anybody believe that rubbish about monkeys throwing coconuts?—trot back to the starting place, and I resume my crouch for days and days.

A Murder That Didn't Jell

During such days I sometimes examine a clot of pages which is headed Ideas for Possible Stories. Among others, I find the following:

Bath water in Princeton or Florida.
Plot—suicide, indulgence, hate, liver and circumstance.
Snubbing or having somebody.
Dancer who found she could fly.

Oddly enough, all these are intelligible, if not enlightening, suggestions to me. But they are all old—old. I am as apt to be stimulated by them as by my signature or the beat of my feet pacing the floor. There is one that for years has puzzled me, that is as great a mystery as Boopsie Dee.

Story: THE WINTER WAS COLD

CHARACTERS

Victoria Cuomo
Mark de Vinci
Jason Tenweather
Ambulance surgeon
Stark, a watchman

What was this about? Who were these people? I have no doubt that one of them was to be murdered or else be a murderer. But all else about the plot I have forgotten long ago.

I turn over a little. Here is something over which I linger longer; a false start that wasn't bad, that might have been run out.

WORDS

When you consider the more expensive article and finally decide on the cheaper one, the salesman is usually thoughtful enough to make it all right for you. "You'll probably get the most wear out of this," he says consolingly, or even, "That's the one I'd choose myself."

The Trimbles were like that. They were specialists in the neat promotion of the next best into the best.

"It'll do to wear around the house," they used to say; or, "We want to wait until we can get a really nice one."

It was at this point that I decided I couldn't write about the Trimbles. They were very nice and I would have enjoyed somebody else's story of how they made out, but I couldn't get under the surface of their lives—what kept them content to make the best of things instead of changing things. So I gave them up.

There is the question of dog stories. I like dogs and would like to write at least one dog story in the style of Mr. Terhune, but see what happens when I take pen in hand:

DOG

THE STORY OF A LITTLE DOG

Only a newsboy with a wizened face, selling his papers on the corner. A big dog fancier, standing on the curb, laughed contemptuously and twitched up the collar of his Airedale coat. Another rich dog man gave a little bark of scorn from a passing taxicab.

But the newsboy was interested in the animal that had crept close to his feet. He was only a cur; his fuzzy coat was inherited from his mother, who had been a fashionable poodle, while in stature he resembled his father, a Great Dane. And somewhere there was a canary concerned, for a spray of yellow feathers projected from his backbone—

You see, I couldn't go on like that. Think of dog owners writing in to the editors from all over the country, protesting that I was no man for that job.

I am thirty-six years old. For eighteen years, save for a short space during the war, writing has been my chief interest in life, and I am in every sense a professional.

Yet even now when, at the recurrent cry of "Baby needs shoes," I sit down facing my sharpened pencils and block of legal-sized paper, I have a feeling of utter helplessness. I may write my story in three days or, as is more frequently the case, it may be six weeks before I have assembled anything worthy to be sent out. I can open a volume from a criminal-law library and find a thousand plots. I can go into highway and byway, parlor and kitchen, and listen to personal revelations that, at the hands of other writers, might endure forever. But all that is nothing—not even enough for a false start.

Twice-Told Tales

Mostly, we authors must repeat ourselves—that's the truth. We have two or three great and moving experiences in our lives—experiences so great and moving that it doesn't seem at the time that anyone else has been so caught up and pounded and dazzled and astonished and beaten and broken and rescued and illuminated and rewarded and humbled in just that way ever before.

Then we learn our trade, well or less well, and we tell our two or three stories—each time in a new disguise—maybe ten times, maybe a hundred, as long as people will listen.

If this were otherwise, one would have to confess to having no individuality at all. And each time I honestly believe that, because I have found a new background and a novel twist, I have really got away from the two or three fundamental tales I have to tell. But it is rather like Ed Wynn's famous anecdote about the painter of boats who was begged to paint some ancestors for a client. The bargain was arranged, but with the painter's final warning that the ancestors would all turn out to look like boats.

When I face the fact that all my stories are going to have a certain family resemblance, I am taking a step toward avoiding false starts. If a friend says he's got a story for me and launches into a tale of being robbed by Brazilian pirates in a swaying straw hut on the edge of a smoking volcano in the Andes, with his fiancée bound and gagged on the roof, I can well believe there were various human emotions involved; but having successfully avoided pirates, volcanoes and fiancées who get themselves bound and gagged on roofs, I can't feel them. Whether it's something that happened twenty years ago or only yesterday, I must start out with an emotion—one that's close to me and that I can understand.

It's an Ill Wind

Last summer I was hauled to the hospital with high fever and a tentative diagnosis of typhoid. My affairs were in no better shape than yours are, reader. There was a story I should have written to pay my current debts, and I was haunted by the fact that I hadn't made a will. If I had really had typhoid I wouldn't have worried about such things, nor made that scene at the hospital when the nurses tried to plump me into an ice bath. I didn't have either the typhoid or the bath, but I continued to rail against my luck that just at this crucial moment I should have to waste two weeks in bed, answering the baby talk of nurses and getting nothing done at all. But three days after I was discharged I had finished a story about a hospital.

The material was soaking in and I didn't know it. I was profoundly moved by fear, apprehension, worry, impatience; every sense was acute, and that is the best way of accumulating material for a story. Unfortunately, it does not always come so easily. I say to myself—looking at the awful blank block of paper—"Now, here's this man Swankins that I've known and liked for ten years. I am privy to all his private affairs, and some of them are wows. I've threatened to write about him, and he says to go ahead and do my worst."

But can I? I've been in as many jams as Swankins, but I didn't look at them the same way, nor would it ever have occurred to me to extricate myself from the Chinese police or from the clutches of that woman in the way Swankins chose. I could write some fine paragraphs about Swankins, but build a story around him that would have an ounce of feeling in it—impossible.

Or into my distraught imagination wanders a girl named Elsie about whom I was almost suicidal for a month, in 1916.

"How about me?" Elsie says. "Surely you swore to a lot of emotion back there in the past. Have you forgotten?"

"No, Elsie, I haven't forgotten."

"Well, then, write a story about me. You haven't seen me for twelve years, so you don't know how fat I am now and how boring I often seem to my husband."

"No, Elsie, I—"

"Oh, come on. Surely I must be worth a story. Why, you used to hang around saying good-bye with your face so miserable and comic that I thought I'd go crazy myself before I got rid of you. And now you're afraid even to start a story about me. Your feeling must have been pretty thin if you can't revive it for a few hours."

"No, Elsie; you don't understand. I have written about you a dozen times. That funny little rabbit curl to your lip, I used it in a story six years ago. The way your face all changed just when you were going to laugh—I gave that characteristic to one of the first girls I ever wrote about. The way I stayed around trying to say good night, knowing that you'd rush to the phone as soon as the front door closed behind me—all that was in a book that I wrote once upon a time."

"I see. Just because I didn't respond to you, you broke me into bits and used me up piecemeal."

"I'm afraid so, Elsie. You see, you never so much as kissed me, except that once with a kind of a shove at the same time, so there really isn't any story."

Plots without emotions, emotions without plots. So it goes sometimes. Let me suppose, however, that I have got under way; two days' work, two thousand words are finished and being typed for a first revision. And suddenly doubts overtake me.

A Jury of One

What if I'm just horsing around? What's going on in this regatta anyhow? Who could care what happens to the girl, when the sawdust is obviously leaking out of her moment by moment? How did I get the plot all tangled up? I am alone in the privacy of my faded blue room with my sick cat, the bare February branches waving at the window, an ironic paper weight that says Business is Good, a New England conscience—developed in Minnesota—and my greatest problem:

"Shall I run it out? Or shall I turn back?"

Shall I say:

"I know I had something to prove, and it may develop farther along in the story?"

Or:

"This is just bullheadedness. Better throw it away and start over."

The latter is one of the most difficult decisions that an author must make. To make it philosophically, before he has exhausted himself in a hundred-hour effort to resuscitate a corpse or disentangle innumerable wet snarls, is a test of whether or not he is really a professional. There are often occasions when such a decision is doubly difficult. In the last stages of a novel, for instance, where there is no question of junking the whole, but when an entire favorite character has to be hauled out by the heels, screeching, and dragging half a dozen good scenes with him.

It is here that these confessions tie up with a general problem as well as with those peculiar to a writer. The decision as to when to quit, as to when one is merely floundering around and causing other people trouble, has to be made frequently in a lifetime. In youth we are taught the rather simple rule never to quit, because we are presumably following programs made by people wiser than ourselves. My own conclusion is that when one has embarked on a course that grows increasingly doubtful and feels the vital forces beginning to be used up, it is best to ask advice, if decent advice is within range. Columbus didn't and Lindbergh couldn't. So my statement at first seems heretical toward the idea that it is pleasantest to live with—the idea of heroism. But I make a sharp division between one's professional life, when, after the period of apprenticeship, not more than 10 per cent of advice is worth a hoot, and one's private and worldly life, when often almost anyone's judgment is better than one's own.

Once, not so long ago, when my work was hampered by so many false starts that I thought the game was up at last, and when my personal life was even more thoroughly obfuscated, I asked an old Alabama Negro:

"Uncle Bob, when things get so bad that there isn't any way out, what do you do then?"

Homely Advice, But Sound

The heat from the kitchen stove stirred his white sideburns as he warmed himself. If I cynically expected a platitudinous answer, a reflection of something remembered from Uncle Remus, I was disappointed.

"Mr. Fitzgerald," he said, "when things get that-away I wuks."

It was good advice. Work is almost everything. But it would be nice to be able to distinguish useful work from mere labor expended. Perhaps that is part of work itself—to find the difference. Perhaps my frequent, solitary sprints around the track are profitable. Shall I tell you about another one? Very well. You see, I had this hunch— But in counting the pages, I find that my time is up and I must put my book of mistakes away. On the fire? No! I put it weakly back in the drawer. These old mistakes are now only toys—and expensive ones at that—give them a toy's cupboard and then hurry back into the serious business of my profession. Joseph Conrad defined it more clearly, more vividly than any man of our time:

"My task is by the power of the written word to make you hear, to make you feel—it is, before all, to make you see."

It's not very difficult to run back and start over again—especially in private. What you aim at is to get in a good race or two when the crowd is in the stand.

Outside the Cabinet-Maker's

THIS delicate little story was printed in *The Century Magazine* in December, 1928. It belongs to the period when the Fitzgeralds were living at Ellerslie, in Wilmington, and their daughter was six. In its essential feelings as well as in a good many particulars, the story is a characteristic example of the way Fitzgerald transmuted actuality to make it true: Fitzgerald's love for his daughter was as intense and as incommunicable as this man's and the Murphys' doll's house was as actual as the Murphys.

The story has the basic simplicity of plan and the care to be explicit, to make no unnecessary mysteries for the reader, that Fitzgerald always aimed at. The very real sense in which the world the hero longs to live in with his daughter is represented by the fairy story and the hopelessness of his trying to communicate his love to her are underlined carefully ("You're my good fairy." "Yes. Look, Daddy! What is that man?"). But the relation between the fairy story and actuality is nonetheless not simple. What is the narrator?—the old king killed? Certainly he is not the young Prince who could share her world: "For a moment he closed his eyes and tried to see with her but he couldn't see—those ragged blinds were drawn against him forever." He could only remember that he once could see. All he can do now is buy her the doll's house which he cannot help knowing is only an expensive piece of cabinet-making and not a fairy castle, and imagine for her mysteries "whose luster and texture he could never see or touch any more himself." " 'I love you.' 'I love you too,' said the little girl, smiling politely."

This is a brilliant, early manifestation of the acceptance of the loss Fitzgerald would never cease to feel, of the understanding which he described by saying he had now necessarily to see himself as a professional writer.

T HE automobile stopped at the corner of Sixteenth and some dingy-looking street. The lady got out. The man and the little girl stayed in the car.

"I'm going to tell him it can't cost more than twenty dollars," said the lady.

"All right. Have you the plans?"

"Oh, yes"—she reached for her bag in the back seat—"at least I have now."

"Dites qu'il ne faut pas avoir les forts placards," said the man. "Ni le bon bois."

"All right."

"I wish you wouldn't talk French," said the little girl.

"Et il faut avoir un bon 'height.' L'un des Murphys était comme ça."

He held his hand five feet from the ground. The lady went through a door lettered "Cabinet-Maker" and disappeared up a small stairs.

The man and the little girl looked around unexpectantly. The neighborhood was red brick, vague, quiet. There were a few darkies doing something or other up the street and an occasional automobile went by. It was a fine November day.

"Listen," said the man to the little girl, "I love you."

"I love you too," said the little girl, smiling politely.

"Listen," the man continued. "Do you see that house over the way?"

The little girl looked. It was a flat in back of a shop. Curtains masked most of its interior, but there was a faint stir behind them. On one window a loose shutter banged from back to forth every few minutes. Neither the man nor the little girl had ever seen the place before.

"There's a Fairy Princess behind those curtains," said the man. "You can't see her but she's there, kept concealed by an Ogre. Do you know what an Ogre is?"

"Yes."

"Well, this Princess is very beautiful with long golden hair."

They both regarded the house. Part of a yellow dress appeared momentarily in the window.

"That's her," the man said. "The people who live there are guarding her for the Ogre. He's keeping the King and Queen prisoner ten thousand miles below the earth. She can't get out until the Prince finds the three—" He hesitated.

"And what, Daddy? The three what?"

"The three—Look! There she is again."

"The three what?"

"The three—the three stones that will release the King and Queen."

He yawned.

"And what then?"

"Then he can come and tap three times on each window and that will set her free."

The lady's head emerged from the upper story of the cabinet-maker's.

"He's busy," she called down. "Gosh, what a nice day!"

"And what, Daddy?" asked the little girl. "Why does the Ogre want to keep her there?"

"Because he wasn't invited to the christening. The Prince has already found one stone in President Coolidge's collar-box. He's looking for the second in Iceland. Every time he finds a stone the room where the Princess is kept turns blue. *Gosh!*"

"What, Daddy?"

"Just as you turned away I could see the room turn blue. That means he's found the second stone."

"Gosh!" said the little girl. "Look! It turned blue again, that means he's found the third stone."

Aroused by the competition the man looked around cautiously and his voice grew tense.

"Do you see what I see?" he demanded. "Coming up the street—there's the Ogre himself, disguised—you know: transformed, like *Mombi* in 'The Land of Oz.'"

"I know."

They both watched. The small boy, extraordinarily small and taking very long steps, went to the door of the flat and knocked; no one answered but he didn't seem to expect it or to be greatly disappointed. He took some chalk from his pocket and began drawing pictures under the door-bell.

"He's making magic signs," whispered the man. "He wants to be sure that the Princess doesn't get out this door. He must know that the Prince has set the King and Queen free and will be along for her pretty soon."

The small boy lingered for a moment; then he went to a window and called an unintelligible word. After a while a woman threw the window open and made an answer that the crisp wind blew away.

"She says she's got the Princess locked up," explained the man.

"Look at the Ogre," said the little girl. "He's making magic signs under the window too. And on the sidewalk. Why?"

"He wants to keep her from getting out, of course. That's why he's dancing. That's a charm too—it's a magic dance."

The Ogre went away, taking very big steps. Two men crossed the street ahead and passed out of sight.

"Who are they, Daddy?"

"They're two of the King's soldiers. I think the army must be gathering over on Market Street to surround the house. Do you know what 'surround' means?"

"Yes. Are those men soldiers too?"

"Those too. And I believe that the old one just behind is the King himself. He's keeping bent down low like that so that the Ogre's people won't recognize him."

"Who is the lady?"

"She's a Witch, a friend of the Ogre's."

The shutter blew closed with a bang and then slowly opened again.

"That's done by the good and bad fairies," the man explained. "They're invisible, but the bad fairies want to close the shutter so nobody can see in and the good ones want to open it."

"The good fairies are winning now."

"Yes." He looked at the little girl. "You're my good fairy."

"Yes. Look, Daddy! What is that man?"

"He's in the King's army too." The clerk of Mr. Miller, the jeweler, went by with a somewhat unmartial aspect. "Hear the whistle? That means they're gathering. And listen—there goes the drum."

"There's the Queen, Daddy. Look at there. Is that the Queen?"

"No, that's a girl called Miss Television." He yawned. He began to think of something pleasant that had happened yesterday. He went into a trance. Then he looked at the little girl and saw that she was quite happy. She was six and lovely to look at. He kissed her.

"That man carrying the cake of ice is also one of the King's soldiers," he said. "He's going to put the ice on the Ogre's head and freeze his brains so he can't do any more harm."

Her eyes followed the man down street. Other men passed. A darky in a yellow darky's overcoat drove by with a cart marked The Del Upholstery Co. The shutter banged again and then slowly opened.

"See, Daddy, the good fairies are winning again."

The man was old enough to know that he would look back to that time—the tranquil street and the pleasant weather and the mystery playing before the child's eyes, mystery which he had created, but whose luster and texture he could never see or touch any more himself. Again he touched his daughter's cheek instead and in payment fitted another small boy and limping man into the story.

"Oh, I love you," he said.

"I know, Daddy," she answered, abstractedly. She was staring at the house. For a moment he closed his eyes and tried to see with her but he couldn't see—those ragged blinds were drawn against him forever. There were only the occasional darkies and the small boys and the weather that reminded him of more glamorous mornings in the past.

The lady came out of the cabinet-maker's shop.

"How did it go?" he asked.

"Good. Il dit qu'il a fait les maisons de poupée pour les Du Ponts. Il va le faire."

"Combien?"

"Vingt-cinq. I'm sorry I was so long."

"Look, Daddy, there go a lot more soldiers!"

They drove off. When they had gone a few miles the man turned around and said, "We saw the most remarkable thing while you were there." He summarized the episode. "It's too bad we couldn't wait and see the rescue."

"But we did," the child cried. "They had the rescue in the next street. And there's the Ogre's body in that yard there. The King and Queen and Prince were killed and now the Princess is queen."

He had liked his King and Queen and felt that they had been too summarily disposed of.

"You had to have a heroine," he said rather impatiently.

"She'll marry somebody and make him Prince."

They rode on abstractedly. The lady thought about the doll's house, for she had been poor and had never had one as a child, the man thought how he had almost a million dollars and the little girl thought about the odd doings on the dingy street that they had left behind.

One Trip Abroad

THIS story was printed in *The Saturday Evening Post*, October 11, 1930. It is Fitzgerald's first attempt to come to terms with his life after Zelda's breakdown the previous spring had forced him to take stock. He has moved a long way from the sense of their European experience which governed "How to Live on Practically Nothing a Year" six years earlier; he is still a certain distance from the attitude which will inform *Tender Is the Night* three years later. The connection between the novel and the story is, however, close, as the identity of the heroines' names most obviously indicates.

Fitzgerald never had any real confidence that, once you were "worn away inside," you could do anything about it; that feeling governs both the novel and the story. With the most innocent intentions in the world, Nicole and Nelson "lose peace and love and health." Fitzgerald understood very clearly the earnest and at the same time irresponsible American desire to have the rewards of serious achievement, especially intellectual and artistic achievement, without making the effort and asserting the discipline the achievement itself requires. In their earnest innocence, Nicole and Nelson gradually become the kind of people who need "half a dozen drinks really to open the eyes and stiffen the mouth up to normal." *Tender Is the Night* is largely concerned to realize what it felt like to be in these verdurous glooms and winding mossy ways. This story is largely concerned with how it felt to be fading away into the forest dim. It takes us, as it were, behind the manner which, as Dick Diver says, remains intact for some time after the morale cracks and thus shows us something about Fitzgerald's mature perception of life that the novel it anticipates does not.

I N THE afternoon the air became black with locusts, and some of the women shrieked, sinking to the floor of the motorbus and covering their hair with traveling rugs. The locusts were coming north, eating everything in their path, which was not so much in that part of the world; they were flying silently and in straight lines, flakes of black snow. But none struck the windshield or tumbled into the car, and presently humorists began holding out their hands, trying to catch some. After ten minutes the cloud thinned out, passed, and the women emerged from the blankets, disheveled and feeling silly. And everyone talked together.

Everyone talked; it would have been absurd not to talk after having been through a swarm of locusts on the edge of the Sahara. The Smyrna-American talked to the British widow going down to Biskra to have one last fling with an as-yet-unencountered sheik. The member of the San Francisco Stock Exchange talked shyly to the author. "Aren't you an author?" he said. The father and daughter from Wilmington talked to the cockney airman who was going to fly to Timbuctoo. Even the French chauffeur turned about and explained in a loud, clear voice: "Bumblebees," which sent the trained nurse from New York into shriek after shriek of hysterical laughter.

Amongst the unsubtle rushing together of the travelers there was one interchange more carefully considered. Mr. and Mrs. Liddell Miles, turning as one person, smiled and spoke to the young American couple in the seat behind:

"Didn't catch any in your hair?"

The young couple smiled back politely.

"No. We survived that plague."

They were in their twenties, and there was still a pleasant touch of bride and groom upon them. A handsome couple; the man rather intense and sensitive, the girl arrestingly light of hue in eyes and hair, her face without shadows, its living freshness modulated by a lovely confident calm. Mr. and Mrs. Miles did not fail to notice their air of good breeding, of a specifically "swell" background, expressed both by their unsophistication and by their ingrained reticence that was not stiffness. If they held aloof, it was because they were sufficient to each other, while Mr. and Mrs. Miles' aloofness toward the other passengers was a conscious mask, a social attitude, quite as public an affair in its essence as the ubiquitous advances of the Smyrna-American, who was snubbed by all.

The Mileses had, in fact, decided that the young couple were "possible" and, bored with themselves, were frankly approaching them.

"Have you been to Africa before? It's been so utterly fascinating! Are you going on to Tunis?"

The Mileses, if somewhat worn away inside by fifteen years of a particular set in Paris, had undeniable style, even charm, and before the evening arrival at the little oasis town of Bou Saada they had all four become companionable. They uncovered mutual friends in New York and, meeting for a cocktail in the bar of the Hotel Transatlantique, decided to have dinner together.

As the young Kellys came downstairs later, Nicole was conscious of a certain regret that they had accepted, realizing that now they were probably committed to seeing a certain amount of their new acquaintances as far as Constantine, where their routes diverged.

In the eight months of their marriage she had been so very happy that it seemed like spoiling something. On the Italian liner that had brought them to Gibraltar they had not joined the groups that leaned desperately on one another in the bar; instead, they seriously studied French, and Nelson worked on business contingent on his recent inheritance of half a million dollars. Also he painted a picture of a smokestack. When one member of the gay crowd in the bar disappeared permanently into the Atlantic just this side of the Azores, the young Kellys were almost glad, for it justified their aloof attitude.

But there was another reason Nicole was sorry they had committed themselves. She spoke to Nelson about it: "I passed that couple in the hall just now."

"Who—the Mileses?"

"No, that young couple—about our age—the ones that were on the other motorbus, that we thought looked so nice, in Bir Rabalou after lunch, in the camel market."

"They did look nice."

"Charming," she said emphatically; "the girl and man, both. I'm almost sure I've met the girl somewhere before."

The couple referred to were sitting across the room at dinner, and Nicole found her eyes drawn irresistibly toward them. They, too, now had companions, and again Nicole, who had not talked to a girl of her own age for two months, felt a faint regret. The Mileses, being formally sophisticated and frankly snobbish, were a different matter. They had been to an alarming number of places and seemed to know all the flashing phantoms of the newspapers.

They dined on the hotel veranda under a sky that was low and full of the presence of a strange and watchful God; around the corners of the hotel the night already stirred with the sounds of which they had so often read but that were even so hysterically unfamiliar —drums from Senegal, a native flute, the selfish, effeminate whine of a camel, the Arabs pattering past in shoes made of old automobile tires, the wail of Magian prayer.

At the desk in the hotel, a fellow passenger was arguing monotonously with the clerk about the rate of exchange, and the inappropriateness added to the detachment which had increased steadily as they went south.

Mrs. Miles was the first to break the lingering silence; with a sort of impatience she pulled them with her, in from the night and up to the table.

"We really should have dressed. Dinner's more amusing if people dress, because they feel differently in formal clothes. The English know that."

"Dress here?" her husband objected. "I'd feel like that man in the ragged dress suit we passed today, driving the flock of sheep."

"I always feel like a tourist if I'm not dressed."

"Well, we are, aren't we?" asked Nelson.

"I don't consider myself a tourist. A tourist is somebody who gets up early and goes to cathedrals and talks about scenery."

Nicole and Nelson, having seen all the official sights from Fez to Algiers, and taken reels of moving pictures and felt improved, confessed themselves, but decided that their experiences on the trip would not interest Mrs. Miles.

"Every place is the same," Mrs. Miles continued. "The only thing that matters is who's there. New scenery is fine for half an hour, but after that you want your own kind to see. That's why some places have a certain vogue, and then the vogue changes and the people move on somewhere else. The place itself really never matters."

"But doesn't somebody first decide that the place is nice?" objected Nelson. "The first ones go there because they like the place."

"Where were you going this spring?" Mrs. Miles asked.

"We thought of San Remo, or maybe Sorrento. We've never been to Europe before."

"My children, I know both Sorrento and San Remo, and you won't stand either of them for a week. They're full of the most awful English, reading the Daily Mail and waiting for letters and talking about the most incredibly dull things. You might as well go to Brighton or Bournemouth and buy a white poodle and a sunshade and walk on the pier. How long are you staying in Europe?"

"We don't know; perhaps several years." Nicole hesitated. "Nelson came into a little money, and we wanted a change. When I was young, my father had asthma and I had to live in the most depressing health resorts with him for years; and Nelson was in the fur business in Alaska and he loathed it; so when we were free we came abroad. Nelson's going to paint and I'm going to study singing." She looked triumphantly at her husband. "So far, it's been absolutely gorgeous."

Mrs. Miles decided, from the evidence of the younger woman's clothes, that it was quite a bit of money, and their enthusiasm was infectious.

"You really must go to Biarritz," she advised them. "Or else come to Monte Carlo."

"They tell me there's a great show here," said Miles, ordering champagne. "The Ouled Naïls. The concierge says they're some kind of tribe of girls who come down from the mountains and learn to be dancers, and what not, till they've collected enough gold to go back to their mountains and marry. Well, they give a performance tonight."

Walking over to the Café of the Ouled Naïls afterward, Nicole regretted that she and Nelson were not strolling alone through the ever-lower, ever-softer, ever-brighter night. Nelson had reciprocated the bottle of champagne at dinner, and neither of them was accustomed to so much. As they drew near the sad flute she didn't want to go inside, but rather to climb to the top of a low hill where a white mosque shone clear as a planet through the night. Life was better than any show; closing in toward Nelson, she pressed his hand.

The little cave of a café was filled with the passengers from the two busses. The girls—light-brown, flat-nosed Berbers with fine, deep-shaded eyes—were already doing each one her solo on the platform. They wore cotton dresses, faintly reminiscent of Southern mammies; under these their bodies writhed in a slow nautch, culminating in a stomach dance, with silver belts bobbing wildly and their strings of real gold coins tinkling on their necks and arms. The flute player was also a comedian; he danced, burlesquing the girls. The drummer, swathed in goatskins like a witch doctor, was a true black from the Sudan.

Through the smoke of cigarettes each girl went in turn through the finger movement, like piano playing in the air—outwardly facile, yet, after a few moments, so obviously exacting—and then through the very simply languid yet equally precise steps of the feet—these were but preparation to the wild sensuality of the culminated dance.

Afterward there was a lull. Though the performance seemed not quite over, most of the audience gradually got up to go, but there was a whispering in the air.

"What is it?" Nicole asked her husband.

"Why, I believe—it appears that for a consideration the Ouled Naïls dance in more or less—ah—Oriental style—in very little except jewelry."

"Oh."

"We're all staying," Mr. Miles assured her jovially. "After all, we're here to see the real customs and manners of the country; a little prudishness shouldn't stand in our way."

Most of the men remained, and several of the women. Nicole stood up suddenly.

"I'll wait outside," she said.

"Why not stay, Nicole? After all, Mrs. Miles is staying."

The flute player was making preliminary flourishes. Upon the raised dais two pale brown children of perhaps fourteen were taking off their cotton dresses. For an instant Nicole hesitated, torn between repulsion and the desire not to appear to be a prig. Then she saw another young American woman get up quickly and start for the door. Recognizing the attractive young wife from the other bus, her own decision came quickly and she followed.

Nelson hurried after her. "I'm going if you go," he said, but with evident reluctance.

"Please don't bother. I'll wait with the guide outside."

"Well—" The drum was starting. He compromised: "I'll only stay a minute. I want to see what it's like."

Waiting in the fresh night, she found that the incident had hurt her—Nelson's not coming with her at once, giving as an argument the fact that Mrs. Miles was staying. From being hurt, she grew angry and made signs to the guide that she wanted to return to the hotel.

Twenty minutes later, Nelson appeared, angry with the anxiety at finding her gone, as well as to hide his guilt at having left her. Incredulous with themselves, they were suddenly in a quarrel.

Much later, when there were no sounds at all in Bou Saada and the nomads in the market place were only motionless bundles rolled up in their burnouses, she was asleep upon his shoulder. Life is progressive, no matter what our intentions, but something was harmed, some precedent of possible nonagreement was set. It was a love match, though, and it could stand a great deal. She and Nelson had passed lonely youths, and now they wanted the taste and smell of the living world; for the present they were finding it in each other.

A month later they were in Sorrento, where Nicole took singing lessons and Nelson tried to paint something new into the Bay of Naples. It was the existence they had planned and often read about. But they found, as so many have found, that the charm of idyllic interludes depends upon one person's "giving the party"—which is to say, furnishing the background, the experience, the patience, against which the other seems to enjoy again the spells of pastoral tranquillity recollected from childhood. Nicole and Nelson were at once too old and too young, and too American, to fall into immediate soft agreement with a strange land. Their vitality made them restless, for as yet his painting had no direction and her singing no immediate prospect of becoming serious. They said they were not "getting anywhere"—the evenings were long, so they began to drink a lot of *vin de Capri* at dinner.

The English owned the hotel. They were aged, come South for good weather and tranquillity; Nelson and Nicole resented the mild tenor of their days. Could people be content to talk eternally about the weather, promenade the same walks, face the same variant of macaroni at dinner month after month? They grew bored, and Americans bored are already in sight of excitement. Things came to head all in one night.

Over a flask of wine at dinner they decided to go to Paris, settle in an apartment and work seriously. Paris promised metropolitan diversion, friends of their own age, a general intensity that Italy lacked. Eager with new hopes, they strolled into the salon after dinner, when, for the tenth time, Nelson noticed an ancient and enormous mechanical piano and was moved to try it.

Across the salon sat the only English people with whom they had had any connection—Gen. Sir Evelyne Fragelle and Lady Fragelle. The connection had been brief and unpleasant—seeing them walking out of the hotel in peignoirs to swim, she had announced, over quite a few yards of floor space, that it was disgusting and shouldn't be allowed.

But that was nothing compared with her response to the first terrific bursts of sound from the electric piano. As the dust of years trembled off the keyboard at the vibration, she shot galvanically forward with the sort of jerk associated with the electric chair. Somewhat stunned himself by the sudden din of Waiting for the Robert

E. Lee, Nelson had scarcely sat down when she projected herself across the room, her train quivering behind her, and, without glancing at the Kellys, turned off the instrument.

It was one of those gestures that are either plainly justified, or else outrageous. For a moment Nelson hesitated uncertainly; then, remembering Lady Fragelle's arrogant remark about his bathing suit, he returned to the instrument in her still-billowing wake and turned it on again.

The incident had become international. The eyes of the entire salon fell eagerly upon the protagonists, watching for the next move. Nicole hurried after Nelson, urging him to let the matter pass, but it was too late. From the outraged English table there arose, joint by joint, Gen. Sir Evelyne Fragelle, faced with perhaps his most crucial situation since the relief of Ladysmith.

" 'T'lee outrageous!—'t'lee outrageous!"

"I beg your pardon," said Nelson.

"Here for fifteen years!" screamed Sir Evelyne to himself. "Never heard of anyone doing such a thing before!"

"I gathered that this was put here for the amusement of the guests."

Scorning to answer, Sir Evelyne knelt, reached for the catch, pushed it the wrong way, whereupon the speed and volume of the instrument tripled until they stood in a wild pandemonium of sound; Sir Evelyne livid with military emotions, Nelson on the point of maniacal laughter.

In a moment the firm hand of the hotel manager settled the matter; the instrument gulped and stopped, trembling a little from its unaccustomed outburst, leaving behind it a great silence in which Sir Evelyne turned to the manager.

"Most outrageous affair ever heard of in my life. My wife turned it off once, and he"—this was his first acknowledgment of Nelson's identity as distinct from the instrument—"he put it on again!"

"This is a public room in a hotel," Nelson protested. "The instrument is apparently here to be used."

"Don't get in an argument," Nicole whispered. "They're old."

But Nelson said, "If there's any apology, it's certainly due to me."

Sir Evelyne's eye was fixed menacingly upon the manager, waiting for him to do his duty. The latter thought of Sir Evelyne's fifteen years of residence, and cringed.

"It is not the habitude to play the instrument in the evening. The clients are each one quiet on his or her table."

"American cheek!" snapped Sir Evelyne.

"Very well," Nelson said; "we'll relieve the hotel of our presence tomorrow."

As a reaction from this incident, as a sort of protest against Sir Evelyne Fragelle, they went not to Paris but to Monte Carlo after all. They were through with being alone.

II

A little more than two years after the Kellys' first visit to Monte Carlo, Nicole woke up one morning into what, though it bore the same name, had become to her a different place altogether.

In spite of hurried months in Paris or Biarritz, it was now home to them. They had a villa, they had a large acquaintance among the spring and summer crowd—a crowd which, naturally, did not include people on charted trips or the shore parties from Mediterranean cruises; these latter had become for them "tourists."

They loved the Riviera in full summer with many friends there and the nights open and full of music. Before the maid drew the curtains this morning to shut out the glare, Nicole saw from her window the yacht of T. F. Golding, placid among the swells of the Monacan Bay, as if constantly bound on a romantic voyage not dependent upon actual motion.

The yacht had taken the slow tempo of the coast; it had gone no farther than to Cannes and back all summer, though it might have toured the world. The Kellys were dining on board that night.

Nicole spoke excellent French; she had five new evening dresses and four others that would do; she had her husband; she had two men in love with her, and she felt sad for one of them. She had her pretty face. At 10:30 she was meeting a third man, who was just beginning to be in love with her "in a harmless way." At one she was having a dozen charming people to luncheon. All that.

"I'm happy," she brooded toward the bright blinds. "I'm young and good-looking, and my name is often in the paper as having been here and there, but really I don't care about shi-shi. I think it's all awfully silly, but if you do want to see people, you might as well see the chic, amusing ones; and if people call you a snob, it's envy, and they know it and everybody knows it."

She repeated the substance of this to Oscar Dane on the Mont Agel golf course two hours later, and he cursed her quietly.

"Not at all," he said. "You're just getting to be an old snob. Do you call that crowd of drunks you run with amusing people? Why, they're not even very swell. They're so hard that they've shifted down through Europe like nails in a sack of wheat, till they stick out of it a little into the Mediterranean Sea."

Annoyed, Nicole fired a name at him, but he answered: "Class C. A good solid article for beginners."

"The Colbys—anyway, her."

"Third flight."

"Marquis and Marquise de Kalb."

"If she didn't happen to take dope and he didn't have other peculiarities."

"Well, then, where are the amusing people?" she demanded impatiently.

"Off by themselves somewhere. They don't hunt in herds, except occasionally."

"How about you? You'd snap up an invitation from every person I named. I've heard stories about you wilder than any you can make up. There's not a man that's known you six months that would take your check for ten dollars. You're a sponge and a parasite and everything—"

"Shut up for a minute," he interrupted. "I don't want to spoil this drive. . . . I just don't like to see you kid yourself," he continued. "What passes with you for international society is just about as hard to enter nowadays as the public rooms at the Casino; and if I can make my living by sponging off it, I'm still giving twenty times more than I get. We dead beats are about the only people in it with any stuff, and we stay with it because we have to."

She laughed, liking him immensely, wondering how angry Nelson would be when he found that Oscar had walked off with his nail scissors and his copy of the New York Herald this morning.

"Anyhow," she thought afterward, as she drove home toward luncheon, "we're getting out of it all soon, and we'll be serious and have a baby. After this last summer."

Stopping for a moment at a florist's, she saw a young woman coming out with an armful of flowers. The young woman glanced at her over the heap of color, and Nicole perceived that she was

extremely smart, and then that her face was familiar. It was someone she had known once, but only slightly; the name had escaped
her, so she did not nod, and forgot the incident until that afternoon.

They were twelve for luncheon: The Goldings' party from the
yacht, Liddell and Cardine Miles, Mr. Dane—seven different nationalities she counted; among them an exquisite young French-
woman, Madame Delauney, whom Nicole referred to lightly as
"Nelson's girl." Noel Delauney was perhaps her closest friend; when
they made up foursomes for golf or for trips, she paired off with
Nelson; but today, as Nicole introduced her to someone as "Nelson's
girl," the bantering phrase filled Nicole with distaste.

She said aloud at luncheon: "Nelson and I are going to get away
from it all."

Everybody agreed that they, too, were going to get away from it
all.

"It's all right for the English," someone said, "because they're doing a sort of dance of death—you know, gayety in the doomed fort,
with the Sepoys at the gate. You can see it by their faces when they
dance—the intensity. They know it and they want it, and they don't
see any future. But you Americans, you're having a rotten time. If
you want to wear the green hat or the crushed hat, or whatever it is,
you always have to get a little tipsy."

"We're going to get away from it all," Nicole said firmly, but
something within her argued: "What a pity—this lovely blue sea,
this happy time." What came afterward? Did one just accept a
lessening of tension? It was somehow Nelson's business to answer
that. His growing discontent that he wasn't getting anywhere ought
to explode into a new life for both of them, or rather a new hope
and content with life. That secret should be his masculine contribution.

"Well, children, good-by."

"It was a great luncheon."

"Don't forget about getting away from it all."

"See you when—"

The guests walked down the path toward their cars. Only Oscar,
just faintly flushed on liqueurs, stood with Nicole on the veranda,
talking on and on about the girl he had invited up to see his stamp
collection. Momentarily tired of people, impatient to be alone, Nicole
listened for a moment and then, taking a glass vase of flowers from

the luncheon table, went through the French windows into the dark, shadowy villa, his voice following her as he talked on and on out there.

It was when she crossed the first salon, still hearing Oscar's monologue on the veranda, that she began to hear another voice in the next room, cutting sharply across Oscar's voice.

"Ah, but kiss me again," it said, stopped; Nicole stopped, too, rigid in the silence, now broken only by the voice on the porch.

"Be careful." Nicole recognized the faint French accent of Noel Delauney.

"I'm tired of being careful. Anyhow, they're on the veranda."

"No, better the usual place."

"Darling, sweet darling."

The voice of Oscar Dane on the veranda grew weary and stopped and, as if thereby released from her paralysis, Nicole took a step—forward or backward, she did not know which. At the sound of her heel on the floor, she heard the two people in the next room breaking swiftly apart.

Then she went in. Nelson was lighting a cigarette; Noel, with her back turned, was apparently hunting for hat or purse on a chair. With blind horror rather than anger, Nicole threw, or rather pushed away from her, the glass vase which she carried. If at anyone, it was at Nelson she threw it, but the force of her feeling had entered the inanimate thing; it flew past him, and Noel Delauney, just turning about, was struck full on the side of her head and face.

"Say, there!" Nelson cried. Noel sank slowly into the chair before which she stood, her hand slowly rising to cover the side of her face. The jar rolled unbroken on the thick carpet, scattering its flowers.

"You look out!" Nelson was at Noel's side, trying to take the hand away to see what had happened.

"*C'est liquide*," gasped Noel in a whisper. "*Est-ce que c'est le sang?*"

He forced her hand away, and cried breathlessly, "No, it's just water!" and then, to Oscar, who had appeared in the doorway: "Get some cognac!" and to Nicole: "You fool, you must be crazy!"

Nicole, breathing hard, said nothing. When the brandy arrived, there was a continuing silence, like that of people watching an operation, while Nelson poured a glass down Noel's throat. Nicole sig-

naled to Oscar for a drink, and, as if afraid to break the silence
without it, they all had a brandy. Then Noel and Nelson spoke at
once:

"If you can find my hat—"

"This is the silliest—"

"—I shall go immediately."

"—thing I ever saw; I—"

They all looked at Nicole, who said: "Have her car drive right up
to the door." Oscar departed quickly.

"Are you sure you don't want to see a doctor?" asked Nelson
anxiously.

"I want to go."

A minute later, when the car had driven away, Nelson came in
and poured himself another glass of brandy. A wave of subsiding
tension flowed over him, showing in his face; Nicole saw it, and
saw also his gathering will to make the best he could of it.

"I want to know just why you did that," he demanded. "No,
don't go, Oscar." He saw the story starting out into the world.

"What possible reason—"

"Oh, shut up!" snapped Nicole.

"If I kissed Noel, there's nothing so terrible about it. It's of absolutely no significance."

She made a contemptuous sound. "I heard what you said to her."

"You're crazy."

He said it as if she were crazy, and wild rage filled her.

"You liar! All this time pretending to be so square, and so particular what I did, and all the time behind my back you've been
playing around with that little—"

She used a serious word, and as if maddened with the sound of it,
she sprang toward his chair. In protection against this sudden attack,
he flung up his arm quickly, and the knuckles of his open hand
struck across the socket of her eye. Covering her face with her hand
as Noel had done ten minutes previously, she fell sobbing to the floor.

"Hasn't this gone far enough?" Oscar cried.

"Yes," admitted Nelson, "I guess it has."

"You go on out on the veranda and cool off."

He got Nicole to a couch and sat beside her, holding her hand.

"Brace up—brace up, baby," he said, over and over. "What are you

—Jack Dempsey? You can't go around hitting French women; they'll sue you."

"He told her he loved her," she gasped hysterically. "She said she'd meet him at the same place. . . Has he gone there now?"

"He's out on the porch, walking up and down, sorry as the devil that he accidentally hit you, and sorry he ever saw Noel Delauney."

"Oh, yes!"

"You might have heard wrong, and it doesn't prove a thing, anyhow."

After twenty minutes, Nelson came in suddenly and sank down on his knees by the side of his wife. Mr. Oscar Dane, reënforced in his idea that he gave much more than he got, backed discreetly and far from unwillingly to the door.

In another hour, Nelson and Nicole, arm in arm, emerged from their villa and walked slowly down to the Café de Paris. They walked instead of driving, as if trying to return to the simplicity they had once possessed, as if they were trying to unwind something that had become visibly tangled. Nicole accepted his explanations, not because they were credible, but because she wanted passionately to believe them. They were both very quiet and sorry.

The Café de Paris was pleasant at that hour, with sunset drooping through the yellow awnings and the red parasols as through stained glass. Glancing about, Nicole saw the young woman she had encountered that morning. She was with a man now, and Nelson placed them immediately as the young couple they had seen in Algeria, almost three years ago.

"They've changed," he commented. "I suppose we have, too, but not so much. They're harder-looking and he looks dissipated. Dissipation always shows in light eyes rather than in dark ones. The girl is *tout ce qu'il y a de chic*, as they say, but there's a hard look in her face too."

"I like her."

"Do you want me to go and ask them if they are that same couple?"

"No! That'd be like lonesome tourists do. They have their own friends."

At that moment people were joining them at their table.

"Nelson, how about tonight?" Nicole asked a little later. "Do you think we can appear at the Goldings' after what's happened?"

"We not only can but we've got to. If the story's around and we're not there, we'll just be handing them a nice juicy subject of conversation. . . . Hello! What on earth—"

Something strident and violent had happened across the café; a woman screamed and the people at one table were all on their feet, surging back and forth like one person. Then the people at the other tables were standing and crowding forward; for just a moment the Kellys saw the face of the girl they had been watching, pale now, and distorted with anger. Panic-stricken, Nicole plucked at Nelson's sleeve.

"I want to get out, I can't stand any more today. Take me home. Is everybody going crazy?"

On the way home, Nelson glanced at Nicole's face and perceived with a start that they were not going to dinner on the Goldings' yacht after all. For Nicole had the beginnings of a well-defined and unmistakable black eye—an eye that by eleven o'clock would be beyond the aid of all the cosmetics in the principality. His heart sank and he decided to say nothing about it until they reached home.

III

There is some wise advice in the catechism about avoiding the occasions of sin, and when the Kellys went up to Paris a month later they made a conscientious list of the places they wouldn't visit any more and the people they didn't want to see again. The places included several famous bars, all the night clubs except one or two that were highly decorous, all the early-morning clubs of every description, and all summer resorts that made whoopee for its own sake—whoopee triumphant and unrestrained—the main attraction of the season.

The people they were through with included three-fourths of those with whom they had passed the last two years. They did this not in snobbishness, but for self-preservation, and not without a certain fear in their hearts that they were cutting themselves off from human contacts forever.

But the world is always curious, and people become valuable merely for their inaccessibility. They found that there were others in Paris who were only interested in those who had separated from the many. The first crowd they had known was largely American, salted with Europeans; the second was largely European, peppered with Americans. This latter crowd was "society," and here and there it touched the ultimate *milieu*, made up of individuals of high position, of great fortune, very occasionally of genius, and always of power. Without being intimate with the great, they made new friends of a more conservative type. Moreover, Nelson began to paint again; he had a studio, and they visited the studios of Brancusi and Leger and Deschamps. It seemed that they were more part of something than before, and when certain gaudy rendezvous were mentioned, they felt a contempt for their first two years in Europe, speaking of their former acquaintances as "that crowd" and as "people who waste your time."

So, although they kept their rules, they entertained frequently at home and they went out to the houses of others. They were young and handsome and intelligent; they came to know what did go and what did not go, and adapted themselves accordingly. Moreover, they were naturally generous and willing, within the limits of common sense, to pay.

When one went out one generally drank. This meant little to Nicole, who had a horror of losing her *soigné* air, losing a touch of bloom or a ray of admiration, but Nelson, thwarted somewhere, found himself quite as tempted to drink at these small dinners as in the more frankly rowdy world. He was not a drunk, he did nothing conspicuous or sodden, but he was no longer willing to go out socially without the stimulus of liquor. It was with the idea of bringing him to a serious and responsible attitude that Nicole decided after a year in Paris, that the time had come to have a baby.

This was coincidental with their meeting Count Chiki Sarolai. He was an attractive relic of the Austrian court, with no fortune or pretense to any, but with solid social and financial connections in France. His sister was married to the Marquis de la Clos d'Hirondelle, who, in addition to being of the ancient noblesse, was a successful banker in Paris. Count Chiki roved here and there, frankly sponging, rather like Oscar Dane, but in a different sphere.

His penchant was Americans; he hung on their words with a pathetic eagerness, as if they would sooner or later let slip their mysterious formula for making money. After a casual meeting, his interest gravitated to the Kellys. During Nicole's months of waiting he was in the house continually, tirelessly interested in anything that

concerned American crime, slang, finance or manners. He came in
for a luncheon or dinner when he had no other place to go, and with
tacit gratitude he persuaded his sister to call on Nicole, who was
immensely flattered.

It was arranged that when Nicole went to the hospital he would
stay at the *appartement* and keep Nelson company—an arrangement
of which Nicole didn't approve, since they were inclined to drink
together. But the day on which it was decided, he arrived with news
of one of his brother-in-law's famous canal-boat parties on the Seine,
to which the Kellys were to be invited and which, conveniently
enough, was to occur three weeks after the arrival of the baby. So,
when Nicole moved out to the American Hospital Count Chiki
moved in.

The baby was a boy. For a while Nicole forgot all about people
and their human status and their value. She even wondered at the
fact that she had become such a snob, since everything seemed trivial
compared with the new individual that, eight times a day, they
carried to her breast.

After two weeks she and the baby went back to the apartment,
but Chiki and his valet stayed on. It was understood, with that
subtlety the Kellys had only recently begun to appreciate, that he
was merely staying until after his brother-in-law's party, but the
apartment was crowded and Nicole wished him gone. But her old
idea, that if one had to see people they might as well be the best,
was carried out in being invited to the De la Clos d'Hirondelles'.

As she lay in her chaise longue the day before the event, Chiki explained the arrangements, in which he had evidently aided.

"Everyone who arrives must drink two cocktails in the American
style before they can come aboard—as a ticket of admission."

"But I thought that very fashionable French—Faubourg St. Ger-
main and all that—didn't drink cocktails."

"Oh, but my family is very modern. We adopt many American
customs."

"Who'll be there?"

"Everyone! Everyone in Paris."

Great names swam before her eyes. Next day she could not resist
dragging the affair into conversation with her doctor. But she was
rather offended at the look of astonishment and incredulity that
came into his eyes.

"Did I understand you aright?" he demanded. "Did I understand you to say that you were going to a ball tomorrow?"

"Why, yes," she faltered. "Why not?"

"My dear lady, you are not going to stir out of the house for two more weeks; you are not going to dance or do anything strenuous for two more after that."

"That's ridiculous!" she cried. "It's been three weeks already! Esther Sherman went to America after—"

"Never mind," he interrupted. "Every case is different. There is a complication which makes it positively necessary for you to follow my orders."

"But the idea is that I'll just go for two hours, because of course I'll have to come home to Sonny—"

"You'll not go for two minutes."

She knew, from the seriousness of his tone, that he was right, but, perversely, she did not mention the matter to Nelson. She said, instead, that she was tired, that possibly she might not go, and lay awake that night measuring her disappointment against her fear. She woke up for Sonny's first feeding, thinking to herself: "But if I just take ten steps from a limousine to a chair and just sit half an hour—"

At the last minute the pale green evening dress from Callets, draped across a chair in her bedroom, decided her. She went.

Somewhere, during the shuffle and delay on the gangplank while the guests went aboard and were challenged and drank down their cocktails with attendant gayety, Nicole realized that she had made a mistake. There was, at any rate, no formal receiving line and, after greeting their hosts, Nelson found her a chair on deck, where presently her faintness disappeared.

Then she was glad she had come. The boat was hung with fragile lanterns, which blended with the pastels of the bridges and the reflected stars in the dark Seine, like a child's dream out of the Arabian Nights. A crowd of hungry-eyed spectators were gathered on the banks. Champagne moved past in platoons like a drill of bottles, while the music, instead of being loud and obtrusive, drifted down from the upper deck like frosting dripping over a cake. She became aware presently that they were not the only Americans there— across the deck were the Liddell Mileses, whom she had not seen for several years.

Other people from that crowd were present, and she felt a faint disappointment. What if this was not the marquis' best party? She remembered her mother's second days at home. She asked Chiki, who was at her side, to point out celebrities, but when she inquired about several people whom she associated with that set, he replied vaguely that they were away, or coming later, or could not be there. It seemed to her that she saw across the room the girl who had made the scene in the Café de Paris at Monte Carlo, but she could not be sure, for with the faint almost imperceptible movement of the boat, she realized that she was growing faint again. She sent for Nelson to take her home.

"You can come right back, of course. You needn't wait for me, because I'm going right to bed."

He left her in the hands of the nurse, who helped her upstairs and aided her to undress quickly.

"I'm desperately tired," Nicole said. "Will you put my pearls away?"

"Where?"

"In the jewel box on the dressing table."

"I don't see it," said the nurse after a minute.

"Then it's in a drawer."

There was a thorough rummaging of the dressing table, without result.

"But of course it's there." Nicole attempted to rise, but fell back, exhausted. "Look for it, please, again. Everything is in it—all my mother's things and my engagement things."

"I'm sorry, Mrs. Kelly. There's nothing in this room that answers to that description."

"Wake up the maid."

The maid knew nothing; then, after a persistent cross-examination, she did know something. Count Sarolai's valet had gone out, carrying his suitcase, half an hour after madame left the house.

Writhing in sharp and sudden pain, with a hastily summoned doctor at her side, it seemed to Nicole hours before Nelson came home. When he arrived, his face was deathly pale and his eyes were wild. He came directly into her room.

"What do you think?" he said savagely. Then he saw the doctor. "Why, what's the matter?"

"Oh, Nelson, I'm sick as a dog and my jewel box is gone, and Chiki's valet has gone. I've told the police. . . . Perhaps Chiki would know where the man—"

"Chiki will never come in this house again," he said slowly. "Do you know whose party that was? Have you got any idea whose party that was?" He burst into wild laughter. "It was our party—our party, do you understand? We gave it—we didn't know it, but we did."

"Maintenant, monsieur, il ne faut pas exciter madame—" the doctor began.

"I thought it was odd when the marquis went home early, but I didn't suspect till the end. They were just guests—Chiki invited all the people. After it was over, the caterers and musicians began to come up and ask me where to send their bills. And that damn Chiki had the nerve to tell me he thought I knew all the time. He said that all he'd promised was that it would be his brother-in-law's sort of party, and that his sister would be there. He said perhaps I was drunk, or perhaps I didn't understand French—as if we'd ever talked anything but English to him."

"Don't pay!" she said. "I wouldn't think of paying."

"So I said, but they're going to sue—the boat people and the others. They want twelve thousand dollars."

She relaxed suddenly. "Oh, go away!" she cried. "I don't care! I've lost my jewels and I'm sick, sick!"

IV

This is the story of a trip abroad, and the geographical element must not be slighted. Having visited North Africa, Italy, the Riviera, Paris and points in between, it was not surprising that eventually the Kellys should go to Switzerland. Switzerland is a country where very few things begin, but many things end.

Though there was an element of choice in their other ports of call, the Kellys went to Switzerland because they had to. They had been married a little more than four years when they arrived one spring day at the lake that is the center of Europe—a placid, smiling spot with pastoral hillsides, a backdrop of mountains and waters of postcard blue, waters that are a little sinister beneath the surface with all the misery that has dragged itself here from every corner of

Europe. Weariness to recuperate and death to die. There are schools, too, and young people splashing at the sunny plages; there is Boni-vard's dungeon and Calvin's city, and the ghosts of Byron and Shelley still sail the dim shores by night; but the Lake Geneva that Nelson and Nicole came to was the dreary one of sanatoriums and rest hotels.

For, as if by some profound sympathy that had continued to exist beneath the unlucky destiny that had pursued their affairs, health had failed them both at the same time; Nicole lay on the balcony of a hotel coming slowly back to life after two successive opera-tions, while Nelson fought for life against jaundice in a hospital two miles away. Even after the reserve force of twenty-nine years had pulled him through, there were months ahead during which he must live quietly. Often they wondered why, of all those who sought pleasure over the face of Europe, this misfortune should have come to them.

"There've been too many people in our lives," Nelson said. "We've never been able to resist people. We were so happy the first year when there weren't any people."

Nicole agreed. "If we could ever be alone—really alone—we could make up some kind of life for ourselves. We'll try, won't we, Nel-son?"

But there were other days when they both wanted company desperately, concealing it from each other. Days when they eyed the obese, the wasted, the crippled and the broken of all nationalities who filled the hotel, seeking for one who might be amusing. It was a new life for them, turning on the daily visits of their two doctors, the arrival of the mail and newspapers from Paris, the little walk into the hillside village or occasionally the descent by funicular to the pale resort on the lake, with its *Kursaal*, its grass beach, its tennis clubs and sight-seeing busses. They read Tauchnitz editions and yellow-jacketed Edgar Wallaces; at a certain hour each day they watched the baby being given its bath; three nights a week there was a tired and patient orchestra in the lounge after dinner, that was all.

And sometimes there was a booming from the vine-covered hills on the other side of the lake, which meant that cannons were shoot-ing at hail-bearing clouds, to save the vineyards from an approaching storm; it came swiftly, first falling from the heavens and then falling again in torrents from the mountains, washing loudly down the roads and stone ditches; it came with a dark, frightening sky and savage filaments of lightning and crashing, world-splitting thunder, while ragged and destroyed clouds fled along before the wind past the hotel. The mountains and the lake disappeared completely; the hotel crouched alone amid tumult and chaos and darkness.

It was during such a storm, when the mere opening of a door admitted a tornado of rain and wind into the hall, that the Kellys for the first time in months saw someone they knew. Sitting downstairs with other victims of frayed nerves, they became aware of two new arrivals—a man and woman whom they recognized as the couple, first seen in Algiers, who had crossed their path several times since. A single unexpressed thought flashed through Nelson and Nicole. It seemed like destiny that at last here in this desolate place they should know them, and watching, they saw other couples eying them in the same tentative way. Yet something held the Kellys back. Had they not just been complaining that there were too many people in their lives?

Later, when the storm had dozed off into a quiet rain, Nicole found herself near the girl on the glass veranda. Under cover of reading a book, she inspected the face closely. It was an inquisitive face, she saw at once, possibly calculating; the eyes, intelligent enough, but with no peace in them, swept over people in a single quick glance as though estimating their value. "Terrible egoist," Nicole thought, with a certain distaste. For the rest, the cheeks were wan, and there were little pouches of ill health under the eyes; these combining with a certain flabbiness of arms and legs to give an impression of unwholesomeness. She was dressed expensively, but with a hint of slovenliness, as if she did not consider the people of the hotel important.

On the whole, Nicole decided she did not like her; she was glad that they had not spoken, but she was rather surprised that she had not noticed these things when the girl crossed her path before.

Telling Nelson her impression at dinner, he agreed with her.

"I ran into the man in the bar, and I noticed we both took nothing but mineral water, so I started to say something. But I got a good look at his face in the mirror and I decided not to. His face is so weak and self-indulgent that it's almost mean—the kind of face that needs half a dozen drinks really to open the eyes and stiffen the mouth up to normal."

After dinner the rain stopped and the night was fine outside. Eager for the air, the Kellys wandered down into the dark garden; on their way they passed the subjects of their late discussion, who withdrew abruptly down a side path.

"I don't think they want to know us any more than we do them," Nicole laughed.

They loitered among the wild rosebushes and the beds of damp-sweet, indistinguishable flowers. Below the hotel, where the terrace fell a thousand feet to the lake, stretched a necklace of lights that was Montreux and Vevey, and then, in a dim pendant, Lausanne; a blurred twinkling across the lake was Evian and France. From some-where below—probably the *Kursaal*—came the sound of full-bodied dance music—American, they guessed, though now they heard American tunes months late, mere distant echoes of what was happening far away.

Over the Dent du Midi, over a black bank of clouds that was the rearguard of the receding storm, the moon lifted itself and the lake brightened; the music and the far-away lights were like hope, like the enchanted distance from which children see things. In their separate hearts Nelson and Nicole gazed backward to a time when life was all like this. Her arm went through his quietly and drew him close.

"We can have it all again," she whispered. "Can't we try, Nelson?"

She paused as two dark forms came into the shadows nearby and stood looking down at the lake below.

Nelson put his arm around Nicole and pulled her closer.

"It's just that we don't understand what's the matter," she said. "Why did we lose peace and love and health, one after the other? If we knew, if there was anybody to tell us, I believe we could try. I'd try so hard."

The last clouds were lifting themselves over the Bernese Alps. Suddenly, with a final intensity, the west flared with pale white lightning. Nelson and Nicole turned, and simultaneously the other couple turned, while for an instant the night was as bright as day. Then darkness and a last low peal of thunder, and from Nicole a sharp, terrified cry. She flung herself against Nelson; even in the darkness she saw that his face was as white and strained as her own.

"Did you see?" she cried in a whisper. "Did you see them?"

"Yes!"

"They're us! They're us! Don't you see?"

Trembling, they clung together. The clouds merged into the dark mass of mountains; looking around after a moment, Nelson and Nicole saw that they were alone together in the tranquil moonlight.

PART IV

"I Didn't Get Over"

THIS story was printed in *Esquire* in October, 1936; it was written the previous August. It is based on the actual swamping of a ferry which was used during maneuvers to get troops across the Talapoosa River near Camp Sheridan, Alabama, where Fitzgerald trained during World War I. Fitzgerald was responsible for saving a number of lives during the accident, but it was his friend, Major Dana Palmer, who got the shell out of the Stokes mortar. Hibbing is, however, the important character. Fitzgerald could see that Hibbing's feeling of inferiority at having missed something mysterious and important in "not getting over" was absurd. But it was a feeling Fitzgerald himself had all his life: he kept a German helmet in his bedroom at Ellerslie and spent a good deal of time trying to learn from books what he believed he would have learned from experience had he got over. The motive for Hibbing's outrageous conduct was all the snubs Fitzgerald had endured in his life: he used to keep lists of them, and was often thrown off by them much as Hibbing was, though not with quite such disastrous consequences (snubbing is one of the ideas for a story mentioned in "One Hundred False Starts"). His feelings in such matters were a part of that social self-consciousness which he understood and was subdued by all his life. "I spent my youth," he said, "in alternately crawling in front of the kitchen maids and insulting the great"; and he once called his mother's family "straight 1850 potato famine Irish," thus demonstrating the very feeling he was trying to explain.

I WAS 'sixteen in college and it was our twentieth reunion this year. We always called ourselves the "War Babies"—anyhow we were all in the damn thing and this time there was more talk about the war than at any previous reunion; perhaps because war's in the air once more.

Three of us were being talkative on the subject in Pete's back room the night after commencement, when a classmate came in and sat down with us. We knew he was a classmate because we remembered his face and name vaguely, and he marched with us in the alumni parade, but he'd left college as a junior and had not been back these twenty years.

"Hello there—ah—Hib," I said after a moment's hesitation. The others took the cue and we ordered a round of beer and went on with what we were talking about.

"I tell you it was kind of moving when we laid that wreath this afternoon." He referred to a bronze plaque commemorating the 'sixteeners who died in the war, "—to read the names of Abe Danzer and Pop McGowan and those fellows and to think they've been dead for twenty years and we've only been getting old."

"To be that young again I'd take a chance on another war," I said, and to the new arrival, "Did you get over, Hib?"

"I was in the army but I didn't get over."

The war and the beer and the hours flowed along. Each of us shot off our mouths about something amusing, or unique, or terrible —all except Hib. Only when a pause came he said almost apologetically:

"I would have gotten over except that I was supposed to have slapped a little boy."

We looked at him inquiringly.

"Of course I didn't," he added. "But there was a row about it." His voice died away but we encouraged him—we had talked a lot and he seemed to rate a hearing.

"Nothing much to tell. The little boy, downtown with his father, said some officer with a blue M. P. band slapped him in the crowd and he picked me! A month afterwards they found he was always accusing soldiers of slapping, so they let me go. What made me think of it was Abe Danzer's name on that plaque this afternoon. They put me in Leavenworth for a couple of weeks while they investigated me, and he was in the next cell to mine."

"Abe *Danzer*!"

He had been sort of a class hero and we all exclaimed aloud in the same breath. "Why he was recommended for the D. S. C.!"

"I know it."

"What on earth was Abe Danzer doing in Leavenworth?"

Again Hibbing became apologetic.

"Oddly enough I was the man who arrested him. But he didn't blame me because it was all in line of duty, and when I turned up in the next cell a few months later he even laughed about it."

We were all interested now.

"What did you have to arrest him for?"

"Well, I'd been put on Military Police in Kansas City and almost the first call I got was to take a detail of men with fixed bayonets to the big hotel there—I forget the name—and go to a certain room. When I tapped on the door I never saw so many shoulder stars and shoulder leaves in my life; there were at least a brace apiece of generals and colonels. And in the center stood Abe Danzer and a girl—

a tart—both of them drunk as monkeys. But it took me a minute's blinking before I realized what else was the matter: the girl had on Abe's uniform overcoat and cap and Abe had on her dress and hat. They'd gone down in the lobby like that and run straight into the divisional commander."

We three looked at him, first incredulous, then shocked, finally believing. We started to laugh but couldn't quite laugh, only looked at Hibbing with silly half-smiles on our faces, imagining ourselves in Abe's position.

"Did he recognize you?" I asked finally.

"Vaguely."

"Then what happened?"

"It was short and sweet. We changed the clothes on them, put their heads in cold water, then I stood them between two files of bayonets and said, forward march."

"And marched old Abe off to prison!" we exclaimed. "It must have been a crazy feeling."

"It was. From the expression in that general's face I thought they'd probably shoot him. When they put me in Leavenworth a couple of months later I was relieved to find he was still alive."

"I can't understand it," Joe Boone said. "He never drank in college."

"That all goes back to his D. S. C.," said Hibbing.

"You know about that too?"

"Oh yes, we were in the same division—we were from the same state."

"I thought you didn't get overseas."

"I didn't. Neither did Abe. But things seemed to happen to him. Of course nothing like what you fellows must have seen—"

"How did he get recommended for the D. S. C.," I interrupted, "—and what did it have to do with his taking to drink?"

"Well, those drownings used to get on his nerves and he used to dream about it—"

"What drownings? For God's sake, man, you're driving us crazy. It's like that story about 'what killed the dog.' "

"A lot of people thought he had nothing to do with the drownings. They blamed the trench mortar."

We groaned—but there was nothing to do but let him tell it his own way.

"Just what trench mortar?" I asked patiently.

"Rather I mean a Stokes mortar. Remember those old stove-pipes, set at forty-five degrees? You dropped a shell down the mouth."

We remembered.

"Well, the day this happened Abe was in command of what they called the 'fourth battalion,' marching it out fifteen miles to the rifle range. It wasn't really a battalion—it was the machine gun company, supply company, medical detachment and Headquarters Company. The H. Q. Company had the trench mortars and the one-pounder and the signal corps, band and mounted orderlies—a whole menagerie in itself. Abe commanded that company but on this day most of the medical and supply officers had to go ahead with the advance, so as ranking first lieutenant he commanded the other companies besides. I tell you he must have been proud that day—twenty-one and commanding a battalion; he rode a horse at the head of it and probably pretended to himself that he was Stonewall Jackson. Say, all this must bore you—it happened on the safe side of the ocean."

"Go on."

"Well, we were in Georgia then, and they have a lot of those little muddy rivers with big old rafts they pull across on a slow cable. You could carry about a hundred men if you packed them in. When Abe's 'battalion' got to this river about noon he saw that the third battalion just ahead wasn't even half over, and he figured it would be a full hour at the rate that boat was going to and fro. So he marched the men a little down the shore to get some shade and was just about to let them have chow when an officer came riding up all covered with dust and said he was Captain Brown and where was the officer commanding Headquarters Company.

" 'That's me, sir,' said Abe.

" 'Well, I just got in to camp and I'm taking command,' the officer said. And then, as if it was Abe's fault, 'I had to ride like hell to catch up with you. Where's the company?'

" 'Right here, sir—and next is the supply, and next is the medical—I was just going to let them eat—'

"At the look in his eye Abe shut up. The captain wasn't going to let them eat yet and probably for no more reason than to show off his authority. He wasn't going to let them rest either—he wanted to see what his company looked like (he'd never seen a Headquarters Company except on paper). He thought for a long time and then he decided that he'd have the trench mortar platoon throw some shells across the river for practice. He gave Abe the evil eye again when Abe told him he only had live shells along; he accepted the suggestion of sending over a couple of signal men to wigwag if any farmers were being bumped off. The signal men crossed on the barge and when they had wigwagged all clear, ran for cover themselves because a Stokes mortar wasn't the most accurate thing in the world. Then the fun began.

"The shells worked on a time fuse and the river was too wide so the first one only made a nice little geyser under water. But the second one just hit the shore with a crash and a couple of horses began to stampede on the ferry boat in midstream only fifty yards down. Abe thought this might hold his majesty the captain but he only said they'd have to get used to shell fire—and ordered another shot. He was like a spoiled kid with an annoying toy.

"Then it happened, as it did once in a while with those mortars no matter what you did—the shell stuck in the gun. About a dozen people yelled, 'Scatter!' all at once and I scattered as far as anybody and lay down flat, and what did that damn fool Abe do but go up and tilt the barrel and spill out the shell. He'd saved the mortar but there were just five seconds between him and eternity and how he got away before the explosion is a mystery to me."

At this point I interrupted Hibbing.

"I thought you said there were some people killed."

"Oh yes—oh but that was later. The third battalion had crossed by now so Captain Brown formed the companies and we marched off to the ferry boat and began embarking. The second lieutenant in charge of the embarking spoke to the captain:

"'This old tub's kind of tired—been over-worked all day. Don't try to pack them in too tight.'

"But the captain wouldn't listen. He sent them over like sardines and each time Abe stood on the rail and shouted:

"'Unbuckle your belts and sling your packs light on your shoulders—' (this without looking at the captain because he'd realized that the captain didn't like orders except his own). But the embarking officer spoke up once more:

"'That raft's low in the water,' he said. 'I don't like it. When you started shooting off that cannon the horses began jumping and the men ran around and unbalanced it.'

" 'Tell the captain,' Abe said. 'He knows everything.'

"The captain overheard this. 'There's just one more load,' he said. 'And I don't want any more discussion about it.'

"It was a big load, even according to Captain Brown's ideas. Abe got up on the side to make his announcement.

" 'They ought to know that by this time,' Captain Brown snapped. 'They've heard it often enough.'

" 'Not this bunch.' Abe rattled it off anyhow and the men unloosened their belts, except a few at the far end who weren't paying attention. Or maybe it was so jammed that they couldn't hear.

"We began to sink when we were half way over, very slowly at first, just a little water around the shoes, but we officers didn't say anything for fear of a panic. It had looked like a small river from the bank but here in the middle and at the rate we were going, it began to look like the widest river in the world.

"In two minutes the water was a yard high in the old soup plate and there wasn't any use concealing things any longer. For once the captain was tongue-tied. Abe got up on the side again and said to stay calm, and not rock the boat and we'd get there, and made his speech one last time about slipping off the packs, and told the ones that could swim to jump off when it got to their hips. The men took it well but you could almost tell from their faces which ones could swim and which couldn't.

"She went down with a big *whush!* just twenty yards from shore; her nose grounded in a mud bank five feet under water.

"I don't remember much about the next fifteen minutes. I dove and swam out into the river a few yards for a view but it all looked like a mass of khaki and water with some sound over it that I remember as a sustained monotone but was composed, I suppose, of cussing, and a few yells of fright, and even a little kidding and laughter. I swam in and helped pull people to shore, but it was a slow business in our shoes . . .

"When there was nothing more in sight in the river (except one corner of the barge which had perversely decided to bob up) Captain Brown and Abe met. The captain was weak and shaking and his arrogance was gone.

" 'Oh God,' he said. 'What'll I do?'

"Abe took control of things—he fell the men in and got squad reports to see if anyone was missing.

"There were three missing in the first squad alone and we didn't wait for the rest—we called for twenty good swimmers to strip and start diving and as fast as they pulled in a body we started a medico working on it. We pulled out twenty-eight bodies and revived seven. And one of the divers didn't come up—he was found floating down the river next day and they gave a medal and a pension to his widow."

Hibbing paused and then added: "But I know that's small potatoes to you fellows in the big time."

"Sounds exciting enough to me," said Joe Boone. "I had a good time in France but I spent most of it guarding prisoners at Brest."

"But how about finishing this?" I demanded. "Why did this drive Abe hell-raising?"

"That was the captain," said Hibbing slowly. "A couple of officers tried to get Abe a citation or something for the trench mortar thing. The captain didn't like that, and he began going around saying that when Abe jumped up on the side of the barge to give the unsling order, he'd hung on to the ferry cable and pulled it out of whack. The captain found a couple of people who agreed with him but there were others who thought it was overloading and the commotion the horses made at the shell bursts. But Abe was never very happy in the army after that."

There was an emphatic interruption in the person of Pete himself who said in no uncertain words:

"Mr. Tomlinson and Mr. Boone. Your wives say they're calling for the last time. They say this has been one night too often, and if you don't get back to the Inn in ten minutes they driving to Philadelphia."

Tommy and Joe Boone arose reluctantly.

"I'm afraid I've monopolized the evening," said Hibbing. "And after what you fellows must have seen."

When they had gone I lingered.

"So Abe wasn't killed in France."

"No—you'll notice all that tablet says is 'died in service.'"

"What did he die of?"

Hibbing hesitated.

"He was shot by a guard trying to escape from Leavenworth. They'd given him ten years."

"God! And what a great guy he was in college."

"I suppose he was to his friends. But he was a good deal of a snob wasn't he?"

"Maybe to some people."

"He didn't seem to even recognize a lot of his classmates when he met them in the army."

"What do you mean?"

"Just what I say. I told you something that wasn't true tonight. That captain's name wasn't Brown."

Again I asked him what he meant.

"The captain's name was Hibbing," he said. "I was that captain, and when I rode up to join my company he acted as if he'd never seen me before. It kind of threw me off—because I used to love this place. Well—good night."

Afternoon of an Author

THIS story—if it can properly be called a story—appeared in *Esquire* in August, 1936. It was written while Fitzgerald was living in an apartment in The Cambridge Arms, across from the Johns Hopkins campus, in Baltimore. It is an account of an actual day in Fitzgerald's life at that time, even down to the minor details. The letter from Paramount asking for a release on a poem is still in his files (the poem was the quotation on the title-page of *The Great Gatsby*: Paramount was taking no chances on Tom D'Invilliers' turning out to be actual). The story of the commandeered locomotive was one of Fitzgerald's favorites, though there is some question whether he did not in fact reach Washington in the usual way. The story about the barber was called "A Change of Class" and was printed in *The Saturday Evening Post*, September 26, 1931.

This story shows again how nearly fabulous Fitzgerald's life always was for him, how intensely he experienced even the smallest movement of feeling and how objectively he could judge it. The details of character in it are undoubtedly as actual as those of external fact, and the irony—first evident in the title's echo of "L'Après-midi d'un Faune"—is the characteristic irony of Fitzgerald's last period. It is in the contrast between the struggle against "fatal facility" fifteen years ago and the absurd charge that the author is "indefatigable" now. It is, above all, in the last paragraph, where the author, having experienced the miracle, sees it with irony professionally, as a possible source of material. "He was quite tired—he would lie down for ten minutes." If this response to being momentarily struck blind is pitiful to the man who lives through it, it is comically ironic to the cool historian who is reporting it to us. This double knowledge of self flows out into the smallest detail of the story: "Never any luck with movies. Stick to your last, boy."

WHEN HE WOKE UP he felt better than he had for many weeks, a fact that became plain to him negatively—he did not feel ill. He leaned for a moment against the door frame between his bedroom and bath till he could be sure he was not dizzy. Not a bit, not even when he stooped for a slipper under the bed.

It was a bright April morning, he had no idea what time because his clock was long unwound but as he went back through the apartment to the kitchen he saw that his daughter had breakfasted and departed and that the mail was in, so it was after nine.

"I think I'll go out today," he said to the maid.

"Do you good—it's a lovely day." She was from New Orleans, with the features and coloring of an Arab.

"I want two eggs like yesterday and toast, orange juice and tea."

He lingered for a moment in his daughter's end of the apartment and read his mail. It was an annoying mail with nothing cheerful in it—mostly bills and advertisements with the diurnal Oklahoma school boy and his gaping autograph album. Sam Goldwyn might do a ballet picture with Spessiwitza and might not—it would all have to wait till Mr. Goldwyn got back from Europe when he might have half a dozen new ideas. Paramount wanted a release on a poem that had appeared in one of the author's books, as they didn't know whether it was an original or quoted. Maybe they were going to get a title from it. Anyhow he had no more equity in that property—he had sold the silent rights many years ago and the sound rights last year.

"Never any luck with movies," he said to himself. "Stick to your last, boy."

He looked out the window during breakfast at the students changing classes on the college campus across the way.

"Twenty years ago I was changing classes," he said to the maid. She laughed her debutante's laugh.

"I'll need a check," she said, "if you're going out."

"Oh, I'm not going out yet. I've got two or three hours' work. I meant late this afternoon."

"Going for a drive?"

"I wouldn't drive that old junk—I'd sell it for fifty dollars. I'm going on the top of a bus."

After breakfast he lay down for fifteen minutes. Then he went into the study and began to work.

The problem was a magazine story that had become so thin in the middle that it was about to blow away. The plot was like climbing endless stairs, he had no element of surprise in reserve, and the characters who started so bravely day-before-yesterday couldn't have qualified for a newspaper serial.

"Yes, I certainly need to get out," he thought. "I'd like to drive down the Shenandoah Valley, or go to Norfolk on the boat."

But both of these ideas were impractical—they took time and energy and he had not much of either—what there was must be conserved for work. He went through the manuscript underlining good phrases in red crayon and after tucking these into a file slowly tore up the rest of the story and dropped it in the waste-basket. Then he walked the room and smoked, occasionally talking to himself.

"Wee-l, let's see—"

"Nau-ow, the next thing—would be—"

"Now let's see, now—"

After awhile he sat down thinking:

"I'm just stale—I shouldn't have touched a pencil for two days."

He looked through the heading "Story Ideas" in his notebook until the maid came to tell him his secretary was on the phone—part time secretary since he had been ill.

"Not a thing," he said. "I just tore up everything I'd written. It wasn't worth a damn. I'm going out this afternoon."

"Good for you. It's a fine day."

"Better come up tomorrow afternoon—there's a lot of mail and bills."

He shaved, and then as a precaution rested five minutes before he dressed. It was exciting to be going out—he hoped the elevator boys wouldn't say they were glad to see him up and he decided to go down the back elevator where they did not know him. He put on his best suit with the coat and trousers that didn't match. He had bought only two suits in six years but they were the very best suits— the coat alone of this one had cost a hundred and ten dollars. As he must have a destination—it wasn't good to go places without a destination—he put a tube of shampoo ointment in his pocket for his barber to use, and also a small phial of luminol.

"The perfect neurotic," he said, regarding himself in the mirror. "By-product of an idea, slag of a dream."

He went into the kitchen and said good-bye to the maid as if he were going to Little America. Once in the war he had commandeered an engine on sheer bluff and had it driven from New York to Washington to keep from being A.W.O.L. Now he stood carefully on the street corner waiting for the light to change, while young people hurried past him with a fine disregard for traffic. On the bus corner under the trees it was green and cool and he thought of Stonewall Jackson's last words: "Let us cross over the river and rest under the shade of the trees." Those Civil War leaders seemed to have realized very suddenly how tired they were—Lee shriveling into another man, Grant with his desperate memoir-writing at the end.

The bus was all he expected—only one other man on the roof and the green branches ticking against each window through whole blocks. They would probably have to trim those branches and it seemed a pity. There was so much to look at—he tried to define the color of one line of houses and could only think of an old opera cloak of his mother's that was full of tints and yet was of no tint— a mere reflector of light. Somewhere church bells were playing "*Venite Adoremus*" and he wondered why, because Christmas was eight months off. He didn't like bells but it had been very moving when they played "*Maryland, My Maryland*" at the governor's funeral.

On the college football field men were working with rollers and a title occurred to him: "Turf-keeper" or else "The Grass Grows," something about a man working on turf for years and bringing up his son to go to college and play football there. Then the son dying in youth and the man's going to work in the cemetery and putting turf over his son instead of under his feet. It would be the kind of piece that is often placed in anthologies, but not his sort of thing—it was sheer swollen antithesis, as formalized as a popular magazine story and easier to write. Many people, however, would consider it excellent because it was melancholy, had digging in it and was simple to understand.

The bus went past a pale Athenian railroad station brought to life by the blue shirted redcaps out in front. The street narrowed as the business section began and there were suddenly brightly dressed girls, all very beautiful—he thought he had never seen such beautiful girls. There were men too but they all looked rather silly, like himself in the mirror, and there were old undecorative women, and presently, too, there were plain and unpleasant faces among the girls; but in general they were lovely, dressed in real colors all the way from six to thirty, no plans or struggles in their faces, only a state of sweet suspension, provocative and serene. He loved life terribly for a minute, not wanting to give it up at all. He thought perhaps he had made a mistake in coming out so soon.

He got off the bus, holding carefully to all the railings and walked a block to the hotel barbershop. He passed a sporting goods store and looked in the window unmoved except by a first baseman's glove which was already dark in the pocket. Next to that was a haberdasher's and here he stood for quite a while looking at the deep shade of shirts and the ones of checker and plaid. Ten years ago on the summer Riviera the author and some others had bought dark blue workmen's shirts, and probably that had started that style. The checkered shirts were nice looking, bright as uniforms and he wished he were twenty and going to a beach club all dolled up like a Turner sunset or Guido Reni's dawn.

The barbershop was large, shining and scented—it had been several months since the author had come downtown on such a mission and he found that his familiar barber was laid up with arthritis; however, he explained to another man how to use the ointment, refused a newspaper and sat, rather happy and sensually content at the strong fingers on his scalp, while a pleasant mingled memory of all the barbershops he had ever known flowed through his mind.

Once he had written a story about a barber. Back in 1929 the proprietor of his favorite shop in the city where he was then living had made a fortune of $300,000 on tips from a local industrialist and was about to retire. The author had no stake in the market, in fact, was about to sail for Europe for a few years with such accumulation as he had, and that autumn hearing how the barber had lost all his fortune he was prompted to write a story, thoroughly disguised in every way yet hinging on the fact of a barber rising in the world and then tumbling; he heard, nevertheless, that the story had been identified in the city and caused some hard feelings.

The shampoo ended. When he came out into the hall an orchestra had started to play in the cocktail room across the way and he stood for a moment in the door listening. So long since he had danced, perhaps two evenings in five years, yet a review of his last book had mentioned him as being fond of night clubs; the same review had also spoken of him as being indefatigable. Something in the sound of the word in his mind broke him momentarily and feeling tears of weakness behind his eyes he turned away. It was like in the beginning fifteen years ago when they said he had "fatal facility," and he labored like a slave over every sentence so as not to be like that.

"I'm getting bitter again," he said to himself. "That's no good, no good—I've got to go home."

The bus was a long time coming but he didn't like taxis and he still hoped that something would occur to him on that upper-deck passing through the green leaves of the boulevard. When it came finally he had some trouble climbing the steps but it was worth it for the first thing he saw was a pair of high school kids, a boy and a girl, sitting without any self-consciousness on the high pedestal of the Lafayette statue, their attention fast upon each other. Their isolation moved him and he knew he would get something out of it professionally, if only in contrast to the growing seclusion of his life and the increasing necessity of picking over an already well-picked past. He needed reforestation and he was well aware of it, and he hoped the soil would stand one more growth. It had never been the very best soil for he had had an early weakness for showing off instead of listening and observing.

Here was the apartment house—he glanced up at his own windows on the top floor before he went in.

"The residence of the successful writer," he said to himself. "I wonder what marvelous books he's tearing off up there. It must be great to have a gift like that—just sit down with pencil and paper. Work when you want—go where you please."

His child wasn't home yet but the maid came out of the kitchen and said:

"Did you have a nice time?"

"Perfect," he said. "I went roller skating and bowled and played around with Man Mountain Dean and finished up in a Turkish Bath. Any telegrams?"

"Not a thing."

"Bring me a glass of milk, will you?"

He went through the dining room and turned into his study, struck blind for a moment with the glow of his two thousand books in the late sunshine. He was quite tired—he would lie down for ten minutes and then see if he could get started on an idea in the two hours before dinner.

Author's House

THIS piece appeared in *Esquire* in July, 1936. It derives from the same impulse as "Afternoon of an Author," the set of feelings which developed in Fitzgerald during that long meditation which followed the experience described in the "Crack-Up" essays, when he learned to live with the despair of these years. As John Peale Bishop's elegy puts it:

> I have . . .
> Heard you cry: *I am lost. But you are lower!*
> And you had that right.
> The damned do not so own to their damnation.

The loss and its remembrance are all here, but so is the clear sense that "in the end . . . it's just like other houses after all" and that this is a gain.

"I lived up here once," the author said after a moment.
"Here? For a long time?"
"No. For just a little while when I was young."
"It must have been rather cramped."
"I didn't notice it."
"Would you like to try it again?"
"No. And I couldn't if I wanted to."
He shivered slightly and closed the windows.

Here the quasi-symbolic method works nearly perfectly, as it does not everywhere in the story. Like Basil, he had once lived in princely glory up there in the wind's trumpeting. Now, like the hero of "Outside the Cabinet-Maker's," he no longer can. Now, too, a part of him does not want to live up there where, continually disregarding the existence of others, he did "things he [could] never repair," and the horror of harm done that comes like a storm in "Sleeping and Waking" can be avoided. He was never completely sure it was worth it to live down here, but it was something gained.

I HAVE SEEN numerous photographs and read many accounts of the houses of Joan Crawford, Virginia Bruce and Claudette Colbert, usually with the hostess done up from behind with a bib explaining how on God's earth to make a Hollywood soufflée or open a can of soup without removing the appendix in the same motion. But it has been a long time since I have seen a picture of an author's house and it occurs to me to supply the deficiency.

Of course I must begin with an apology for writing about authors at all. In the days of the old *Smart Set* Mencken and Nathan had a rejection slip which notified the aspirant that they would not consider stories about painters, musicians and authors—perhaps because these classes are supposed to express themselves fully in their own work and are not a subject for portraiture. And having made the timorous bow I proceed with the portrait.

Rather than leave a somber effect at the end we begin at the bottom, in a dark damp unmodernized cellar. As your host's pale yellow flashlight moves slowly around through the spiderwebs, past old boxes and barrels and empty bottles and parts of old machines you feel a little uneasy.

"Not a bad cellar—as cellars go," the author says. "You can't see it very well and I can't either—it's mostly forgotten."

"What do you mean?"

"It's everything I've forgotten—all the complicated dark mixture of my youth and infancy that made me a fiction writer instead of a fireman or a soldier.

"You see fiction is a trick of the mind and heart composed of as many separate emotions as a magician uses in executing a pass or a palm. When you've learned it you forget it and leave it down here."

"When did you learn it?"

"Oh every time I begin I have to learn it all over again in a way. But the intangibles are down here. Why I chose this God awful metier of sedentary days and sleepless nights and endless dissatisfaction. Why I would choose it again. All that's down here and I'm just as glad I can't look at it too closely. See that dark corner?"

"Yes."

"Well, three months before I was born my mother lost her other two children and I think that came first of all though I don't know how it worked exactly. I think I started then to be a writer."

Your eyes fall on another corner and you give a start of alarm.

"What's that?" you demand.

"That?" The author tries to change the subject, moving around so as to obscure your view of the too recent mound of dirt in the corner that has made you think of certain things in police reports. But you insist.

"That is where it is buried," he says.

"What's buried?"

"That's where I buried my love after—" he hesitates.

"After you *killed* her?"

"After I killed *it*."

"I don't understand what you mean."

The author does not look at the pile of earth.

"That is where I buried my first childish love of myself, my belief that I would never die like other people, and that I wasn't the son of my parents but a son of a king, a king who ruled the whole world."

He breaks off.

"But let's get out of here. We'll go upstairs."

In the living room the author's eye is immediately caught by a scene outside the window. The visitor looks—he sees some children playing football on the lawn next door.

"There is another reason why I became an author."

"How's that?"

"Well, I used to play football in a school and there was a coach who didn't like me for a damn. Well, our school was going to play a game up on the Hudson, and I had been substituting for our climax runner who had been hurt the week before. I had a good day substituting for him so now that he was well and had taken his old place I was moved into what might be called the position of blocking back. I wasn't adapted to it, perhaps because there was less glory and less stimulation. It was cold, too, and I don't stand cold, so instead of doing my job I got thinking how grey the skies were. When the coach took me out of the game he said briefly:

" 'We simply can't depend on you.'

"I could only answer, 'Yes, sir.'

"That was as far as I could explain to him literally what happened—and it's taken me years to figure it out for my own benefit. I had been playing listlessly. We had the other team licked by a couple of touchdowns, and it suddenly occurred to me that I might as well let the opposing end—who hadn't so far made a single tackle—catch a forward pass, but at the last moment I came to life and realized that I couldn't let him catch the pass, but that at least I wouldn't intercept it, so I just knocked it down.

"That was the point where I was taken out of the game. I remember the desolate ride in the bus back to the train and the desolate ride back to school with everybody thinking I had been yellow on the occasion, when actually I was just distracted and sorry for that opposing end. That's the truth. I've been afraid plenty of times but that wasn't one of the times. The point is it inspired me to write a poem for the school paper which made me as big a hit with my father as if I had become a football hero. So when I went home that Christmas vacation it was in my mind that if you weren't able to function in action you might at least be able to tell about it, because you felt the same intensity—it was a back door way out of facing reality."

They go into a dining room now. The author walks through it in haste and a certain aversion.

"Don't you enjoy food?" the visitor asks.

"Food—yes! But not the miserable mixture of fruit juices and milk and whole-wheat bread I live on now."

"Are you dyspeptic?"

"Dyspeptic! I'm simply ruined."

"How so?"

"Well, in the middle west in those days children started life with fried food and waffles and that led into endless malted milks and bacon buns in college and then a little later I jumped to meals at Foyot's and the Castelli dei Caesari and the Escargot and every spice merchant in France and Italy. And under the name of alcohol— Clarets and Burgundys, Chateau Yquems and Champagnes, Pilsener and Dago Red, prohibition Scotch and Alabama white mule. It was very good while it lasted but I didn't see what pap lay at the end." He shivered, "Let's forget it—it isn't dinner time. Now this—" he says opening a door, "is my study."

A secretary is typing there or rather in a little alcove adjoining. As they come in she hands the author some letters. His eye falls on the envelope of the first one, his face takes on an expectant smile and he says to the visitor:

"This is the sequel to something that was rather funny. Let me tell you the first part before I open this. Well, about two weeks ago I got a letter under cover from *The Saturday Evening Post*, addressed not to me but to

Thomas Kracklin,
Saturday Evening post
Philadelphia
pennsylvania Pa

On the envelope were several notations evidently by the *Post's* mail department.

[186]

Not known here
Try a story series in 1930 files
Think this is character in story by X in 1927 files

"This last person had guessed it, for Thomas Kracklin was indeed a character in some stories of mine. Here's what the letter said:

Mr. Kracklin I wonder if you are any kin to mine because my name was Kracklin an I had a brother an he did not see us much any more we was worried about him an I thought when I read your story that you was that Kracklin an I thought if I wrote you I would find out yours truly Mrs. Kracklin Lee.

"The address was a small town in Michigan. The letter amused me and was so different from any that I had received for a long time that I made up an answer to it. It went something like this:

My dear Mrs. Kracklin Lee:
I am indeed your long lost brother. I am now in the Baltimore Penitentiary awaiting execution by hanging. If I get out I will be glad to come to visit you. I think you would find me all right except I cannot be irritated as I sometimes kill people if the coffee is cold. But I think I won't be much trouble except for that but I will be pretty poor when I get out of the penitentiary and will be glad if you can take care of me—unless they string me up next Thursday. Write me care of my lawyer.

"Here I gave my name and then signed the letter 'Sincerely, Thomas Kracklin.' This is undoubtedly the answer."

The author opened the envelope—there were two letters inside. The first was addressed to him by his real name.

Dear Sir I hope my brother has not been hung an I thank you for sending his letter I am a poor woman an have no potatoes this day an can just buy the stamp but I hope my brother has not been hung an if not I would like to see him an will you give him this letter yours truly Mrs. Kracklin Lee.

This was the second letter:

Dear Brother I have not got much but if you get off you can come back here an I could not promise to suply you with much but maybe we could get along cannot really promise anythin but I hope you will get off an wish you the very best always your sister Mrs. Kracklin Lee.

When he had finished reading the author said:

"Now isn't it fun to be so damn smart! Miss Palmer, please write a letter saying her brother's been reprieved and gone to China and put five dollars in the envelope."

"But it's too late," he continued as he and his visitor went upstairs. "You can pay a little money but what can you do for meddling with a human heart? A writer's temperament is continually making him do things he can never repair.

"This is my bedroom. I write a good deal lying down and when there are too many children around, but in summer it's hot up here in the daytime and my hand sticks to the paper."

The visitor moved a fold of cloth to perch himself on the side of a chair but the author warned him quickly:

"Don't touch that! It's just the way somebody left it."

"Oh I beg your pardon."

"Oh it's all right—it was a long long time ago. Sit here for a moment and rest yourself and then we'll go on up."

"Up?"

"Up to the attic. This is a big house you see—on the old-fashioned side."

The attic was the attic of Victorian fiction. It was pleasant, with beams of late light slanting in on piles and piles of magazines and pamphlets and children's school books and college year books and "little" magazines from Paris and ballet programs and the old *Dial* and *Mercury* and *L'Illustration* unbound and the *St. Nicholas* and the journal of the Maryland Historical Society, and piles of maps and guide books from the Golden Gate to Bou Saada. There were files bulging with letters, one marked "letters from my grandfather to my grandmother" and several dozen scrap books and clipping books and photograph books and albums and "baby books" and great envelopes full of unfiled items. . . .

"This is the loot," the author said grimly. "This is what one has instead of a bank balance."

"Are you satisfied?"

"No. But it's nice here sometimes in the late afternoon. This is a sort of a library in its way, you see—the library of a life. And nothing is as depressing as a library if you stay long in it. Unless of course you stay there all the time because then you adjust yourself and become a little crazy. Part of you gets dead. Come on let's go up."

"Where?"

"Up to the cupola—the turret, the watch-tower, whatever you want to call it. I'll lead the way."

It is small up there and full of baked silent heat until the author opens two of the glass sides that surround it and the twilight wind blows through. As far as your eye can see there is a river winding between green lawns and trees and purple buildings and red slums blended in by a merciful dusk. Even as they stand there the wind increases until it is a gale whistling around the tower and blowing birds past them.

"I lived up here once," the author said after a moment.

"Here? For a long time?"

"No. For just a little while when I was young."

"It must have been rather cramped."

"I didn't notice it."

"Would you like to try it again?"

"No. And I couldn't if I wanted to."

He shivered slightly and closed the windows. As they went downstairs the visitor said, half apologetically:

"It's really just like all houses, isn't it?"

The author nodded.

"I didn't think it was when I built it, but in the end I suppose it's just like other houses after all."

Design in Plaster

This story was printed in *Esquire* in November, 1939; it was written the previous July. Its starting point was an accident Fitzgerald had had three years before. In July of 1936 he broke his collar bone during a swan dive from a fifteen-foot board—"trying," as he said, "to show off for Zelda, on the first day I could swim in a year and a half." Several weeks after the original accident, while he was still in a cast, he fell in the bathroom and lay helpless on the floor for a long time. As a result he was in bed for five weeks more. This accident is also used in "Financing Finnegan."

The force of the story is in its understanding of the progress of jealousy. It is in Martin's inability to summon more than a faint irony when he says that his illness is "in a way of becoming my life"; it is in his trying and failing to "go slow," his effort to control what he knows is an irrational preoccupation with Joris; it is in the gradual conquest of his mind by the image of Mary, late at night, dropping her book in her lap and looking up at the ceiling, a conquest which leads him to do the one thing which will make the fantasy come true. Dick Diver found himself victimized in the same way by the fantasy of jealousy when Collis Clay told him the story about Rosemary on the train to Chicago. This perception is one of the keys to his experience for Fitzgerald.

How long does the doctor think now?" Mary asked.

With his good arm Martin threw back the top of the sheet, disclosing that the plaster armor had been cut away in front in the form of a square, so that his abdomen and the lower part of his diaphragm bulged a little from the aperture. His dislocated arm was still high over his head in an involuntary salute.

"This was a great advance," he told her. "But it took the heat wave to make Ottinger put in this window. I can't say much for the view but—have you seen the wire collection?"

"Yes, I've seen it," his wife answered, trying to look amused.

It was laid out on the bureau like a set of surgeons' tools—wires bent to every length and shape so that the nurse could reach any point inside the plaster cast when perspiration made the itching unbearable.

Martin was ashamed at repeating himself.

"I apologize," he said. "After two months you get medical psychology. All this stuff is fascinating to me. In fact—" he added, and with only faint irony, "—it is in a way of becoming my life."

Mary came over and sat beside the bed raising him, cast and all, into her slender arms. He was chief electrical engineer at the studio and his thirty-foot fall wasn't costing a penny in doctor's bills. But that—and the fact that the catastrophe had swung them together after a four months' separation, was its only bright spot.

"I feel so close," she whispered. "Even through this plaster."

"Do you think that's a nice way to talk?"

"Yes."

"So do I."

Presently she stood up and rearranged her bright hair in the mirror. He had seen her do it half a thousand times but suddenly there was a quality of remoteness about it that made him sad.

"What are you doing tonight?" he asked.

Mary turned, almost with surprise.

"It seems strange to have you ask me."

"Why? You almost always tell me. You're my contact with the world of glamour."

"But you like to keep bargains. That was our arrangement when we began to live apart."

"You're being very technical."

"No—but that *was* the arrangement. As a matter of fact I'm not doing anything. Bieman asked me to go to a preview, but he bores me. And that French crowd called up."

"Which member of it?"

She came closer and looked at him.

"Why, I believe you're jealous," she said. "The wife of course. Or *he* did, to be exact, but he was calling for his wife—she'd be there. I've never seen you like this before."

Martin was wise enough to wink as if it meant nothing and let it die away, but Mary said an unfortunate last word.

"I thought you liked me to go with them."

"That's it," Martin tried to go slow, "—with 'them,' but now it's 'he.'"

"They're all leaving Monday," she said almost impatiently. "I'll probably never see him again."

Silence for a minute. Since his accident there were not an un-limited number of things to talk about, except when there was love between them. Or even pity—he was accepting even pity in the past fortnight. Especially their uncertain plans about the future were in need of being preceded by a mood of love.

"I'm going to get up for a minute," he said suddenly. "No, don't help me—don't call the nurse. I've got it figured out."

The cast extended half way to his knee on one side but with a snake-like motion he managed to get to the side of the bed—then rise with a gigantic heave. He tied on a dressing gown, still without assistance, and went to the window. Young people were splashing and calling in the outdoor pool of the hotel.

"I'll go along," said Mary. "Can I bring you anything tomorrow? Or tonight if you feel lonely?"

"Not tonight. You know I'm always cross at night—and I don't like you making that long drive twice a day. Go along—be happy."

"Shall I ring for the nurse?"

"I'll ring presently."

He didn't though—he just stood. He knew that Mary was wearing out, that this resurgence of her love was wearing out. His accident was a very temporary dam of a stream that had begun to overflow months before.

When the pains began at six with their customary regularity the nurse gave him something with codein in it, shook him a cocktail and ordered dinner, one of those dinners it was a struggle to digest since he had been sealed up in his individual bomb-shelter. Then she was off duty four hours and he was alone. Alone with Mary and the Frenchman.

He didn't know the Frenchman except by name but Mary had said once:

"Joris is rather like you—only naturally not formed—rather immature."

Since she said that, the company of Mary and Joris had grown increasingly unattractive in the long hours between seven and eleven. He had talked with them, driven around with them, gone to pictures and parties with them—sometimes with the half comforting ghost of Joris' wife along. He had been near as they made love and even that was endurable as long as he could seem to hear and see them. It was when they became hushed and secret that his stomach winced inside the plaster cast. That was when he had pictures of the Frenchman going toward Mary and Mary waiting. Because he was not sure just how Joris felt about her or about the whole situation.

"I told him I loved you," Mary said—and he believed her, "I told him that I could never love anyone but you."

Still he could not be sure how Mary felt as she waited in her apartment for Joris. He could not tell if, when she said good night at her door, she turned away relieved, or whether she walked around her living room a little and later, reading her book, dropped it in her lap and looked up at the ceiling. Or whether her phone rang once more for one more good night.

Martin hadn't worried about any of these things in the first two months of their separation when he had been on his feet and well.

At half-past eight he took up the phone and called her; the line was busy and still busy at a quarter of nine. At nine it was out of order; at nine-fifteen it didn't answer and at a little before nine-thirty it was busy again. Martin got up, slowly drew on his trousers and with the help of a bellboy put on a shirt and coat.

"Don't you want me to come, Mr. Harris?" asked the bellboy.

"No thanks. Tell the taxi I'll be right down."

When the boy had gone he tripped on the slightly raised floor of the bathroom, swung about on one arm and cut his head against the wash bowl. It was not so much, but he did a clumsy repair job with the adhesive and, feeling ridiculous at his image in the mirror, sat down and called Mary's number a last time—for no answer. Then he went out, not because he wanted to go to Mary's but because he had to go somewhere toward the flame, and he didn't know any other place to go.

At ten-thirty Mary, in her nightgown, was at the phone.

"Thanks for calling. But, Joris, if you want to know the truth I have a splitting headache. I'm turning in."

"Mary, listen," Joris insisted. "It happens Marianne has a headache too and has turned in. This is the last night I'll have a chance to see you alone. Besides, you told me you'd *never* had a headache."

Mary laughed.

"That's true—but I *am* tired."

"I would promise to stay one-half hour—word of honor. I am only just around the corner."

"No," she said and a faint touch of annoyance gave firmness to the word. "Tomorrow I'll have either lunch or dinner if you like, but now I'm going to bed."

She stopped. She had heard a sound, a weight crunching against the outer door of her apartment. Then three odd, short bell rings.

"There's someone—call me in the morning," she said. Hurriedly hanging up the phone she got into a dressing gown.

By the door of her apartment she asked cautiously.

"Who's there?"

No answer—only a heavier sound—a human slipping to the floor.

"Who is it?"

She drew back and away from a frightening moan. There was a little shutter high in the door, like the peephole of a speakeasy, and feeling sure from the sound that whoever it was, wounded or drunk, was on the floor Mary reached up and peeped out. She could see only a hand covered with freshly ripening blood, and shut the trap hurriedly. After a shaken moment, she peered once more.

This time she recognized something—afterwards she could not have said what—a way the arm lay, a corner of the plaster cast—but it was enough to make her open the door quickly and duck down to Martin's side.

"Get doctor," he whispered. "Fell on the steps and broke."

His eyes closed as she ran for the phone.

Doctor and ambulance came at the same time. What Martin had done was simple enough, a little triumph of misfortune. On the first flight of stairs that he had gone up for eight weeks, he had stumbled, tried to save himself with the arm that was no good for anything, then spun down catching and ripping on the stair rail. After that a five minute drag up to her door.

Mary wanted to exclaim, "Why? Why?" but there was no one to hear. He came awake as the stretcher was put under him to carry him to the hospital, repair the new breakage with a new cast, start it over again. Seeing Mary he called quickly. "Don't you come. I don't like anyone around when—when—Promise on your word of honor not to come?"

The orthopedist said he would phone her in an hour. And five minutes later it was with the confused thought that he was already calling that Mary answered the phone.

"I can't talk, Joris," she said. "There was an awful accident—"

"Can I help?"

"It's gone now. It was my husband—"

Suddenly Mary knew she wanted to do anything but wait alone for word from the hospital.

"Come over then," she said. "You can take me up there if I'm needed."

She sat in place by the phone until he came—jumped to her feet with an exclamation at his ring.

"Why? Why?" she sobbed at last. "I offered to go see him at his hotel."

"Not drunk?"

"No, no—he almost never takes a drink. Will you wait right outside my door while I dress and get ready?"

The news came half an hour later that Martin's shoulder was set again, that he was sleeping under the ethylene gas and would sleep till morning. Joris Deglen was very gentle, swinging her feet up on the sofa, putting a pillow at her back and answering her incessant "Why?" with a different response every time—Martin had been delirious; he was lonely; then at a certain moment telling the truth he had long guessed at: Martin was jealous.

"That was it," Mary said bitterly. "We were to be free—only I wasn't free. Only free to sneak about behind his back."

She was free now though, free as air. And later, when he said he wouldn't go just yet, but would sit in the living room reading until she quieted down, Mary went into her room with her head clear as morning. After she undressed for the second time that night she stayed for a few minutes before the mirror arranging her hair and keeping her mind free of all thoughts about Martin except that he was sleeping and at the moment felt no pain.

Then she opened her bedroom door and called down the corridor into the living room:

"Do you want to come and tell me good night?"

PAT HOBBY

BETWEEN September, 1939, and the end of his life, Fitzgerald wrote a series of these short stories about Pat Hobby for *Esquire*; there were seventeen in all. These three appeared in March, April, and November, 1940. Pat Hobby is the controlled projection of one of the recurrent nightmares of Fitzgerald's last years. This is what he thought he might possibly become if he wholly succeeded in cutting his losses and "pasting it together" again. Or, put the other way round, this is the explanation he found in his own nature for the innocently conscienceless characters he saw in Hollywood. He makes the point quite explicitly in *The Crack-Up*:

If you are young and you should write asking to see me and learn how to be a sombre literary man writing pieces upon the state of emotional exhaustion that often overtakes writers in their prime—if you should be so young and so fatuous as to do this, I would not do so much as acknowledge your letter, unless you were related to someone very rich and important indeed. And if you were dying of starvation outside my window, I would go out quickly and give you the smile and the voice (if no longer the hand) and stick around till somebody raised a nickel to phone for the ambulance, that is if I thought there would be any copy in it for me.

As always, he was dead in earnest about the fundamental insight here, but his judgment saw quite clearly its comic aspect: he once described Pat as "a complete rat" but not "sinister." It is characteristic of Fitzgerald that these stories blame Hollywood itself for almost nothing. Like Cecilia, who "knew what you were supposed to think of it but . . . was obstinately unhorrified," he never blames Le Vigne and the rest, but sees them as able, humane, even philosophic ("Talk quick and I'll give you another month at two-fifty. I kinda like having you around"). The failure is all in Pat himself, with his selfishness, his awe of the Big Table, his bold ineffectuality. Yet he is so completely and innocently of his world that we do not really blame him.

Boil Some Water—Lots of It

PAT HOBBY sat in his office in the Writers' Building and looked at his morning's work, just come back from the script department. He was on a "polish job," about the only kind he ever got nowadays. He was to repair a messy sequence in a hurry, but the word "hurry" neither frightened nor inspired him for Pat had been in Hollywood since he was thirty—now he was forty-nine. All the work he had done this morning (except a little changing around of lines so he could claim them as his own)—all he had actually invented was a single imperative sentence, spoken by a doctor.

"Boil some water—lots of it."

It was a good line. It had sprung into his mind full grown as soon as he had read the script. In the old silent days Pat would have used it as a spoken title and ended his dialogue worries for a space, but he needed some spoken words for other people in the scene. Nothing came.

Boil some water, he repeated to himself, lots of it.

The word boil brought a quick glad thought of the commissary. A reverent thought too—for an old-timer like Pat, what people you sat with at lunch was more important in getting along than what you dictated in your office. This was no art, as he often said—this was an industry.

"This is no art," he remarked to Max Leam who was leisurely drinking at a corridor water cooler. "This is an industry."

Max had flung him this timely bone of three weeks at three-fifty.

"Say look, Pat! Have you got anything down on paper yet?"

"Say I've got some stuff already that'll make 'em—" He named a familiar biological function with the somewhat startling assurance that it would take place in the theater.

Max tried to gauge his sincerity.

"Want to read it to me now?" he asked.

"Not yet. But it's got the old guts if you know what I mean."

Max was full of doubts.

"Well, go to it. And if you run into any medical snags check with the doctor over at the First Aid Station. It's got to be right."

The spirit of Pasteur shone firmly in Pat's eyes.

"It will be."

He felt good walking across the lot with Max—so good that he decided to glue himself to the producer and sit down with him at the Big Table. But Max foiled his intention by cooing, "See you later," and slipping into the barbershop.

Once Pat had been a familiar figure at the Big Table; often in his golden prime he had dined in the private canteens of executives. Being of the older Hollywood he understood their jokes, their vanities, their social system with its swift fluctuations. But there were too many new faces at the Big Table now—faces that looked at him with the universal Hollywood suspicion. And at the little tables where the young writers sat they seemed to take work so serious. As for just sitting down anywhere, even with secretaries or extras—Pat would rather catch a sandwich at the corner.

Detouring to the Red Cross Station he asked for the doctor. A girl, a nurse, answered from a wall mirror where she was hastily drawing her lips, "He's out. What is it?"

"Oh. Then I'll come back."

She had finished, and now she turned—vivid and young and with a bright consoling smile.

"Miss Stacey will help you. I'm about to go to lunch."

He was aware of an old, old feeling—left over from the time when he had had wives—a feeling that to invite this little beauty to lunch might cause trouble. But he remembered quickly that he didn't have any wives now—they had both given up asking for alimony.

"I'm working on a medical," he said. "I need some help."

"A medical?"

"Writing it—idea about a doc. Listen—let me buy you lunch. I want to ask you some medical questions."

The nurse hesitated.

"I don't know. It's my first day out here."

"It's all right," he assured her. "Studios are democratic; everybody is just 'Joe' or 'Mary'—from the big shots right down to the prop boys."

He proved it magnificently on their way to lunch by greeting a male star and getting his own name back in return. And in the commissary, where they were placed hard by the Big Table, his producer, Max Leam, looked up, did a little "takem" and winked.

The nurse—her name was Helen Earle—peered about eagerly.

"I don't see anybody," she said. "Except oh, there's Ronald Colman. I didn't know Ronald Colman looked like that."

Pat pointed suddenly to the floor.

"And there's Mickey Mouse!"

She jumped and Pat laughed at his joke—but Helen Earle was already staring starry-eyed at the costume extras who filled the hall with the colors of the First Empire. Pat was piqued to see her interest go out to these nonentities.

"The big shots are at this next table," he said solemnly, wistfully, "directors and all except the biggest executives. They could have

Ronald Colman pressing pants. I usually sit over there but they don't want ladies. At lunch, that is, they don't want ladies."

"Oh," said Helen Earle, polite but unimpressed. "It must be wonderful to be a writer too. It's so very interesting."

"It has its points," he said . . . he had thought for years it was a dog's life.

"What is it you want to ask me about a doctor?"

Here was toil again. Something in Pat's mind snapped off when he thought of the story.

"Well, Max Leam—that man facing us—Max Leam and I have a script about a Doc. You know? Like a hospital picture?"

"I know." And she added after a moment, "That's the reason that I went in training."

"And we've got to have it *right* because a hundred million people would check on it. So this doctor in the script he tells them to boil some water. He says, 'Boil some water—lots of it.' And we were wondering what the people would do then."

"Why—they'd probably boil it," Helen said, and then, somewhat confused by the question, "What people?"

"Well somebody's daughter and the man that lived there and an attorney and the man that was hurt."

Helen tried to digest this before answering.

"—and some other guy I'm going to cut out," he finished.

There was a pause. The waitress set down tuna fish sandwiches.

"Well, when a doctor gives orders they're orders," Helen decided.

"Hm." Pat's interest had wandered to an odd little scene at the Big Table while he inquired absently, "You married?"

"No."

"Neither am I."

Beside the Big Table stood an extra. A Russian Cossack with a fierce mustache. He stood resting his hand on the back of an empty chair between Director Paterson and Producer Leam.

"Is this taken?" he asked, with a thick Central European accent.

All along the Big Table faces stared suddenly at him. Until after the first look the supposition was that he must be some well-known actor. But he was not—he was dressed in one of the many-colored uniforms that dotted the room.

Someone at the table said: "That's taken." But the man drew out the chair and sat down.

"Got to eat somewhere," he remarked with a grin.

A shiver went over the near-by tables. Pat Hobby stared with his mouth ajar. It was as if someone had crayoned Donald Duck into the *Last Supper*.

"Look at that," he advised Helen. "What they'll do to him! Boy!"

The flabbergasted silence at the Big Table was broken by Ned Harman, the Production Manager.

"This table is reserved," he said.

The extra looked up from a menu.

"They told me sit anywhere."

He beckoned a waitress—who hesitated, looking for an answer in the faces of her superiors.

"Extras don't eat here," said Max Leam, still politely. "This is a—"

"I got to eat," said the Cossack doggedly. "I been standing around six hours while they shoot this stinking mess and now I got to eat."

The silence had extended—from Pat's angle all within range seemed to be poised in midair.

The extra shook his head wearily.

"I dunno who cooked it up—" he said—and Max Leam sat forward in his chair—"but it's the lousiest tripe I ever seen shot in Hollywood."

—At his table Pat was thinking why didn't they do something? Knock him down, drag him away. If they were yellow themselves they could call the studio police.

"Who is that?" Helen Earle was following his eyes innocently. "Somebody I ought to know?"

He was listening attentively to Max Leam's voice, raised in anger.

"Get up and get out of here, buddy, and get out quick!"

The extra frowned.

"Who's telling me?" he demanded.

"You'll see." Max appealed to the table at large, "Where's Cushman—where's the Personnel man?"

"You try to move me," said the extra, lifting the hilt of his scabbard above the level of the table. "And I'll hang this on your ear. I know my rights."

The dozen men at the table, representing a thousand dollars an hour in salaries, sat stunned. Far down by the door one of the studio police caught wind of what was happening and started to elbow through the crowded room. And Big Jack Wilson, another director, was on his feet in an instant coming around the table.

But they were too late—Pat Hobby could stand no more. He had jumped up, seizing a big heavy tray from the serving stand nearby. In two springs he reached the scene of action—lifting the tray he brought it down upon the extra's head with all the strength of his forty-nine years. The extra, who had been in the act of rising to meet Wilson's threatened assault, got the blow full on his face and temple and as he collapsed a dozen red streaks sprang into sight through the heavy grease paint. He crashed sideways between the chairs.

Pat stood over him panting—the tray in his hand.

"The dirty rat!" he cried. "Where does he think—"

The studio policeman pushed past; Wilson pushed past—two aghast men from another table rushed up to survey the situation.

"It was a gag!" one of them shouted. "That's Walter Herrick, the writer. It's his picture."

"My God!"

"He was kidding Max Leam. It was a gag I tell you!"

"Pull him out . . . Get a doctor . . . Look out, there!"

Now Helen Earle hurried over; Walter Herrick was dragged out into a cleared space on the floor and there were yells of "Who did it?—Who beaned him?"

Pat let the tray lapse to a chair, its sound unnoticed in the confusion.

He saw Helen Earle working swiftly at the man's head with a pile of clean napkins.

"Why did they have to do this to him?" someone shouted.

Pat caught Max Leam's eye but Max happened to look away at the moment and a sense of injustice came over Pat. He alone in this crisis, real or imaginary, had *acted*. He alone had played the man, while those stuffed shirts let themselves be insulted and abused. And now he would have to take the rap—because Walter Herrick was powerful and popular, a three thousand a week man who wrote hit shows in New York. How could anyone have guessed that it was a gag?

There was a doctor now. Pat saw him say something to the manageress and her shrill voice sent the waitresses scattering like leaves toward the kitchen.

"Boil some water! Lots of it!"

The words fell wild and unreal on Pat's burdened soul. But even though he now knew at first-hand what came next, he did not think that he could go on from there.

Teamed with Genius

"I TOOK A CHANCE in sending for you," said Jack Berners. "But there's a job that you just *may* be able to help out with."

Though Pat Hobby was not offended, either as man or writer, a formal protest was called for.

"I been in the industry fifteen years, Jack. I've got more screen credits than a dog has got fleas."

"Maybe I chose the wrong word," said Jack. "What I mean is, that was a long time ago. About money we'll pay you just what Republic paid you last month—three-fifty a week. Now—did you ever hear of a writer named René Wilcox?"

The name was unfamiliar. Pat had scarcely opened a book in a decade.

"She's pretty good," he ventured.

"It's a man, an English playwright. He's only here in L. A. for his health. Well—we've had a Russian Ballet picture kicking around for a year—three bad scripts on it. So last week we signed up René Wilcox—he seemed just the person."

Pat considered.

"You mean he's—"

"I don't know and I don't care," interrupted Berners sharply. "We think we can borrow Zorina, so we want to hurry things up—do a shooting script instead of just a treatment. Wilcox is inexperienced and that's where you come in. You used to be a good man for structure."

"*Used* to be!"

"All right, maybe you still are." Jack beamed with momentary encouragement. "Find yourself an office and get together with René Wilcox." As Pat started out he called him back and put a bill in his hand. "First of all, get a new hat. You used to be quite a boy around the secretaries in the old days. Don't give up at forty-nine!"

Over in the Writers' Building Pat glanced at the directory in the hall and knocked at the door of 216. No answer, but he went in to discover a blond, willowy youth of twenty-five staring moodily out the window.

"Hello, René!" Pat said. "I'm your partner."

Wilcox's regard questioned even his existence, but Pat continued heartily, "I hear we're going to lick some stuff into shape. Ever collaborate before?"

"I have never written for the cinema before."

While this increased Pat's chance for a screen credit he badly needed, it meant that he might have to do some work. The very thought made him thirsty.

"This is different from playwriting," he suggested, with suitable gravity.

"Yes—I read a book about it."

Pat wanted to laugh. In 1928 he and another man had concocted such a sucker-trap, *Secrets of Film Writing*. It would have made money if pictures hadn't started to talk.

"It all seems simple enough," said Wilcox. Suddenly he took his hat from the rack. "I'll be running along now."

"Don't you want to talk about the script?" demanded Pat. "What have you done so far?"

"I've not done anything," said Wilcox deliberately. "That idiot, Berners, gave me some trash and told me to go on from there. But it's too dismal." His blue eyes narrowed. "I say, what's a boom shot?"

"A boom shot? Why, that's when the camera's on a crane."

Pat leaned over the desk and picked up a blue-jacketed "Treatment." On the cover he read:

BALLET SHOES

A Treatment

by

Consuela Martin

An Original from an idea by Consuela Martin

Pat glanced at the beginning and then at the end.

"I'd like it better if we could get the war in somewhere," he said frowning. "Have the dancer go as a Red Cross nurse and then she could get regenerated. See what I mean?"

There was no answer. Pat turned and saw the door softly closing.

What is this? he exclaimed. What kind of collaborating can a man do if he walks out? Wilcox had not even given the legitimate excuse —the races at Santa Anita!

The door opened again, a pretty girl's face, rather frightened, showed itself momentarily, said "Oh," and disappeared. Then it returned.

"Why it's Mr. Hobby!" she exclaimed. "I was looking for Mr. Wilcox."

He fumbled for her name but she supplied it.

"Katherine Hodge. I was your secretary when I worked here three years ago."

Pat knew she had once worked with him, but for the moment could not remember whether there had been a deeper relation. It did not seem to him that it had been love—but looking at her now, that appeared rather too bad.

"Sit down," said Pat. "You assigned to Wilcox?"

"I thought so—but he hasn't given me any work yet."

"I think he's nuts," Pat said gloomily. "He asked me what a boom shot was. Maybe he's sick—that's why he's out here. He'll probably start throwing up all over the office."

"He's well now," Katherine ventured.

"He doesn't look like it to me. Come on in my office. You can work for *me* this afternoon."

Pat lay on his couch while Miss Katherine Hodge read the script of *Ballet Shoes* aloud to him. About midway in the second sequence he fell asleep with his new hat on his chest.

Except for the hat, that was the identical position in which he found René next day at eleven. And it was that way for three straight days—one was asleep or else the other—and sometimes both. On the fourth day they had several conferences in which Pat again put forward his idea about the war as a regenerating force for ballet dancers.

"Couldn't we *not* talk about the war?" suggested René. "I have two brothers in the Guards."

"You're lucky to be here in Hollywood."

"That's as it may be."

"Well, what's your idea of the start of the picture?"

"I do not like the present beginning. It gives me an almost physical nausea."

"So then, we got to have something in its place. That's why I want to plant the war—"

"I'm late to luncheon," said René Wilcox. "Good-bye, Mike."

Pat grumbled to Katherine Hodge:

"He can call me anything he likes, but somebody's got to write this picture. I'd go to Jack Berners and tell him—but I think we'd both be out on our ears."

For two days more he camped in René's office, trying to rouse him to action, but with no avail. Desperate on the following day—when the playwright did not even come to the studio—Pat took a benzedrine tablet and attacked the story alone. Pacing his office with the treatment in his hand he dictated to Katherine—interspersing the dictation with a short, biased history of his life in Hollywood. At the day's end he had two pages of script.

The ensuing week was the toughest in his life—not even a moment to make a pass at Katherine Hodge. Gradually with many creaks, his battered hulk got in motion. Benzedrine and great drafts of coffee woke him in the morning, whiskey anesthetized him at night. Into his feet crept an old neuritis and as his nerves began to crackle he developed a hatred against René Wilcox, which served him as a sort of *ersatz* fuel. He was going to finish the script by himself and hand it to Berners with the statement that Wilcox had not contributed a single line.

But it was too much—Pat was too far gone. He blew up when he was half through and went on a twenty-four-hour bat—and next morning arrived back at the studio to find a message that Mr. Berners wanted to see the script at four. Pat was in a sick and confused state when his door opened and René Wilcox came in with a typescript in one hand, and a copy of Berners' note in the other.

"It's all right," said Wilcox. "I've finished it."

"*What?* Have you been *working?*"

"I always work at night."

"What've you done? A treatment?"

"No, a shooting script. At first I was held back by personal worries, but once I got started it was very simple. You just get behind the camera and dream."

Pat stood up aghast.

"But we were supposed to collaborate. Jack'll be wild."

"I've always worked alone," said Wilcox gently. "I'll explain to Berners this afternoon."

Pat sat in a daze. If Wilcox's script was good—but how could a first script be good? Wilcox should have fed it to him as he wrote; then they might have *had* something.

Fear started his mind working—he was struck by his first original idea since he had been on the job. He phoned to the script department for Katherine Hodge and when she came over told her what he wanted. Katherine hesitated.

"I just want to *read* it," Pat said hastily. "If Wilcox is there you can't take it, of course. But he just might be out."

He waited nervously. In five minutes she was back with the script. "It isn't mimeographed or even bound," she said.

He was at the typewriter, trembling as he picked out a letter with two fingers.

"Can I help?" she asked.

"Find me a plain envelope and a used stamp and some paste."

Pat sealed the letter himself and then gave directions:

"Listen outside Wilcox's office. If he's in, push it under his door. If he's out get a call boy to deliver it to him, wherever he is. Say it's from the mail room. Then you better go off the lot for the afternoon. So he won't catch on, see?"

As she went out Pat wished he had kept a copy of the note. He was proud of it—there was a ring of factual sincerity in it too often missing from his work.

"Dear Mr. Wilcox:
I am sorry to tell you your two brothers were killed in action today by a long range Tommy-gun. You are wanted at home in England right away.
John Smythe
The British Consulate, New York"

But Pat realized that this was no time for self-applause. He opened Wilcox's script.

To his vast surprise it was technically proficient—the dissolves, fades, cuts, pans and trucking shots were correctly detailed. This simplified everything. Turning back to the first page he wrote at the top:

BALLET SHOES
First Revise
From Pat Hobby and René Wilcox—presently changing this to read: *From René Wilcox and Pat Hobby.*

Then, working frantically, he made several dozen small changes. He substituted the word "Scram!" for "Get out of my sight!", he put "Behind the eight-ball" instead of "in trouble," and replaced "you'll be sorry" with the apt coinage "Or else!" Then he phoned the script department.

"This is Pat Hobby. I've been working on a script with René Wilcox, and Mr. Berners would like to have it mimeographed by half-past three."

This would give him an hour's start on his unconscious collaborator.

"Is it an emergency?"

"I'll say."

"We'll have to split it up between several girls."

Pat continued to improve the script till the call boy arrived. He wanted to put in his war idea but time was short—still, he finally told the call boy to sit down, while he wrote laboriously in pencil on the last page.

CLOSE SHOT: *Boris and Rita*

Rita: *What does anything matter now! I have enlisted as a trained nurse in the war.*

Boris: (moved) *War purifies and regenerates!*

(He puts his arms around her in a wild embrace as the music soars way up and we FADE OUT)

Limp and exhausted by his effort he needed a drink, so he left the lot and slipped cautiously into the bar across from the studio where he ordered gin and water.

With the glow, he thought warm thoughts. He had done *almost* what he had been hired to do—though his hand had accidentally fallen upon the dialogue rather than the structure. But how could Berners tell that the structure wasn't Pat's? Katherine Hodge would say nothing, for fear of implicating herself. They were all guilty but guiltiest of all was René Wilcox for refusing to play the game. Always, according to his lights, Pat had played the game.

He had another drink, bought breath tablets and for awhile amused himself at the nickel machine in the drugstore. Louie, the studio bookie, asked if he was interested in wagers on a bigger scale.

"Not today, Louie."

"What are they paying you, Pat?"

"Thousand a week."

"Not so bad."

"Oh, a lot of us old-timers are coming back," Pat prophesied. "In silent days was where you got real training—with directors shooting off the cuff and needing a gag in a split second. Now it's a sis job. They got English teachers working in pictures! What do they know?"

"How about a little something on 'Quaker Girl'?"

"No," said Pat. "This afternoon I got an important angle to work on. I don't want to worry about horses."

At three-fifteen he returned to his office to find two copies of his script in bright new covers.

BALLET SHOES
from
René Wilcox and Pat Hobby
First Revise

It reassured him to see his name in type. As he waited in Jack Berners' anteroom he almost wished he had reversed the names. With the right director this might be another *It Happened One Night*, and if he got his name on something like that it meant a three or four year gravy ride. But this time he'd save his money— go to Santa Anita only once a week—get himself a girl along the type of Katherine Hodge, who wouldn't expect a mansion in Beverly Hills.

Berners' secretary interrupted his reverie, telling him to go in. As he entered he saw with gratification that a copy of the new script lay on Berners' desk.

"Did you ever—" asked Berners suddenly "—go to a psychoanalyst?"

"No," admitted Pat. "But I suppose I could get up on it. Is it a new assignment?"

"Not exactly. It's just that I think you've lost your grip. Even larceny requires a certain cunning. I've just talked to Wilcox on the phone."

"Wilcox must be nuts," said Pat, aggressively. "I didn't steal anything from him. His name's on it, isn't it? Two weeks ago I laid out all his structure—every scene. I even wrote one whole scene—at the end about the war."

"Oh yes, the war," said Berners as if he was thinking of something else.

"But if you like Wilcox's ending better—"

"Yes, I like his ending better. I never saw a man pick up this work so fast." He paused. "Pat, you've told the truth just once since you came in this room—that you didn't steal anything from Wilcox."

"I certainly did not. I *gave* him stuff."

But a certain dreariness, a grey *malaise*, crept over him as Berners continued:

"I told you we had three scripts. You used an old one we discarded a year ago. Wilcox was in when your secretary arrived, and he sent one of them to you. Clever, eh?"

Pat was speechless.

"You see, he and that girl like each other. Seems she typed a play for him this summer."

"They like each other," said Pat incredulously. "Why, he—"

"Hold it, Pat. You've had trouble enough today."

"He's responsible," Pat cried. "He wouldn't collaborate—and all the time—"

"—he was writing a swell script. And he can write his own ticket if we can persuade him to stay here and do another."

Pat could stand no more. He stood up.

"Anyhow thank you, Jack," he faltered. "Call my agent if anything turns up." Then he bolted suddenly and surprisingly for the door.

Jack Berners signaled on the Dictograph for the President's office.

"Get a chance to read it?" he asked in a tone of eagerness.

"It's swell. Better than you said. Wilcox is with me now."

"Have you signed him up?"

"I'm going to. Seems he wants to work with Hobby. Here, you talk to him."

Wilcox's rather high voice came over the wire.

"Must have Mike Hobby," he said. "Grateful to him. Had a quarrel with a certain young lady just before he came, but today Hobby brought us together. Besides I want to write a play about him. So give him to me—you fellows don't want him any more."

Berners picked up his secretary's phone.

"Go after Pat Hobby. He's probably in the bar across the street. We're putting him on salary again but we'll be sorry."

He switched off, switched on again.

"Oh! Take him his hat. He forgot his hat."

No Harm Trying

Pat hobby's apartment lay athwart a delicatessen shop on Wilshire Boulevard. And there lay Pat himself, surrounded by his books— the *Motion Picture Almanac* of 1928 and *Barton's Track Guide, 1939*—by his pictures, authentically signed photographs of Mabel Normand and Barbara LaMarr (who, being deceased, had no value in the pawn-shops)—and by his dogs in their cracked leather oxfords, perched on the arm of a slanting settee.

Pat was at "the end of his resources"—though this term is too ominous to describe a fairly usual condition in his life. He was an old-timer in pictures; he had once known sumptuous living, but for the past ten years jobs had been hard to hold—harder to hold than glasses.

"Think of it," he often mourned. "Only a writer—at forty-nine."

All this afternoon he had turned the pages of *The Times* and *The Examiner* for an idea. Though he did not intend to compose a motion picture from this idea, he needed it to get him inside a studio. If you had nothing to submit it was increasingly difficult to pass the gate. But though these two newspapers, together with *Life*, were the sources most commonly combed for "originals," they yielded him nothing this afternoon. There were wars, a fire in Topanga Canyon, press releases from the studios, municipal corruptions, and always the redeeming deeds of "The Trojuns," but Pat found nothing that competed in human interest with the betting page.

—If I could get out to Santa Anita, he thought—I could maybe get an idea about the nags.

This cheering idea was interrupted by his landlord, from the delicatessen store below.

"I told you I wouldn't deliver any more messages," said Nick, "and *still* I won't. But Mr. Carl Le Vigne is telephoning in person from the studio and wants you should go over right away."

The prospect of a job did something to Pat. It anesthetized the crumbled, struggling remnants of his manhood, and inoculated him instead with a bland, easygoing confidence. The set speeches and attitudes of success returned to him. His manner as he winked at a studio policeman, stopped to chat with Louie, the bookie, and presented himself to Mr. Le Vigne's secretary, indicated that he had been engaged with momentous tasks in other parts of the globe. By saluting Le Vigne with a facetious "Hel-*lo* Captain!" he behaved almost as an equal, a trusted lieutenant who had never really been away.

"Pat, your wife's in the hospital," Le Vigne said. "It'll probably be in the papers this afternoon."

Pat started.

"My wife?" he said. "What wife?"

"Estelle. She tried to cut her wrists."

"Estelle!" Pat exclaimed. "You mean *Estelle*? Say, I was only married to her three weeks!"

"She was the best girl you ever had," said Le Vigne grimly.

"I haven't even heard of her for ten years."

"You're hearing about her now. They called all the studios trying to locate you."

"I had nothing to do with it."

"I know—she's only been here a week. She had a run of hard luck wherever it was she lived—New Orleans? Husband died, child died, no money . . ."

Pat breathed easier. They weren't trying to hang anything on him.

"Anyhow she'll live," Le Vigne reassured him superfluously, "—and she was the best script girl on the lot once. We'd like to take care of her. We thought the way was give you a job. Not exactly a job, because I know you're not up to it." He glanced into Pat's red-rimmed eyes. "More of a sinecure."

Pat became uneasy. He didn't recognize the word, but "sin" disturbed him and "cure" brought a whole flood of unpleasant memories.

"You're on the payroll at two-fifty a week for three weeks," said Le Vigne, "—but one-fifty of that goes to the hospital for your wife's bill."

"But we're divorced!" Pat protested. "No Mexican stuff either. I've been married since, and so has—"

"Take it or leave it. You can have an office here, and if anything you can do comes up we'll let you know."

"I never worked for a hundred a week."

"We're not asking you to work. If you want you can stay home."

Pat reversed his field.

"Oh, I'll work," he said quickly. "You dig me up a good story and I'll show you whether I can work or not."

Le Vigne wrote something on a slip of paper.

"All right. They'll find you an office."

Outside Pat looked at the memorandum.

"Mrs. John Devlin," it read, "Good Samaritan Hospital."

The very words irritated him.

"Good Samaritan!" he exclaimed. "Good gyp joint! One hundred and fifty bucks a week!"

Pat had been given many a charity job but this was the first one that made him feel ashamed. He did not mind not *earn*ing his salary, but not getting it was another matter. And he wondered if other people on the lot who were obviously doing nothing, were being fairly paid for it. There were, for example, a number of beautiful young ladies who walked aloof as stars, and whom Pat took for stock girls, until Eric, the callboy, told him they were imports from Vienna and Budapest, not yet cast for pictures. Did half their pay checks go to keep husbands they had only had for three weeks!

The loveliest of these was Lizzette Starheim, a violet-eyed little blonde with an ill-concealed air of disillusion. Pat saw her alone at tea almost every afternoon in the commissary—and made her acquaintance one day by simply sliding into a chair opposite.

"Hello, Lizzette," he said. "I'm Pat Hobby, the writer."

"Oh, hel*lo*!"

She flashed such a dazzling smile that for a moment he thought she must have heard of him.

"When they going to cast you?" he demanded.

"I don't know." Her accent was faint and poignant.

"Don't let them give you the run-around. Not with a face like yours." Her beauty roused a rusty eloquence. "Sometimes they just keep you under contract till your teeth fall out, because you look too much like their big star."

"Oh no," she said distressfully.

"Oh yes!" he assured her. "I'm telling *you*. Why don't you go to another company and get borrowed? Have you thought of that idea?"

"I think it's wonderful."

He intended to go further into the subject but Miss Starheim looked at her watch and got up.

"I must go now, Mr.——"

"Hobby. Pat Hobby."

Pat joined Dutch Waggoner, the director, who was shooting dice with a waitress at another table.

"Between pictures, Dutch?"

"Between pictures hell!" said Dutch. "I haven't done a picture for six months and my contract's got six months to run. I'm trying to break it. Who was the little blonde?"

Afterwards, back in his office, Pat discussed these encounters with Eric the callboy.

"All signed up and no place to go," said Eric. "Look at this Jeff Manfred, now—an associate producer! Sits in his office and sends notes to the big shots—and I carry back word they're in Palm Springs. It breaks my heart. Yesterday he put his head on his desk and boo-hoo'd."

"What's the answer?" asked Pat.

"Changa management," suggested Eric, darkly. "Shake-up coming."

"Who's going to the top?" Pat asked, with scarcely concealed excitement.

"Nobody knows," said Eric. "But wouldn't I like to land uphill! Boy! I want a writer's job. I got three ideas so new they're wet behind the ears."

"It's no life at all," Pat assured him with conviction. "I'd trade with you right now."

In the hall next day he intercepted Jeff Manfred who walked with the unconvincing hurry of one without a destination.

"What's the rush, Jeff?" Pat demanded, falling into step.

"Reading some scripts," Jeff panted without conviction.

Pat drew him unwillingly into his office.

"Jeff, have you heard about the shake-up?"

"Listen now, Pat—" Jeff looked nervously at the walls. "What shake-up?" he demanded.

"I heard that this Harmon Shaver is going to be the new boss," ventured Pat, "Wall Street control."

"Harmon Shaver!" Jeff scoffed. "He doesn't know anything about pictures—he's just a money man. He wanders around like a lost soul." Jeff sat back and considered. "Still—if you're *right*, he'd be a man you could get to." He turned mournful eyes on Pat. "I haven't been able to see Le Vigne or Barnes or Bill Behrer for a month. Can't get an assignment, can't get an actor, can't get a story." He broke off. "I've thought of drumming up something on my own. Got any ideas?"

"Have I?" said Pat. "I got three ideas so new they're wet behind the ears."

"Who for?"

"Lizzette Starheim," said Pat, "with Dutch Waggoner directing —see?"

"I'm with you all a hundred per cent," said Harmon Shaver. "This is the most encouraging experience I've had in pictures." He had a bright bond-salesman's chuckle. "By God, it reminds me of a circus, we got up when I was a boy."

They had come to his office inconspicuously like conspirators— Jeff Manfred, Waggoner, Miss Starheim and Pat Hobby.

"You like the idea, Miss Starheim?" Shaver continued.

"I think it's wonderful."

"And you, Mr. Waggoner?"

"I've heard only the general line," said Waggoner with director's caution, "but it seems to have the old emotional socko." He winked at Pat. "I didn't know this old tramp had it in him."

Pat glowed with pride. Jeff Manfred, though he was elated, was less sanguine.

"It's important nobody talks," he said nervously. "The Big Boys would find some way of killing it. In a week, when we've got the script done we'll go to them."

"I agree," said Shaver. "They have run the studio so long that— well, I don't trust my own secretaries—I sent them to the races this afternoon."

Back in Pat's office Eric, the callboy, was waiting. He did not know that he was the hinge upon which swung a great affair.

"You like the stuff, eh?" he asked eagerly.

"Pretty good," said Pat with calculated indifference.

"You said you'd pay more for the next batch."

"Have a heart!" Pat was aggrieved. "How many callboys get seventy-five a week?"

"How many callboys can write?"

Pat considered. Out of the two hundred a week Jeff Manfred was advancing from his own pocket, he had naturally awarded himself a commission of sixty per cent.

"I'll make it a hundred," he said. "Now check yourself off the lot and meet me in front of Benny's bar."

At the hospital, Estelle Hobby Devlin sat up in bed, overwhelmed by the unexpected visit.

"I'm glad you came, Pat," she said, "you've been very kind. Did you get my note?"

"Forget it," Pat said gruffly. He had never liked this wife. She had loved him too much—until she found suddenly that he was a poor lover. In her presence he felt inferior.

"I got a guy outside," he said.

"What for?"

"I thought maybe you had nothing to do and you might want to pay me back for all this jack—"

He waved his hand around the bare hospital room.

"You were a swell script girl once. Do you think if I got a typewriter you could put some good stuff into continuity?"

"Why—yes. I suppose I could."

"It's a secret. We can't trust anybody at the studio."

"All right," she said.

"I'll send this kid in with the stuff. I got a conference."

"All right—and—oh Pat—come and see me again."

"Sure, I'll come."

But he knew he wouldn't. He didn't like sickrooms—he lived in one himself. From now on he was done with poverty and failure. He admired strength—he was taking Lizzette Starheim to a wrestling match that night.

In his private musings Harmon Shaver referred to the showdown as "the surprise party." He was going to confront Le Vigne with a *fait accompli* and he gathered his coterie before phoning Le Vigne to come over to his office.

"What for?" demanded Le Vigne. "Couldn't you tell me now —I'm busy as hell."

This arrogance irritated Shaver—who was here to watch over the interests of Eastern stockholders.

"I don't ask much," he said sharply, "I let you fellows laugh at me behind my back and freeze me out of things. But now I've got something and I'd like you to come over."

"All right—all right."

Le Vigne's eyebrows lifted as he saw the members of the new production unit but he said nothing—sprawled into an arm chair with his eyes on the floor and his fingers over his mouth.

Mr. Shaver came around the desk and poured forth words that had been fermenting in him for months. Simmered to its essentials, his protest was: "You would not let me play, but I'm going to play anyhow." Then he nodded to Jeff Manfred—who opened the script and read aloud. This took an hour, and still Le Vigne sat motionless and silent.

"There you are," said Shaver triumphantly. "Unless you've got any objection I think we ought to assign a budget to this proposition and get going. I'll answer to my people."

Le Vigne spoke at last.

"You like it, Miss Starheim?"

"I think it's wonderful."

"What language you going to play it in?"

To everyone's surprise Miss Starheim got to her feet.

"I must go now," she said with her faint poignant accent.

"Sit down and answer me," said Le Vigne. "What language are you playing it in?"

Miss Starheim looked tearful.

"Wenn I gute teachers hätte konnte ich dann thees rôle gut spielen," she faltered.

"But you like the script."

She hesitated.

"I think it's wonderful."

Le Vigne turned to the others.

"Miss Starheim has been here eight months," he said. "She's had three teachers. Unless things have changed in the past two weeks she can say just three sentences. She can say, 'How do you do'; she can say, 'I think it's wonderful'; and she can say, 'I must go now.' Miss Starheim has turned out to be a pinhead—I'm not insulting her because she doesn't know what it means. Anyhow—there's your Star."

He turned to Dutch Waggoner, but Dutch was already on his feet.

"Now Carl—" he said defensively.

"You force me to it," said Le Vigne. "I've trusted drunks up to a point, but I'll be goddam if I'll trust a hophead."

He turned to Harmon Shaver.

"Dutch has been good for exactly one week apiece on his last four pictures. He's all right now but as soon as the heat goes on he reaches for the little white powders. Now Dutch! Don't say anything you'll regret. We're carrying you in *hopes*—but you won't get on a stage till we've had a doctor's certificate for a year."

Again he turned to Harmon.

"There's your director. Your supervisor, Jeff Manfred, is here for one reason only—because he's Behrer's wife's cousin. There's nothing against him but he belongs to silent days as much as—as much as—" His eyes fell upon a quavering broken man, "—as much as Pat Hobby."

"What do you mean?" demanded Jeff.

"You trusted Hobby, didn't you? That tells the whole story." He turned back to Shaver. "Jeff's a weeper and a wisher and a dreamer. Mr. Shaver, you have bought a lot of condemned building material."

"Well, I've bought a good story," said Shaver defiantly.

"Yes. That's right. We'll make that story."

"Isn't that something?" demanded Shaver. "With all this secrecy how was I to know about Mr. Waggoner and Miss Starheim? But I do know a good story."

"Yes," said Le Vigne absently. He got up. "Yes—it's a good story. . . . Come along to my office, Pat."

He was already at the door. Pat cast an agonized look at Mr. Shaver as if for support. Then, weakly, he followed.

"Sit down, Pat."

"That Eric's got talent, hasn't he?" said Le Vigne. "He'll go places. How'd you come to dig him up?"

Pat felt the straps of the electric chair being adjusted.

"Oh—I just dug him up. He—came in my office."

"We're putting him on salary," said Le Vigne. "We ought to have some system to give these kids a chance."

He took a call on his Dictograph, then swung back to Pat.

"But how did you ever get mixed up with this goddam Shaver. *You*, Pat—an old-timer like you."

"Well, I thought—"

"Why doesn't he go back East?" continued Le Vigne disgustedly. "Getting all you poops stirred up!"

Blood flowed back into Pat's veins. He recognized his signal, his dog-call.

"Well, I got you a story, didn't I?" he said, with almost a swagger. And he added, "How'd you know about it?"

"I went down to see Estelle in the hospital. She and this kid were working on it. I walked right in on them."

"Oh," said Pat.

"I knew the kid by sight. Now, Pat, tell me this—did Jeff Manfred think you wrote it—or was he in on the racket?"

"Oh God," Pat mourned. "What do I have to answer that for?"

Le Vigne leaned forward intensely.

"Pat, you're sitting over a trap door!" he said with savage eyes. "Do you see how the carpet's cut? I just have to press this button and drop you down to hell! Will you *talk*?"

Pat was on his feet, staring wildly at the floor.

"Sure I will!" he cried. He believed it—he believed such things.

"All right," said Le Vigne relaxing. "There's whiskey in the sideboard there. Talk quick and I'll give you another month at two-fifty. I kinda like having you around."

News of Paris—Fifteen Years Ago

THE manuscript of this story was among Fitzgerald's papers. It was printed in *Furioso*, Winter, 1947. The story was apparently written in 1940. Fitzgerald had it typed on yellow paper and triple-spaced, an almost sure sign with him that he thought it had real possibilities and that he meant to work on it further; it is easy to see how it might have been filled out, episode by episode, and given a neat plot.

But it is not so easy to think that what is best in the story would have been made better by such revision. The taxis with their phrase from Debussy, the draperies with their peacocks stirring in the April wind—these beautifully evocative details would lose something in a context of more commonplace ones. The story fully reveals, as it stands, the twenties' sense that, though they are—they are happy to feel—somewhat unconventional, they know what they are doing and think it good. The Fitzgerald of 1925 knew that Henry and Bessie leaving the Bois would feel "like escaping children"; he was capable, too, of the joke about becoming a contemptible drone. But perhaps only the Fitzgerald of 1940 knew the full force of the truth embedded in this joke, as perhaps only he knew the full force of the observation that Henry "had been a romantic four years ago" and now was jealous of the reporter. This is the loss of faith and confidence he explored in Dick Diver and Martin Harris. Only the Fitzgerald of the last years would have known all it meant and would have placed it as he does here.

WE SHOULDN'T both be coming from the same direction," Ruth said. "A lot of people know we're at the same hotel."

Henry Haven Dell smiled and then they both laughed. It was a bright morning in April and they had just turned off the Champs Elysées toward the English Church.

"I'll walk on the other side of the street," he said, "and then we'll meet at the door."

"No, we oughtn't even to sit together. I'm a countess—laugh it off but anything I do will be in that damn 'Boulevardier.'"

They stopped momentarily.

"But I hate to leave you," he said. "You look so lovely."

"I hate to leave you too," she whispered. "I never knew how nice you were. But good-bye."

Half way across the street, he stopped to a great screech of auto horns playing Debussy.

"We're lunching," he called back.

She nodded, but continued to walk looking straight ahead on her sidewalk. Henry Haven Dell continued his crossing and then walked quickly, from time to time throwing a happy glance at the figure across the way.

—I wonder if they have telephones in churches, he thought. After the ceremony he would see.

He stood in a rear row, catching Ruth's eye from time to time, teasing her. It was a very fashionable wedding. As the bride and groom came down the aisle the bride caught his arm and took him with them down the street.

"Isn't it fun," the bride said. "And just think, Henry, I almost married you."

Her husband laughed.

—at what, Henry thought. I could have had her if she'd really been the one.

Aloud he said:

"I have to telephone before the reception."

"The hotel's full of phones. Come and stand beside me. I want you to be the first to know."

He got to the phone only after an hour.

"The *Paris* is delayed," said the Compagnie Transatlantique. "We can't give you an exact hour. Not before four."

"Oh, no, Monsieur—not possibly."

Good. In the lobby he joined a party of wedding guests and repaired to the Ritz on the man's part of the bar. You couldn't be with women incessantly.

"How long will you be in Paris, Henry?"

"That's not a fair question. I can always tell you how long I'll be in New York or London."

He had two cocktails—each at a different table. A little before one when the confusion and din were at their height he went out into the Rue Cambon. There was not a taxi to be had—the doormen were chasing them all the way up to the Rue de Rivoli. One sailed into port with a doorman on the running board but a lovely little brunette in pale green was already waiting.

"Oh, look," begged Henry. "You're not by any chance going near the Bois?"

He was getting into the cab as he spoke. His morning coat was a sort of introduction. She nodded.

"I'm lunching there."

"I'm Henry Dell," he said, lifting his hat.

"Oh, it's you—at last," she said eagerly. "I'm Bessie Wing—born Leighton. I know all your cousins."

"Isn't this nice," he exclaimed and she agreed.

"I'm breaking my engagement at luncheon," she said. "And I'll name you."

"Really breaking your engagement?"

"At the Café Dauphine—from one to two."

"I'll be there—from time to time I'll look at you."

"What I want to know is—does he take me home afterward. I'm not Emily Posted."

On impulse he said:

"No, I do. You may be faint or something. I'll keep an eye on you."

She shook her head.

"No—it wouldn't be reverend this afternoon," she said. "But I'll be here weeks."

"This afternoon," he said. "You see, there's a boat coming in."

After a moment's reluctance she answered:

"I do *almost* know you. Leave it this way. If you see me talk shaking a spoon back and forth I'll meet you in front in five minutes."

Ruth was waiting at table. Henry talked lazily to her for ten minutes, watching her face and the spring light upon the table. Then with a casual glance he located Bessie Wing across the room, deep in conversation with a man of twenty-six, his own age.

"We'll have this afternoon—and then good-bye," said Ruth.

"Not even this afternoon," he answered solemnly, "I'm meeting the boat in an hour."

"I'm sorry, Henry. Hasn't it been fun?"

"Lots of fun. So much fun." He felt sincerely sad.

"It's just as well," said Ruth with a little effort, "I have fittings that I've postponed. Remember me when you go to the Opera or out to St.-Germain."

"I'll do my best to forget you."

A little later he saw the spoon waving.

"Let me go first," he said. "I somehow couldn't bear to sit here and see you walk off."

"All right, I'll sit here and think."

Bessie was waiting under a pear tree in front—they crammed hastily into a taxi like escaping children.

"Was it bad?" he asked. "I watched you. There were tears in his eyes."

She nodded.

"It was pretty bad."

"Why did you break it?"

"Because my first marriage was a flop. There were so many men around that when I married I didn't know who I loved any more. So there didn't seem to be any point if you know what I mean. Why should it have been Hershell Wing?"

"How about this other man?"

"It would have been the same way only now it would be my fault because I know."

They sat in the cool American drawing room of her apartment and had coffee.

"For anyone so beautiful—" he said, "there must be many times like those. When there isn't a man—there's just men."

"There was a man once," she said, "when I was sixteen. He looked like you. He didn't love me."

Henry went and sat beside her on the fauteuil.

"That happens too," said Henry. "Perhaps the safest way is 'Ships that pass in the night.'"

She held back a little.

"I don't want to be old-fashioned but we don't know each other."

"Sure we do—remember—we met this morning."

She laughed.

"Sedative for a broken engagement!"

"The specific one," he said.

It was quiet in the room. The peacocks in the draperies stirred in the April wind.

Later they stood on her balcony arm in arm and looked over a sea of green leaves to the Arc de Triomphe.

"Where is the phone?" he asked suddenly. "Never mind—I know."

He went inside, picked up the phone beside her bed.

"Compagnie Générale? . . . How about the boat train from the *Paris*?"

"Oh, she has not docked in Havre yet, monsieur. Call in several hours. The delay has been at Southampton."

Returning to the balcony Henry said:

"All right—let's do go to the Exposition."

"I have to, you see," she said. "This woman, Mary Tolliver I told you about—she's the only person I can go to with what I did at luncheon. She'll understand."

"Would she understand about us too?"

"She'll never know. She's been an ideal of mine since I was six-teen."

She was not much older than Bessie, Henry thought as they met her in the Crillon lobby—she was a golden brown woman, very trim and what the French call "soignée"—which means washed and something more. She had an American painter and an Austrian sculptor with her and Henry gathered that they were both a little in love with her, or else exploiting her for money—money evident in the Renault town car that took them to the exhibition of decora-tive arts that ringed the Seine.

They walked along through the show, passed the chromium rails, the shining economy of steel that was to change the furniture of an era. Henry, once art editor of the Harvard Lampoon, was not without a seeing eye but he let the painter and sculptor talk. When they sat down for an apéritif afterwards, Bessie sat very close to him—Mary Tolliver smiled and saw. She looked appraisingly at Henry.

"Have you two known each other long?" she asked.

"Years," said Henry. "She is a sister to me. And now I must leave you all—after a charming afternoon."

Bessie looked at him reproachfully, started to rise with him—con-trolled herself.

"I told you there was a boat," he said gently.

"Ship," she answered.

As he walked away he saw the painter move to the chair he had vacated by her side.

The *Paris* was still delayed at Southampton and Henry consid-ered what to do. When you have been doing nothing in a pleasant way a long time it is difficult to fill in stray hours. More difficult than for one who works. In the country he might have exercised—here there were only faces over tables. And there must continue to be faces over tables.

—I am become a contemptible drone, he thought. I must give at least a thought to duty.

He taxied over to the left bank—to the Rue Nôtre-Dame des Champs—to call on a child he had endowed just after the war. A beautiful little orphan who begged in front of the Café du Dôme, Henry had sent her for three years to convent. He saw her once or twice each summer—not now for almost a year.

"Hélène is out," said a new concierge whom Henry did not know. "How should I guess where she is? At the Café des Lilas? At Lipps?"

He was faintly shocked—then faintly reassured when he found her at Lipps, the beer place which was, at least, a step more respectable than the Dôme or the Rotonde. She left the two Americans with whom she was sitting and embraced him shyly.

"What are you preparing to do, Hélène?" he demanded kindly. "What profession do the nuns teach you?"

She shrugged her shoulders.

"I shall marry," she said. "A rich American if I can. That young man I just left for example—he is on the staff of the New York Herald Tribune."

"Reporters are not rich," he reproved her, "and that one doesn't look very promising."

"Oh, he is drunk now," said Hélène, "but at times he is all one would desire."

Henry had been a romantic four years ago—right after the war. He had in no sense brought up this girl to marry or for anything else. Yet the thought was in his mind then, What if she could continue to be a great beauty. And now as he looked at her he felt a surge of jealousy toward the reporter.